READY FOR IT

ML NYSTROM

HOT TREE PUBLISHING

DRAGON RUNNERS MC

Mute

Stud

Blue

Table

Brick

MACATEER BROTHERS

Run With It

Ready For It

Hold It Close

Risk It All

Give It To Me

For information, contact the publisher, Hot Tree Publishing.

www.hottreepublishing.com

Editing: Hot Tree Editing

Cover Designer: BookSmith Design

E-book ISBN: 978-1-922359-36-0

Paperback ISBN: 978-1-922359-38-4

To all those women who have ever dealt with sexual harassment, assault, bullying, and any other unfair sexism whether in the workplace, home, or public arena, you're not alone.
#MeToo.

CHAPTER ONE

I CHECKED MY WATCH, AND THE HANDS HAD ONLY moved three ticks from the last time I looked. The principal droned on, his voice low with forgettable words, and I started to nod off. Planning discussions were a necessary evil for the faculty, but the school year had ended, final grades were already turned in, graduation done, and the classrooms emptied. The students had left for family beach vacationing, rafting the rivers, or working summer jobs.

I fanned my face with the agenda paper. *Why did our illustrious leader have to have this meeting in June after maintenance turned off the air-conditioning in the building?* I looked at my watch again. Another three ticks. *God, this is taking so freaking long!*

My eyes met those of my best friend ever, Beverly

Archer. Correction, Beverly MacAteer. She got married last year to Connor, the man who had moved in next door. I couldn't have picked a better man for my BFF. After watching them for a year, I knew she made the right call in finally admitting she liked him. They were perfect together, and Connor made the perfect stepdad for Bevvie's four children. Brave woman to be a divorced mom raising her kids alone. Connor slipped into her heart when she wasn't looking, and now her life was nothing short of wedded bliss.

She rolled her eyes and sighed in commiseration. She taught chorus, played the piano, and was one of the most talented people I'd ever met. I teach Algebra One and Two and help coach the ultimate nerds on the Mathletes team. Big yawn to some people, but I love my job.

I snuck another glance at my watch, and a burning eruption hit my throat. *Fuck me, not again!* I fished for a berry-flavored Tums somewhere in the vast recesses of my luggage sized purse. I'd been eating the damn things like candy all weekend. The heartburn attack I had on Friday was the worst one I'd ever experienced, and already I'd consumed two little travel rolls of the tablets. This morning on the way to this mandatory boringness, I stopped by the drug store and picked up an economy-sized bottle.

I crunched on the chalky rounds and saw only five more minutes had passed. *Surely, this shit can't go on much longer.* The burn in my throat eased when I swallowed the masticated mass. It was probably the sausage and egg biscuit I'd eaten earlier. I was a single female who lived alone and didn't cook. At all. I was, however, a wiz at microwaving frozen instant food. My fridge was an empty wasteland, while my freezer was stocked with a wide variety of Lean Cuisine, Stouffer's dinners, and single-serve Ben and Jerry's ice cream.

"The grounds improvements begin on June 18 with the installation of our new flagpole court. The dedication ceremony for this will take place the week of…"

The principal's voice faded as my chin bumped against my chest. The man had a real talent. I'd bet my left breast his speeches had the ability to put my ADHD kids asleep with only a few sentences. I jerked my head back up and caught Bevvie suppressing a grin in my direction. *Bitch,* I mouthed at her, and her grin got bigger. If the droning man hadn't been frowning at me, I'd have shot her a bird.

What the fuck was wrong with me? I hadn't been feeling very well lately. In fact, I'd been tired as hell and sluggish the last few weeks of school, but I'd slogged on through to the end. It figured I'd catch another kid virus just before school let out. Even if I swam in a vat of hand sanitizer on a daily basis, when working with an army of viral-laden children, something was bound to get me eventually.

The watch hands hadn't moved, and I tapped the face to see if I had a dead battery. *Another fifteen minutes, and I swear I'm walking out!*

My stomach rumbled and twisted in on itself unexpectedly. The burn in my throat came back with a vengeance, and there was no stopping it.

Oh, shit! I ran out of the media center and barely made it to the bathroom before the greasy Jimmy Dean biscuit made an encore appearance. I heaved again and again until it wouldn't surprise me if last night's lo mein takeout came back up too. *God, I hate vomiting!*

"Hey, Mellie? You okay?" Bev's call echoed off the tile floors and cinderblock walls.

"Ugh, yeah, I think so." I spat into the toilet and tried not to think of the dirt on the floor and my white Vera Wang pants. I didn't care how many times housekeeping came through to clean the bathroom, they always smelled of sweaty kid bodies. That thought had me gagging again.

"You don't sound okay. The Alley twins had strep through graduation. Think you caught it?"

"I don't know what I caught, but I'm ready as hell to give it back. I don't even *have* the Alley twins in any of my classes. I need this meeting to be over, like a half hour ago."

I flushed and got off my knees and brushed at the gray circles on my pants. Ugh, that was enough to make me want to throw up again. I loved these pants!

Bevvie leaned against a sink when I exited the stall. I turned on the water to rinse my mouth and wash my hands. "I'll be fine once this day is over and I can get to the mall. After the last week of exams, I need some retail therapy. Wanna come?"

She shook her head. "I can't today. Connor is working in the woodshop with the two youngest kids, but he can't actually do much with Mattie underfoot. Sarah keeps her nose in a book at all times now so she's no problem. Jacob is hanging with his buddies at the Y, and Abby took off to the beach this week with her friend Autumn. Maybe sometime this weekend." She looked at my pale face and squinted. "Mellie, you look terrible. I think you need to skip the mall and go see the doctor."

I wiped my hands on a brown paper towel that barely sucked up any moisture. "I'm fine, mother hen.

Nothing more than end-of-the-year stress. I need a vacation badly, and even more, I need to get out of this stinky bathroom."

"You are such a PITA."

"You're a pain in the ass, too."

"Yet you still love me."

"You're the mother of my beautiful godchildren. I have to love you."

We made kissy noises at each other as we sauntered down the hallway back to the media center. The meeting was over, as evidenced by the exiting teachers. They double timed it out of the stuffy building, ready to start their own summer break. More like summer recovery.

Bevvie hefted her handbag over her shoulder in preparation to leave. "Thank God, it's over. I really need to get home and rescue Connor. Come by for dinner on Thursday. It's laundry and taco night." She gave me her best game show host voice and expression.

"Oh, the excitement!" I laughed in response and moved to hug my BFF. *Jeez, my breasts hurt!* I expected my favorite time of the month (not!) to come any day now.

"Miss Miser, may I have a word?" The principal

said right behind me. It was a real effort not to groan in irritation. *What the hell does he want now?*

"Yes, Mr. Bradshaw." I waved at the amused Beverly before turning to face the man who had become my nemesis. He was old enough to have already retired, and in my opinion, should have. He disapproved of just about everything, and we had clashed more than once during the school year.

"The testing scores in your classes were extremely high this year. Exceptionally so." He took off his wire rims and began to polish the lenses with a handkerchief. "The records show you didn't have any failing students. Not one. This is highly unusual for advanced math courses."

I blinked in surprise. I didn't consider Algebra to be advanced math, as it was a standard course. The AP calculus, trigonometry, and statistics classes better fit that category. "Why would this be a problem? Aren't we supposed to push for higher scores? You laid out a very clear goal with the new testing standard that came out last year."

He put the glasses back on his nose and adjusted the few white hairs that combed over his shiny pate. "Yes, the goal was straightforward. However, your students in particular showed the most improvement in grades."

I still didn't understand. "I don't see the problem." I guess I should have added *sir* to the end of that sentence. I didn't.

"There's no real problem, Miss Miser. However, there is some speculation as to how you achieved this level of success."

I shook my head in bafflement. My students and I worked hard this year. After-school tutoring, group study sessions, lots of weekend emails to ask and answer questions. The kids in my class were diligent in their work, and I was just as diligent in helping them. Then it dawned on me what the slimy weasel was hinting, and my back snapped ramrod straight. My fatigue disappeared, replaced by heated anger.

"I hope you are not implying anyone cheated. My students worked damn hard all year for those grades and deserved every one of them."

"Is there a possibility they got the test answers ahead of time?"

Oh no, he didn't! "Mr. Bradshaw, as per state requirements, the test booklets stayed locked in the guidance storeroom next to your office until testing day. Only the head guidance counselor and you have an access key, and everyone, *everyone,* in the main office has a line of sight to that storeroom. If you are proposing I somehow magically stole a key from you or Ms. Bunting, unlocked that closet in full view of the office staff, and somehow covered myself in Harry Potter's invisibility cloak to avoid detection from you and the entire guidance department, I can say you are sadly and badly mistaken. *Sir.*"

I'm a tall woman, and some say my height is intimidating. My sarcasm can be as well. I admit my mouth has gotten me into trouble more than once, but in this case, Mr. Bradshaw retreated. The man in front of me shrank into his bargain basement suit like a turtle. "No, no, Miss Miser. I… uh… I only wanted to compliment you on a job well done."

Yeah, right. "Thank you, Mr. Bradshaw. If there is nothing else, I'm still not feeling well and would like to go home."

"Yes, yes, by all means, yes."

Asshole! That man was a throwback to a bygone era that truly needed to be bygone. He'd made little remarks throughout the year about girls and dress code violations, female teachers acting too mannish, and the biggest one for me personally, why girls didn't need to be in higher math and science classes. It still burned me up when I overheard him say to a male colleague that girls didn't need physics to balance a grocery budget.

I got to my red Audi and paused as dizziness hit

and my stomach roiled again. *Jeez, what the hell? Maybe I should take Bevvie's advice and go see the doctor today.* I decided to go home instead of to the mall. I didn't even open the top of my car as I drove. Normally, I'd be whipping around the curves of the road leading to my place, but in deference to my funky stomach, I slowed to a sedate pace. My condo complex sat up on one of the many mountains that overlooked the city of Asheville, North Carolina. It wasn't a cheap place, and on my teacher's salary, there was no way I could have afforded the luxury real estate. My lifestyle came from a trust fund, and if I stayed careful, it would last me the rest of my life. I owned a snazzy car, high-end housing, and kept a vast wardrobe. As long as I didn't go crazy and buy a yacht, a mansion in Maui, or start wearing only haute couture, I was set.

I entered my condo and rushed to the bathroom to dry heave into the white porcelain. *Fuck, this was getting old.* My mouth tasted awful. I stood up and weakly opened the medicine cabinet to get my toothbrush and toothpaste. The box of condoms caught my eye, and my brain clicked into overdrive. Sore, sensitive breasts, bloatedness, and some irritability were all typical signs that I was gearing up for the great monthly purge. Vomiting, fatigue, and constant heartburn added something else to that glorious time.

Usually I didn't pay attention to dates and times, but I remembered my last period was during the last round of mathletes competition. I pulled up Google calendar on my phone and counted backward, my heart speeding up. Four. Five. Six weeks. Almost seven.

Oh, shit! My knees gave out, and I sat abruptly on the floor with a soft thump as the truth dawned on me. *I'm fucking pregnant!*

CHAPTER TWO

OWEN FINISHED HIS PEANUT BUTTER SANDWICH AND swallowed the last of his Coke. Break was over, and work needed to get done. Done, as in this was the last week of his contract with this construction company, and the end of it loomed in sight. They were building houses in an upscale development in Nashville, and the work had become repetitive and boring. Same four house designs repeated over and over, but he only got to work on the framing. His twin, Garrett, had finished his contract with the company and left to visit their older brother, Connor, in Asheville for a few days before heading up to New Jersey to join the rest of the brothers and their father for some independent work. Their sister lived in Bryson City but was currently out of town with her husband and their three daughters for a bike rally.

"You need to speak up more, Owen," his twin said before he departed. "You have more ideas and talent than those bozos to get stuck on framing the same damn pattern over and over again."

"It's easy work and *mood gunny*." His face turned red. "Good money."

Garrett didn't blink an eye at his brother's word reversal. "Good money but grunt work. You can make better money if you'd do more designing. That's all I'm saying."

Owen's speech problems had been around a long time and had been a lifelong embarrassment for him. During their childhood years, Garrett often finished his brother's sentences so Owen wouldn't have to deal with the teasing and ridicule of other kids at school. He started speech therapy as a very young child, but that stopped when their mother passed away. Their father, Fergus, didn't keep it up, and Owen grew from a large lumbering child who didn't speak much to a large lumbering man who still didn't speak much. Because of his quiet nature, Owen got overlooked most of the time for the finer, more complicated finish work. He had the talent to calculate spatial relationships just by looking at a project, but few recognized that gift. Instead, framing was the job he got stuck with over and over.

Owen sighed and lifted his hard hat to set it back on his head. Garrett had left, and there were only a few more days until his own contract completed.

"Owen MacAteer!"

He turned to see the project foreman coming towards him. "Need you to finish up lots four and six today. The plumbing's goin' in tomorrow mornin', and they need the final frames up."

"Tubs in?"

"Notchyet. Got back ordered. You just get the framing done. Them other guys will take care o' the rest."

Owen blinked at the man. Framing the bathroom areas didn't work if the tubs and other pieces weren't in place yet. These weren't regular standard tubs, they were the large triangular jetted ones that held four people at one time. If they weren't there to frame around, it would be next to impossible to put the units in place once they completed the interiors. He opened his mouth to point out the problem, and his brain seized up. His jaw moved up and down, but no sound came out. The squat man in front of him waited a few seconds, his eyebrows raised, then he nodded and moved away.

"Yep, don't you worry 'bout the horses, jus' load the wagon. Get them frames done. Nothin' else."

Owen pressed his dry lips together and watched silently while the man waddled away. He had a better way of making this job work, but he couldn't express it. Sometimes he stuttered if he spoke over three or four words at a time. Sometimes he reversed sounds. Sometimes he froze up and had trouble finding words at all. Frustrated, he picked up his tool belt and walked to lot four. *Not my problem if they have to tear out framing and waste a day redoing everything. I'm getting paid and I'm done.*

He paused in front of the lot and pulled out his phone. Several other workers were already in the house interior. He saw them moving through the forest of two-by-fours, adding additional wood to the frames for the future sheetrock ceiling. He tapped open the screen and sent a quick text to Connor.

Owen: Contract almost done. I should be able to leave by Friday. Be there in time for dinner. Garrett left already?

It took a few minutes, but the three little dots started bouncing.

Connor: Yes. He took off this morning. Joy is on a tear about something and Garrett needed to get up there to make her happy. I don't get what he sees in that woman. I'll get steaks for the grill. What you got lined up next for work?

Owen: Whatever Garrett and Da have booked next month. Not sure if I will take it. I'm sick to death of cutting and framing. What do you have coming up?

Connor: Got some people wanting decks built. Custom stuff around pools. A couple gazebos and pergolas. I'm getting a lot of calls about them and I need an extra pair of hands for a few weeks. You want to summer here and do something different for a while? The kids would love to see their uncle.

Owen debated for a few minutes as he read the text. Garrett had mentioned the new job was more of the same as this one. More framing for a large housing development. Cookie cutter work. He always got paid well, but the unchallenging work had lost any appeal to him, not to mention the stress of working with his father. Connor's projects would be a nice change of pace, and he wasn't under any contractual obligation.

Owen: Do I get to design or just build?

Connor: I'm getting calls for both. Pick what you want as long as the jobs get done on time.

Owen: I'll help out at least a week or two. You got a place to park my camper?

Connor: I think it will fit in the backyard once I clear the brush on the side of the woodshop. Bev won't care. She leaves all the yard work up to me. No trouble though for you to sleep in the house. We have the room.

Owen: Depends on how long I stay. Only a week, I'll take the room. More than one, I'll hook up to the house. Fair?

Connor: Great. You'll be saving me a lot of overtime. Seriously, think about sticking around for a while. I need extra help I can count on.

Owen swiped the screen closed and slipped the slim phone in his back pocket. *Four more days, then I'm building something special.* It would be nice to take a break and enjoy his nieces and nephews. Each one had a unique personality, and he loved watching them grow up. There was another person in Asheville he wouldn't mind seeing, but that dream had long since faded.

"Hey, Owen! You gonna stand around with your thumb up your ass? Get to work!"

Owen started the air compressor, and the loud chugging drowned out the foreman's voice. He rarely indulged himself in anger, as he didn't see a point in it.

Especially since in four days he would be in Asheville eating steaks with his family and starting something new. He kept his mouth shut, loaded the nail gun, and resumed work.

CHAPTER THREE

I sat in my car outside Beverly's remodeled home, inhaling huge breaths through my nose and exhaling slowly through my mouth. After I had my panic attack on Monday afternoon, I drove straight to the closest CVS for a pregnancy test. It took me about four point zero seconds to step back out of the store and drive home empty-handed. What was I thinking? The clerk was a former student of mine, and I avoided buying tampons and condoms when he was working. A pregnancy test? No way. I ended up going back home and ordering two from Amazon. The box arrived yesterday, and I took the test this morning.

The red plus sign had mocked me from the plastic wand, and I took the second one just to make sure the first one wasn't defective. *Fuck! This is real.*

Beverly's house had been two side-by-side duplexes, with her and her kids crammed into one side and Connor in the other. When they married, Connor redesigned both sides into one house with six bedrooms, a large open kitchen and den area, a game room, and a deck in the back. It was still a crowded house with four kids and two adults, but they made it work.

My hands tightened on the padded steering wheel. It had to be close to dinnertime before I made myself loosen my grip and exit my vehicle. I had told no one yet about my condition, still coming to grips with it myself. I wasn't ready to share, but I needed advice. Scratch that. I needed help.

"Hey, Auntie M!" Mattie, Beverly's youngest son, answered the door. The blue ring around his seven-year-old mouth told me he had been in the ice pops. "Watch this!" He ran through the den in his socked feet and surfed over the smooth linoleum floor. I'd seen him pull this move before, usually with a crash into a cabinet or the fridge.

"Mattie-boo, you'll make a fine surfer dude someday."

"Coolio! Mom's out back with Connor. Uncle Owen is coming tonight."

Fuck, why me? I hadn't seen Owen since last year,

when he, his twin, Garrett, and their sister, Eva, were helping with the redesign and construction of the house. I had flirted outrageously with both of them, but neither took the bait. Owen wouldn't even speak to me. The ginger-haired giant just looked at me with his greenish-blue eyes and kept silent. I asked questions, flipped my hair, laughed, pulled at my earlobe. No response from either of them. It was embarrassing.

"Oh, I'd better leave then. I don't want to get in the middle of family night. Tell your mom I'll call her later."

"You will not. Come on out back and sit your butt down. Connor's cooking steaks, and we have extra." Beverly came through the back door and pulled a bag of marinating meat from the fridge. "Abby decided this morning she wanted to be vegetarian. A few days at the beach and she is 'in love' with some boy she and Autumn met there." She used her fingers to make air quotes. "He claims to be vegetarian, therefore she *needs* to be vegetarian too."

One look at the bloody plastic bag and an unpleasant wave ran through my middle. *Jeez, not now!* I swallowed several times. "I'll be in the way."

"You've never been in the way. Besides, didn't you break up with Peter? No date night for you tonight."

"Um… yes, about a month ago."

"I think you said he works as a clerk in the courthouse archives." She pulled the steaks out and dropped them on a platter. "Tax records, births, deaths. People are just dying to work with him, eh?"

I didn't attempt to rebut her lame joke with one of my own. I was trying to deal with the wet, sloppy sound the meat made when it hit the large dish. She looked at me with concern. "You okay? You look a little green."

"The pollen is thick right now. That's all."

Mattie ran by with Jacob chasing him. Both were screaming like banshees.

"Give it back!"

"It's mine!"

"No, it's not!"

"It is too!"

Muttface, the family dog, followed, barking his head off. Bev lifted the loaded platter high in the air and let the two bodies streak past her. She was an old hand at this and didn't blink an eye. "You have other plans tonight? Clubbing at Saddle 'n' Spurs?"

Saliva filled my mouth, and I nearly choked on it. My head pounded with the noise.

"No. I'm not going clubbing anytime soon." *Probably never again.*

She put the platter down on the counter and opened the fridge to pull out a big bowl of green salad and a smaller one of potato salad. "Boys, if you're gonna fight over… whatever it is you're fighting over, I'll take it away from both of you. Go outside and take the dog with you."

"But, Mom!"

"No buts. Out."

"I need—"

"You heard me."

Mattie surfed across the kitchen floor. "Do I hafta put shoes on?"

"Might be a good idea, since Muttface leaves doggie bombs in the backyard."

"What if I stay on the deck?"

Bev pulled an aluminum-covered casserole dish from the oven. "What are the chances that will happen?"

Mattie regarded her for a moment and sprinted to find his shoes.

"No peeing off the deck either!" she called after him while pulling off the foil with a rattle. Steam rose from the bubbling mac and cheese. "I caught them last week trying to see who could squirt further. I thought Mattie would poop himself, as hard as he was straining."

Girl. I should definitely have a girl. There's no way I can handle a boy.

"I'm not eating anything but the green salad, Mom." Abby sauntered into the kitchen in a long skirt, loose T-shirt, and bare feet. A long braid hung down her back, and no makeup showed on her face. The distraction helped. Normally, she never graced anyone with her presence unless she was fully coiffed, made up, and dressed to the nines. The girl had made a one-eighty turn with this new natural hippie chick look.

Beverly pulled a spoon from a drawer and started to stir the thick pasta concoction. "Mac and cheese and the potato salad are vegetarian, aren't they?"

Abby huffed and expertly rolled her eyes. "Mom, how many times to I have to repeat myself. It's *vegan*. Not vegetarian. No animal products at all. It's inhumane."

"Says the girl who spent yesterday scarfing down cheese pizza at the pool."

"Mom! You just don't get it." Abby stomped off.

Boy. Definitely a boy.

Mattie, now clad in his sneakers, ran through the kitchen with Muttface at his heels and slammed open the back screen door. The sound exploded in my head.

"Don't break my house, you mini hooligan!"

Beverly called out, further exacerbating the war going on in my skull.

Boy. Girl. Was there another option?

The spoon made a sticky squelching noise as Beverly moved the mac and cheese around. My eyes burned as I looked at the oozing meat still on the platter in a puddle. A raw odor hit my nostrils. The sound, the sight, the smell, all of it became too much for me to handle.

Oh, shit! I covered my mouth and made a beeline for the downstairs powder room. The door was closed and locked.

"I'm busy in here! Wait your turn!" Sarah's muffled voice came from the other side.

I gagged twice and rushed for the front door. Bev's concerned voice followed me, but her words didn't register. I made it to the porch and hit a wall. Literally.

Strong arms came around me as I lost my balance. My head flew back, and I saw Owen's face swim in front of me. He said nothing, but his eyes showed concern. I should have said something, I suppose, but I didn't have time for niceties. I jerked away from him, leaned over the rail, and proceeded to embarrass the shit out of myself.

Two broad hands swept the sides of my face and gently pulled my hair out of the way. *Shit!* Owen was holding back my blonde mane while I was sick. The gesture was sweet. Still, it was humiliating that he saw me like this. Of all the people to watch me vomit up whatever I had left inside me, the last person I'd pick would be him.

"What the hell, Melanie? What's wrong?" Bev rushed out to the front porch and handed me a glass of cold water. I kept my head down as I swished and spat. My temples pounded, and I grew dizzy. *Fuck, is this what I have to look forward to for nine long-ass months?* I pressed two fingers to my forehead and closed my eyes. I needed to tell my BFF what was happening. I needed to think about my life. I needed... I needed... fuck, I needed to sit down before I fell down.

The glass slipped from my limp fingers and broke into a thousand sparkling pieces on the porch. I followed it but didn't hit the ground. Two strong arms scooped me up and cradled me against a hard chest. Passing out seemed to be my best option, so I went with that.

I DIDN'T KNOW HOW LONG I WAS OUT. IT MIGHT HAVE been a few minutes or a few hours. I woke up to the concerned faces of Bev, Sarah, and Abby. The furnishings showed I was in the guest room, lying on the bed. Bev sat at my side and was stroking my hands. Abby was standing behind Sarah, holding the younger girl against her hips. A groan burst from my mouth as the memory of my gastric explosion and who saw it came back to me. I rolled over and wanted nothing more than to hide.

"Mom, what's wrong with Melanie?" Sarah's tearful voice tugged at my heart.

"I'm not sure, sweetheart. I think I may have an idea what it is, but Melanie will tell me when she's ready."

"Is she going to die?"

"No, she's not going to die."

"Is it brain cancer?"

"No, it's not brain cancer. This isn't any kind of cancer."

"What is it?"

"Right now, it's private. I'm sure Connor has the steaks ready now. You girls go tell him Melanie is awake and feeling better. I'll come down soon. Make sure the boys eat. Abby, you take charge of cleanup. Sarah, you help her."

"I wanna stay with Melanie."

"Melanie will be down in a minute too. Just give

her some time to get her breath and drink something. Now scoot."

The two girls grumbled as they left the room, and Beverly tapped my shoulder. "Quit playing possum. The coast is clear for now. Sit up, drink this, and don't argue. I already had to break up one fight tonight. Connor wanted to call an ambulance, and Owen wanted to put you in his truck and drive you to the hospital emergency room himself. It was a crapshoot to see which one would turn green and burst through his shirt. First time I've ever seen Owen get mad at anything. I convinced them at least for now that you aren't in any immediate danger of dying."

She handed me a glass of something carbonated, and I sipped at the liquid. The bright taste of ginger ale crossed my tongue.

"You want a few crackers? I have some saltines here. I can't guarantee they aren't a little stale, but it's what I have on hand."

I drank more of the soda and waited to see if my stomach behaved. It seemed to accept the ginger ale. Damn, if this stuff kept me from hugging the porcelain bowl all fucking day, I'd go buy a case. Two. Three. Did it come in a keg? "No crackers right now. Maybe in a little while." *Fuck, when did I get so weak sounding?*

Stop this now, Mel. You're a strong woman. In control. Rough and tough.

"So how far are along are you?"

I promptly burst into tears.

"That far, eh?" Her hug made me cry even harder.

"I'mb ad leezed seven, maybe aaighd weeks I thinck." *Damnit, now my nose plugged up.* I hate crying almost as much as I hate vomiting. "I toog the test this mornding. Id'z for real. I'mb knocked up. How'joo figure it oud?"

"From the faculty meeting vomitorium and the beautiful reprise a little while ago. I put two and two together and came up with two: you and baby onboard."

I sobbed on her shoulder. She just held me and let me get it out. *God, I love my BFF!* She was my safe place.

When I got enough control over myself, I leaned back and picked up the glass again. I was sure my nose was red and my face blotchy. Bev plucked three tissues from a box on the nightstand and handed them to me. I took them and wiped myself off, attempting to preserve a tiny bit of dignity. "Seriously, what gave it away?"

She smiled. "I have a little experience with

morning sickness, as you well know. Was it food smells or noise?"

I shuddered. "Both, I think."

She nodded. "With Abby, it was meat. Beef, to be exact. The sight and smell drove me to the bathroom every time I was around it. I was constantly sick all day. Jacob had me craving sweets, but not a lot of morning sickness. Only for a week or two. Sarah was my easiest. No morning sickness at all, but I couldn't go to any football or basketball games at school, because noisy crowds got to me. Mattie's was morning sickness for three weeks and then tired, all the time. He had nothing in particular he wanted to eat, but I snacked a lot. Have you seen a doctor yet?"

I blew my nose. The wet sound bothered me, but my stomach had settled enough I didn't have to give an encore performance. "No, I've been staring at the test stick all fucking day thinking about what to do."

"I'm guessing you haven't told... um... Peter, I guess?"

The uncertainty in her tone was warranted. I'm not exactly Miss Chastity. I dated a lot of men and slept with most of them at least once. Sometimes I strung along two simultaneously. I tried to time it so that just before they genuinely got into me, I'd break it off. Commitment-phobic? Absolutely. Plays hard to get?

Definitely. Grade A bitch? Guilty at times. I let no one close enough to me to learn why. Not even Bev.

"It can only be his."

"Are you going to tell him? I think you should."

"Yeah, I will. I don't want to, but you're right, I should. I'll think of something to say."

My stomach gurgled. *Fucking thing!* It rejected everything I put in it all day, and now it wanted to be fed. *Grrr!*

Bev got up from the bed. "Come on, Mellie-Jellie. Let's go downstairs before the testosterone brigade gets more worried and decides to make an appearance. I have chicken noodle soup, crackers, and bananas. All good foods for bad stomachs. Even if it comes back up, you still need to keep drinking liquids so you don't get dehydrated. I still have the bible, and I'll just give it to you. Not much has changed in the newer editions."

I swallowed the last of the ginger ale and sucked a piece of ice into my mouth. "I have a Bible somewhere already."

"Not that Bible. The mom bible, *What to Expect When You're Expecting*. Read it this weekend, and on Monday, you'll come here for breakfast and we'll get a plan together for you. Dr. Reule is the OB-GYN I used. Terrible bedside manner, but one of the best for prenatal care. Your general practitioner may have a referral you like better. No more drinking, and stay away from smokers as much as you can."

"Yes, Mother." The word resonated in my head. *Mother. Omigod! I'm gonna be one. I'm gonna be a mother. Fuck!*

The panic must have shown, as Beverly leaned down and folded me in her embrace again. "It's gonna be fine, Mellie. You have a lotta love in this family. We're all with you one hundred percent. Now go brush your teeth, 'cause your breath is worse than Muttface's. Take a few minutes and come outside. Better now?"

I laughed and tried not to direct it at her face. "Yeah, I'll be fine. I'm not sure if I can stay, though. I think I may just go home."

"You sure you're steady enough to drive? Maybe you should sleep here tonight. I can pull out the futon in the game room for Owen, or he can use his camper. I don't think he'll mind giving up the guest room for you."

"Thanks for the offer, Bevvie, but I want to be in my own space in my own bed. Besides, the kids will ask questions, and I'm not ready to give them answers right now."

She nodded and stood up. "Come outside when

you're ready. Take your time and holler for me if you need help."

"Thanks for everything, Bevvie."

She put on a soft face and spoke with genuine conviction. "I'm happy for you, Mellie. Now go get those teeth brushed."

She left, and I shuffled into the bathroom to find my toothbrush sitting in the flowery ceramic holder. I spent enough time in this house that it made sense for me to keep one here. The strong mint flavor helped clear my head. I spat in the sink, rinsed, and spat again. My reflection looked back at me. My eyes had the beginnings of dark fatigue circles. I leaned in closer and squinted. Make that fatigue circles helped along by smeared mascara. Home sounded great. Bed sounded better.

"Fuck me," I told my glass image. "I have to tell my parents. That's gonna be a fucking circus."

I could cuss to my heart's content since the kids were outside, but I probably should start tempering that now. I didn't want my baby's first words to be "dammit" or "fuck off."

Is this how mothers think? Shit, I have a lot of work to do.

I put a dab of lotion on my finger from Bev's pump dispenser and wiped away the traces of mascara smudges. This method worked better than water and would help keep wrinkles at bay. At thirty-six, I wasn't old, but I had every intention of fighting the aging process with every weapon in my arsenal. As long as people regularly told me I didn't look my age, I thought I was winning. I left the bathroom and made my way downstairs.

Owen was there at the bottom, watching me as I carefully descended with my hand on the rail. His eagle eyes and grim face told me of his concern. I thought it sweet, but I was still embarrassed. The times a man had held back my hair while I puked numbered exactly one, and I didn't care to keep a scorecard. I smiled and bounced down the steps like I didn't just faint in his arms. I'd gotten good at faking over the years.

"Thanks for catching me. Not one of my more notable moments, eh? I'm okay now, but I think I'm gonna just go home."

"I'll drive."

Huh, this is new. "No, thanks, O-man. I can manage."

He shook his head.

"What? I'm not going home? I beg to differ."

"I'll drive." The words were soft but sounded like a command.

Tendrils of anger drifted up my spine. "You'll

drive? Yeah, you'll drive me up the wall. I'm fine. I can take care of myself."

"Not alone."

Jeez, what is with this guy? "I don't need a fucking nanny, Owen."

"What's going on?" Connor appeared, along with Beverly. I breathed a sigh of relief that the kids were still outside. I really needed to start watching my language.

"Your brother thinks he's gonna drive me home."

"Not a bad idea. You still look a bit shaky," Bev chimed in while handing me a plastic grocery bag. "Here's a can of soup, a sleeve of crackers, and some bananas. Put a few crackers on your nightstand and grab them in the morning before you get out of bed. That will help with mor—ah… if your stomach's still bad tomorrow."

So she hadn't told Connor yet. That was a relief. I love my BFF for not telling on me, although I didn't need to keep this a secret. Pregnancy becomes rather hard to hide, eventually.

"Either he drives you or I drive you." Connor's declaration was both irritating and endearing. I liked that he was concerned about me, but I was used to being on my own.

"I can handle it. I've been sick by myself before and lived to tell the tale."

"You're not by yourself anymore. You're a capable woman, but *I'd* feel better if you'd let one of them take you home." Bevvie's logic kicked in and defused my temper before it flared.

"Owen, then." *At least he won't ask a lot of questions.*

The giant man grunted once, plucked the keys from my hand, turned, and walked out the door.

Well, fuck, I guess I'm leaving now.

I hugged Bevvie. "Thank you for the soup and stuff. You're my favorite person, even if you do get bossy."

"And you're my favorite PITA."

I shot her the bird by scratching the side of my nose with my middle finger before I followed Owen's retreating back.

"I guess you'll take an Uber back here?" I said to the behemoth next to me. He had to be over six feet tall. I was five foot eight, and he towered over me. Broad back, broad shoulders, short buzz cut, close beard. Bear. The man was a bear.

"Yeah."

He may be a bear, but definitely not the cuddly type. More like a grizzly in a bad mood. I supposed being folded up in a sports car wouldn't make anyone his size very happy.

The drive to my condo took the longest fifteen minutes of my life. The only words spoken came from me as I gave directions. By the time we pulled up to my place, I was so ready for him to be gone and me to be on my couch with a bottle of wine and Netflix. Scratch that. No more wine. Chicken soup and bananas. Uh, yummy? Not!

The condos were in sets of four to a building, and mine was the one on the upper left. It took two sets of stairs to get to my unit. The architect had designed these condos in accordance with the topography of the mountainside. They were built at odd angles to each other and the driveways were a bitch to get into. I loved the beautiful view of the city, but someday my knees would ask why I couldn't have picked a home that had an elevator.

"I'm up there." I pointed to my cozy condo. "You want to come up while you call an Uber?"

I didn't particularly want Owen in my space, but it was the right thing to do. He did drive me home, even if he didn't want to talk to me.

He grunted, which seemed to be his major form of communication. Lovely.

Truthfully, it was good to have him there. I worked out at the complex gym regularly and had a Stairmaster machine in my bedroom that I actually used for daily cardio workouts and not as a handy clothes hanger. Normally, climbing these stairs didn't faze me at all, but after a day of fasting and vomiting, the task became laborious. By the time I got to my front door, I was huffing and puffing and slightly dizzy. Owen carried the bag of soup and crackers, as I couldn't even lift that bit of weight. He probably would have carried me if I'd let him. He still had my keys and opened the door with a deft twist.

I flopped on my overstuffed plush sofa, breathing hard and watching the room spin. "Do what you gotta do, O-man. I need a minute." I leaned my head back and closed my eyes with every intention of just resting. Sometime later, I woke up to Owen's concerned face. He leaned over me with one hand on my shoulder and a tray of soup, crackers, and a banana in the other. It looked like he'd made himself at home in my kitchen.

Anyone else going through my stuff uninvited would have pissed me off. For some reason, Owen's exploration didn't bother me. Probably because he was trying to feed and take care of me. I could count on one hand the number of people who did this in my life and still have fingers leftover.

I sat up and took the tray from his hand and set it

on the glass coffee table in front of me. "Thank you. That's so sweet."

He nodded and lowered his wide frame into one of the low-slung matching chairs. I flashed a picture in my head of him settling into an oversized recliner, picking up the TV remote, and relaxing after a long and hard day's work. Very domestic.

Instead of the remote, he opened his phone and began typing. How did those gigantic thumbs manage a tiny digital keyboard? I shook my head and grabbed the remote to click on the TV. A mindless sitcom appeared. Not one I watched, but I let it play simply to have some noise in the room. Owen kept at his phone, while I slowly ate the soup and crackers. My stomach did a happy dance now that I was putting something in it that would stay down.

I glanced at the man ensconced in my chair. Even though his knees were almost at his chin, he seemed comfortable. He concentrated on his phone, and I guessed he was texting someone. I realized I knew very little about the man other than that he was Connor's brother, had a twin named Garrett, two other brothers, a sister, and worked construction. That was it.

Time to do a little recon. "So, Owen. How long are you in town?"

His focus stayed on the screen, and he shrugged.

"Do you like the city?"

He put out a hand and waggled it in a so-so gesture.

"Think you'll stay and find work?"

Another shrug. *Fuck me, I figured out a long time ago he doesn't talk much, but this is ridiculous.*

"Is it just me you don't want to talk to, or are you naturally shy?"

He raised his eyes to meet mine. Damn, he was a good-looking man.

"Shy." The low rumble of his voice spread from my ears to my toes in a delicious thrill.

I couldn't help myself. I burst into laughter. "Good one. At least you're honest."

He rewarded me with a big grin. "Better?"

I thought he was asking if I felt better. "I'm good. You don't have to babysit me anymore. Did you call that Uber yet?"

"Cancelled."

"Why?"

"Sick."

"You're not feeling well?"

"You."

"You planning on spending the night?"

"Yes."

"Not happening, big guy."

"Sick."

He was either the most stubborn man in the world or the most obtuse. If I flipped a coin, either side would be right. "I'm not that sick."

"Worried."

"I'm not worried at all."

"Me."

I got it. He was worried about me. I could've burred up and gotten angry, but his face showed genuine concern, and I had to admit, it was nice. "That's really sweet, and I'm flattered that you're anxious about me, but I can promise you, I'm fine. I've eaten the soup. I'm drinking the water, and I'm not running to the bathroom in *vomitus delirium*. Don't get me wrong, but right now, I need my own company more than I need yours, okay? My plans are to crash in the next ten minutes with a good book."

No reaction from him other than to hand me his cell phone. "Number. Text if t-trouble."

I laughed. Most of the time when a guy asks me for my number, he has some cheesy line to go with it. Owen wasn't asking me on a date or flirting. He simply wanted my number so he could check on me. "Okay, big guy." I typed in my number and handed him the phone back.

He looked at the name I listed, chuffed, and grinned. *My Favorite Girl.*

I grinned back. "You know it's true. Now get that Uber back and get outta here so I can go pee and get to bed."

OWEN LAY BACK ON THE CREAKING BED AND PUT HIS hands behind his head. Beverly hadn't waited for him to return before going to bed. She had kept a plate warm for him since he hadn't eaten yet, and he made a mental note to thank her for the consideration. He couldn't ask for a better sister-in-law. Connor had stayed up long enough for Owen to get in the door and eat. He kept talking to a minimum, as both of them were tired and ready to crash for the night. No mention of Melanie's condition came up, but Owen already knew. He stared at the ceiling and replayed the conversation.

"I'm about six or eight weeks, I think. I took the test this morning. It's for real. I'm knocked up."

He hadn't meant to overhear something private. He had been outside the door, worried about Melanie's state, and when he heard her crying, he'd had to stop himself from running in and doing... doing... what?

Owen flopped to his side, and the bed shuddered. The queen-sized frame barely fit him.

Yeah, what could he do? Stand over her staring? His stuttering speech kept him from talking much. Part of it was psychological and came and went depending on whom he was conversing with at the time. He spoke longer without tripping over his words to people he knew well, but these were very few beyond his family. It was also something that embarrassed him to the point he'd rather not talk at all. One- and two-word sentences were usually safe. Three pushed it. Four words… well… that was when something when wrong.

My favorite girl. If only she realized the truth of it. *Beautiful.* The word rolled through his thoughts. *Smart. Funny. Sad. Hurting.* And the big one: *Pregnant.*

A light scent of something spicy and exotic wafted up from his pillow, and he inhaled deep. Melanie's perfume. Jesus, Mary, and Joseph, she smelled so good. He admitted he had a crush on his sister-in-law's best friend and also that he could do nothing about it. Melanie had never noticed him in that way, and he had resolved that she never would. The closest he would ever get to touching his dream had been when he lifted her limp form in his arms. The fear for her safety still sat in his heart, and he wished like hell she had let him stay. He wanted to take care of her, even if only for one night.

What was the baby's father's name? Peter? Owen knew Melanie dated a lot of men, and this Peter fellow was another man in a long line of them leading to her bedroom door. Did it bother him that she changed partners so often? Maybe a little. She was an independent woman and had the right to make her own decisions, but his concern centered more on why she never settled on just one man. When she had insisted on being by herself tonight, he hadn't liked it, but he'd backed off. Respect was something he understood and lived by. She deserved it as much as anyone else.

Hmph. This Peter fellow was so damned lucky. *If I had a shot at being Melanie's man, I'd fight tooth and nail to stay there.*

The long day took its toll, and Owen drifted off to sleep with his nose buried in his pillow, breathing in the scent of unreachable dreams.

CHAPTER FOUR

I TURNED THE COLORFUL COFFEE CUP ON THE TABLE and glanced at my watch. Eleven fifteen, and he still hadn't called, texted, or shown up. His constant tardiness was one of several reasons I broke up with Peter. He had a law degree, but instead of practicing in a firm, he chose to work in the courthouse basement archives, pushing and filing a mountain of papers. The job paid well, but it was boring. Totally mind-numbing boring.

Peter agreed to meet me at the Double D coffee shop. The converted double-decker bus had the coffee shop in the lower level, tables in the upper, and a few patio sets. It was as eclectic and fun as the downtown part of the city. Plus the owners treated coffee making as an art form.

I sat outside at a tall bistro table and sipped at the cup of decaf. Normally, I regarded coffee without caffeine as a sin, but I didn't know if that would be a problem for the baby. Already, I had given up my nightly glass of wine. Weekend bottle binges were out of the question.

"Sorry I'm late." Peter's tall, lanky form bent down and kissed me on the cheek. "I'll go order something and be right back."

I only smiled and nodded. Damn, he looked good. Jacket and tie, styled short dark hair, crisp blue eyes, runner's build. My physical attraction to him hadn't gone away. I picked up my napkin and began tearing it into little pieces.

He returned and sat across from me. "I'm so glad you called me, Mel. I've truly missed you."

Truthfully, I kinda missed him too. Even if he did have the most mundane job in the world, he was a sweet, smart man and always treated me with respect. In bed, he was not very adventurous, but still generous enough with his attention that I usually came. He maintained a beautiful and precision-sculpted body by visiting an upscale private gym daily before work or running as weather permitted. Why did I break up with him again?

It didn't take me long to remember.

It took him three attempts to settle his chair the way he wanted it and several minutes to prepare his coffee and Danish. Three packs of sugar and three creamers stirred three times clockwise and then three times counterclockwise. Three taps of the wooden stirrer on the edge of the cup. Three sips, and he was ready to hear me.

He took a bite of his Danish, chewed three times, and swallowed before speaking. "I wasn't expecting to hear from you again. You made it clear you weren't ready for a long-term relationship." He wiped his fingers of the sticky sugar and took my hand in both of his across the table. "Dare I hope you've changed your mind about us? We run in the same circles with the same class of people. We make a great couple. I care for you so much, Melanie. I'd do anything for you to take me back into your life."

Fuck, I have to do this! I'd rehearsed my speech several times over the last few days and had my words down pat. Now that I was facing the task of telling Peter he would be a father, my tongue stuck to the roof of my dry mouth. My stomach spun and threatened, but I'd become an expert with morning sickness. Make that all-day sickness.

"Peter, I have to tell you something." I hesitated. The hope in his eyes was so obvious. He thought we were getting back together, and I was about to burst his bubble. "Fuck, this is hard."

"Just tell me, darling." His voice cajoled softly and tenderly.

Oh, God, someone shoot me. Please! "I'm pregnant."

A sudden bath of ice water dumped on his head couldn't have frozen him any faster. He reared back in the chair, his face going slack. The tone of his voice changed from pretty fluff to diamond hard. "Say again?"

"I'm pregnant. I thought you should know."

"So you think it's mine?"

I wasn't expecting that. "Uh, yeah. Who else's could it be?"

He let go of my hand and leaned back, taking three more sips of his drink. "Well, you don't lead a celibate lifestyle, and your commitment phobia is legendary."

Seriously? So much for the sweet boyfriend, pining away because he cares about me so much. My eyes narrowed. "Exactly what are you implying?"

"You've never been committed to one man long-term, nor have you wasted time mourning a broken heart."

"What the fuck are you talking about?"

He took three more sips and another bite of the flaky pastry. "Oh, come on, Melanie. Everyone in the city knows you go through men like water. Couple of weeks, no more than a month of hard banging, and you're done. Hell, you fucked two other men at my gym before dating me."

Crumbs fell from his mouth to land on his blazer. He made a half-hearted attempt to brush them away. "One more week with you, and I would have won. There's a betting pool going at the gym to see who lasts the longest. The pot is up to seventeen hundred dollars now. Besides, we used condoms every time we fucked, since you wouldn't take the pill."

I was taken aback by his reaction to my news and the sudden one-eighty from hopeful lover to asshole ex. I guess I had expected him to be the kind, loving man I remembered. *Betting pool? Longest?* My spine stiffened, and angry heat infused my body. "I told you I can't take the pill or any other hormonal birth control. It messes me up too much. Do you remember we thought the condom might have broken once?"

"Yeah, once. Only once. And it was just a little tear."

"That's all it takes."

He sighed and continued his ritual of three sips per one Danish bite. "So what are you going to do about it?"

I ignored the *you* instead of *we*. "I have an appointment with a doctor this afternoon."

He nodded. "It's for the best. Neither of us wants to be parents."

It didn't take a genius to figure out what he was assuming. I realized the thought had not even occurred to me. It took me zero-point-zero seconds to dismiss it. I'd always been pro-choice and still was, but for the last five days, I'd done a lot of thinking and planning. I wanted this baby.

"Not that kind of appointment."

He frowned. "Adoption?"

Now I was getting irritated. *Must be the hormones, right?* "No, I'm keeping the baby."

His faced twisted up, and he banged his coffee cup down on the table hard enough to knock over the snowy-white mountain of paper bits I'd built. "Is this some joke? You? A mother?"

Forget irritated. I was mad. Red-hot angry mad. "Yes, me. A mother. What's wrong with that?"

"Everything. You like to drink. You go out to bars and clubs like some people go to church. You sleep around. A lot. You cuss like a sailor. None of that says mother material."

How dare he be so fucking judgmental? "So when a man drinks, goes out clubbing, and sleeps with a lot of different women, he's a fucking rock star. His friends congratulate him on winning *longevity* betting pools.

When a woman does it, she's a slut. Double standard much?"

He shrugged. "It's the way it is, and you can't possibly need money from me either."

"What the fuck do you mean now?"

He threw the last of the Danish into his mouth and chomped on it. No careful threes this time. "You know exactly what I mean. Your family has a shit ton of money, and you get a monthly cut of it. In fact, you'll be rich the rest of your life and not have to lift a goddamned finger. You were born with a fucking silver spoon in your mouth, and you're still sucking on it. If this is your ploy to get child support from me, get ready to fight, baby. You have to prove I'm the father, and I can drag this out until that kid graduates college."

Oh, no. I'm so done with this!

I stood up and threw my cold coffee at his face. "I don't want a goddamned thing from you, asshole! This is *my* kid, and I'd rather raise him alone than deal with your fucking lame ass."

He spluttered, and the chair screeched as he pushed back. His knees knocked into the edge of the table and raised it a few inches, and the noise caught the attention of several passers-by.

"Bitch!" His yell was to my back, as I'd already

turned and walked away. Bitch was right. It stood for Being-In-Total-Control-of-Herself. I'd wear the title proudly.

My rage kept me going until I got to my car, started it, and drove away. Only then did I let the tears roll down my cheeks.

"Fuck that asshole!" The clock on my dashboard said I had an hour before my appointment, and I wasted time and gas driving in circles around the city. I had expected the conversation with Peter to go differently and longer. His anger shocked me, as I thought he would try to convince me to stay with him for the baby's sake, or perhaps want to coparent with me. I never dreamed he would attack me as he did. His words repeated on a loop in my head while I drove around on autopilot.

"Is this some joke? You? A mother?"

"You like to drink. You go out to bars and clubs like some people go to church. You sleep around. You cuss like a sailor. None of that says mother material."

"You were born with a fucking silver spoon in your mouth, and you're still sucking on it."

My hands clenched the steering wheel. Yes, I liked to go out. I was single. What else was I going to do? Stay home and knit a closet full of blankets and scarves while waiting for the Saturday night HBO movie feature? A fucking betting pool? How many men had betting pools on how long *they* lasted in a relationship? Hurt, frustration, and anger all rolled into a big iron ball and sat in my gut. The silver spoon remark bugged me the most. I might have come from money and had a lot in my bank account, but dammit, I still worked like everyone else in the world. So what if my money paid for college without taking out massive school loans? I didn't go to an uber-fancy private high school or Ivy League college. I graduated with honors from a state university, and I earned my degrees with hours of studying and classes. Teaching was a calling, not a hobby to fill a rich girl's time. I worked hard every fucking day for my students and spent huge amounts of time tutoring and coaching. I cared about my students with a passion.

Fuck, I wanted to call Bevvie so bad. I'd do that later after this appointment. Thank God I had one person in the world that didn't judge me. Make that six, as her kids and Connor didn't either. Owen's name popped into my mind. He'd carried me to the guest bedroom, driven me home, made sure I ate, and argued about leaving me alone. I took a big breath and let it go along with some of the anxiety roiling in my gut as I added another tick on my side.

CHAPTER FIVE

THE HOUR WAS UP, AND I DASHED AWAY MY TEARS AS I drove into the parking lot of the OB-GYN. I decided to try my BFF's recommendation, since her guy was in our insurance network and delivered all of her kids. The doctor's office was clean and cool with a nice grayish blue décor in the waiting room. A TV mounted on one wall played some random talk show with a host spouting about recipes using chickpeas. I sat in a row of chairs and filled out a clipboard full of medical forms.

Across from me sat two women with huge stomachs who looked like they were ready to pop. I couldn't help but hear their loud conversation.

"I gained ninety-five pounds with ma first one an'

seventy-five with ma second. This is ma third an' the doctor don't want me gainin' nothin' at all."

"This is my first, and I haven't gained a lot, but my ankles have swelled up bigger than my calves. I have to wear flip-flops all the time 'cause I cain't wear no shoes."

Oh jeez, is this what I'm in for? I kept my head down and marked the bubbles on the form. Damn, these questions got extremely personal. Thank God for HIPPA privacy rules!

"It's easier the second time round. The first one done stretched me all out so's I had no trouble at all pushin' out ma next one. Took no time at all. Only a couple hours in labor an' done. Almost had her in the truck on the way to the hospital. I reckon this'n gonna come fast too. He's been wrestling against ma bladder somethin' fierce. I gotta pee all the time even when I just went."

Please stop talking! I wished my ears came with switches so I could turn them off. Or at least mute. This was getting a little TMI-ish.

"The doctor said I might have to have a C-section. I hear when they open you up, they put all your guts in big bowls while they get the baby out. Is that true?"

"I don' know 'bout that, but I kinda wisht I had C-sections. Both a mine have been natural. Ma first was nine pounds an' ma second was eleven. Let me tell you, I got tore up good. Doctor had to stitch me up stern to stem on that one."

God, please make them stop talking! My gorge rose. I'd read about the episiotomy cut, tearing, stitches… Fuck me, I wanted to run screaming from the office.

"Miss Miser? You can come on back."

No, I'm so not ready for this! "Thank you."

I got up on shaky knees and wobbled after the squat older nurse. Her wide hips swayed with every step as she walked back to the labyrinth of examination rooms.

"Step on the scale, please."

To my surprise, the scale showed a weight loss. I was six pounds lighter than my normal one hundred forty-seven. At five foot eight, I was right in the middle of what normal should be for my height and weight. "The book said I would gain weight."

"It's not unusual for you to lose a little in the beginning. Don't worry, you'll gain it back."

"That woman out there in the lobby said she gained ninety-five pounds with her first pregnancy."

The nurse made a *tching* noise and gave me a wry look. "Yeah, not all of that was baby. She put on nearly a hundred pounds and had a nine pounder. I'm sure you can do the math. She'll sit out there and tell everyone she's an expert in child birthing and rearing, when she and everyone else knows each pregnancy is different. Just eat right, no alcohol or smoking, drink lots of water, lighten up on caffeine, and take your prenatal vitamins. Rule of thumb is around a twenty-five-pound gain, give or take."

Babies are complicated. I kept my mouth shut while she took my blood pressure, temperature, and asked all the triage questions I just answered on the forms. *Redundant much?*

She left me alone with instructions for me to strip naked and put on the ugly hospital gown, open to the front. "The doctor will give you a full examination. That include belly, breasts, abdomen, and pelvic."

Shit's getting real. I could still get off the table, get dressed, and run. I didn't know what good it would do, but I had that option, right?

As I was contemplating the benefits of going home to crawl in bed and ignore the world, Dr. Reule knocked on the door and entered. Damn, how close to retirement was this guy? His thin, slightly stooped form and shuffling gait didn't inspire a lot of confidence, but Bevvie trusted the man. The nurse followed him and pulled out the sock-covered stirrups.

He picked up the clipboard full of notes and squinted at it while his reading glasses stayed perched on his head. "Good afternoon, Miss Miser. How many times a day do you move your bowels?"

Bev warned me about his bedside manner. I grinned and acted cheeky to lighten my mood. Or maybe hide my fear. "Gee, doc. I usually get a few dinners and a bottle or two of wine before I share that kind of personal knowledge."

By the confused look on his face, my joke fell flat. I didn't try again and kept my comments to myself.

The next half hour was the most intimate and thorough doctor's examination I'd ever had. There wasn't a place on my body that didn't get poked, prodded, touched, and measured. I had to joke with myself as I answered the questions he asked and the nurse typed the information on a portable computer cart.

"Do you have regular periods?"

"Yes." *But only at the end of sentences.*

"Hemorrhoids?"

"No." *Not counting my pain-in-the-ass boss at school.*

"Any history of diabetes in the family?"

"Not that I'm aware." *My family isn't very sweet.*

If I didn't find any humor in something, I would melt into a big emotional ball of tears like the Wicked Witch of the West. *What the fuck am I doing? A mom? Who in the hell do I think I am? I can't do this. Bevvie is the mom. She's great at it. How am I supposed to measure up when everything in my fucking life is shit?*

"Hmmm. Seven weeks or so? Might be a little soon, but let's see if we can hear it." The nurse handed him a wand-looking thing while the doctor spread a wet, clear gel on my stomach.

"Hear what?"

"The heartbeat."

Heartbeat? There's a heartbeat already?

He pressed the wand into my lower abdomen and slid it around. The room became quiet except for a soft *quooh-quooh-quooh.* "There it is. Strong and steady. Right now the fetus is about the size of an egg. We'll set up an ultrasound in a few weeks."

His voice faded away, and my whirling thoughts stilled. The only sound I focused on was the heartbeat of my child.

My child!

In less than nine months, I would have another person in my life. One who would totally depend on me. One who would stay with me all day, every day. One I would be responsible to teach, nurture, and shape into an adult. One who would love me without condition. One who would never abandon me. Fuck, I'm going to be a mother!

Quooh-quooh-quooh.

Tears filled my eyes as I listened to the pulse of my new future. *Fuck, when did I get to be such a fucking crybaby?* I dashed them away with a flick of my fingers and nodded at whatever the doctor said.

"You okay, hon?" The nurse helped me up after the man wandered out of the room.

"Yes, I'm fine. I'm just a little… I'm…" *God, where are my words?*

She patted my arm in a show of empathy. I was sure she had seen and heard it all working here. "Overwhelmed?"

I looked her square in the eye and made a statement that rarely came from my mouth. "I think I'm happy."

OWEN RAISED HIS EYES TO THE THICK GRAY CLOUDS overhead. The summer humidity and falling temperatures of twilight meant an evening rain shower, and he'd timed it to finish the day's work by when the first drop hit.

The owner picked out the octagonal design with built-in benches on the railings. Owen had showed him a different flooring pattern, where the slats were cut and laid in a Celtic knot, made even more noticeable by a different color stain. The time to complete the project had increased, but so did the pay.

Owen picked up a two-by-six board and glanced at the spot where the next piece would go. His chop saw started with the flick of a switch. He lowered his safety glasses before lining up the board and bringing the spinning blade down. The wood barely hissed as the saw cut clean through in one push. Owen took the fitted slat and slipped it into the open track. Perfect. Owen anchored it in with several deck nails and stood up to look at the finished flooring. Benches would go in tomorrow as long as the rain kept to the evenings and didn't bleed over into the days.

"Hey there, Owen." A man dressed in a blazer and tie walked toward him from the driveway. "I just got home from work. This looks amazing."

The man, Jerry Harris, worked as a manager at a large car dealership. His pudgy stomach and hanging chin looked like he spent more time behind an office desk than walking the lot. "You've been at this all day I see. Very nice, very nice. When do you think you will finish?"

"Three days."

"Wonderful. Randy Steagall is our district manager, and he wants you to see about building him something on his back porch. I think he wants an extension and then a screened-in part. Mind if I give him your number?"

Owen nodded his go ahead but stayed quiet.

"Excellent. I appreciate the fast turnaround. The last guy I hired to work on the house took three weeks to put on a roof. Three weeks! He gave me every excuse in the book. Back strains, sprained toes, something about license plates and his car getting impounded by mistake, girlfriend and wife problems at the same time, the dog getting sick and needing emergency surgery. I get that life happens, but every other day it seemed he had something happen that kept him from finishing the work. After he finally got done, I found out he doesn't even have a dog and his domestic problems stemmed from him trying to meet other women on one of those singles meeting sites. Nice to find someone that has some integrity."

"Thanks." Owen started coiling the drop lines from the power tools. It was a pain in the ass to put them away and load the truck every night by himself, but it was better than taking chances of them getting ruined by rain or stolen, or even worse, an accident from the man's kids playing with the equipment when he wasn't there.

Jerry shifted from foot to foot in agitation. "Um, say, Owen, the wife wants me to find out if you'd be interested in meeting her sister. She just got her final divorce papers and is planning on moving here in a month or two."

Owen lifted his rip saw and put it in the case along with his drill and power driver. "No time to date."

"Bertie is a lot of fun now that she's in the land of the living again. She and Karl were pretty stagnant as a couple. She's younger than Jodie and nice to look at and a hard worker like you. You really should meet her. At least just once. She's gonna need friends more than anything else, and she's a real hoot to be around."

Owen flipped a tarp over the remaining lumber to keep it dry overnight. He'd already covered the semi-finished deck railings. "Not now."

Jerry didn't give up. He put on his best salesman smile. "Ah, come on, Owen. You got time to think about it. Just for one date, and it's far enough in the future, you'll change your mind. You can do the dinner thing or the movie thing, and that's it. My wife will be ecstatic and stop hounding me about setting up her sister. Besides, Bertie has this big plan to open a bed-and-breakfast, and the places she is looking at need some serious renovations. You can think of the date as more of a business meeting, yeah?"

Owen opened his mouth to protest again, and nothing came out. The words just didn't happen, and

Jerry took that as a sign of acquiescence. "Great, I'll tell Jodie tonight and get her off my ass for a change. Fantastic, man. Really 'preciate you."

The man smiled huge and turned to leave. He whirled back with a finger in the air. "Oh, yeah. One more thing. Jodie wants you to build her a she shed kinda thing in the basement. The unfinished part. I'm not sure what a she shed is, but whatever my sweetie wants, she gets. Know what I mean?"

He laughed and sauntered in the house, leaving Owen on the half-finished deck with his mouth still open.

CHAPTER SIX

"Mellie-Jellie, what's up? You busy today? I'm headed to the mall with Abby and her posse. Meet me at Starbucks? Please?"

There rang a slight note of desperation in Bevvie's voice. It had the message of please-rescue-me-from-being-alone-with-a-bunch-of-teenage-girls-in-mall-mode. "I've already had my real coffee quota for the day. Starbucks decaf is a real thing, right?"

"Yes, Starbucks decaf exists, and you can handle it. I'll buy if you come save me."

Who could resist an invitation like that?

I headed to my second home, Asheville Mall. As a kid and then a teenager, I spent entire Saturdays here, shopping, examining the kiosks, eating junk food, and sometimes just sitting in the food court reading books. My home away from home, and I liked it a lot better. Not much had changed over the years, as kids still considered this the place to hang out and be seen. Groups of teenage girls and boys circled the stores, eyeing each other as much as the store items. I spotted Abby and her friends through the window of Old Navy. Abby treated clothes shopping like I did, as an Olympic event. Bevvie treated it like a torturous chore. She used to get a lot of her clothes from Goodwill because of money issues. She didn't have to now, but she still didn't get the finesse of modern style.

Bevvie sat at one table just inside the coffee shop and waved when I entered. She already had a cup for me plus a chocolate brownie. I loved my BFF!

She sipped at the frothy latte. "Abby is in Old Navy looking at jeans. I expect I'll have to send a search party if she goes more than an hour in there."

I smiled. "You don't understand the complexities of jeans shopping. There's skinny, high rise, low rise, straight leg, boot cut, relaxed fit…."

She stuck her fingers in her ears and recited, "La-la-la-la."

My laugh came out, and with that, the rest of my tension. "Where are the other kids?"

"Connor has them at the pool. We drew straws to

see which one of us got Abby and the girls or swimming. I lost."

I laughed as I broke off a part of the brownie and stuffed it into my mouth. Her mouth grew pensive. "Any news about Peter?"

I shook my head and swallowed. "That ship has sailed so far, it's fallen off the edge of flat earth. He's not interested and plans on signing any paternal rights away as soon as possible."

"I'm sorry, Mellie-Jellie."

I waved a hand as I gulped at the coffee. Decaf? Not too bad. "I don't need that shit to deal with, anyway. I'm better off on my own than trying to coparent with an asshole like him."

Bevvie picked her plastic stirring stick to bend and twist it in her fingers. "I'm still sorry you had to go through that meeting with him, but, you know, we are at the mall. I'm not the expert on the intricacies of teenage fashion, but I'm very familiar with maternity clothes. If you're game, we can go look at mommy and baby stuff."

I hadn't thought about that yet. The upcoming changes meant a whole new wardrobe. "Bevvie-Levvie, you are my hero. My credit card balance is currently at zero. Time to load it up. Let's go."

I never imagined in my wildest dreams there would

be such a plethora of stylish clothes for pregnant women. I always thought maternal wear was comprised of tent-like shirts and stretchy yoga pants. I was wrong. Skirts, jackets, pants, dresses, lots of clothes designed with growing bellies in mind. I bought a pile of new stuff including some T-shirts with cute sayings like Baby on Board and Under Construction with an arrow pointing to my belly button. Even though my condition didn't show yet, it didn't hurt to be prepared, right?

The baby clothes were even cuter. Yellow floral gowns, green striped onesies, zip-up fuzzy pajamas with feet, tiny socks with lacy frills, pink bows, blue baseball shirts…. With this many options, my kid would be the best-dressed newborn ever. This was a whole new world of shopping. Time to give my Amazon Prime account a serious workout.

Bevvie picked up a doll-sized pink shirt that said Spoiled Princess on the front. "Which do you want? Boy or girl?"

I lifted and displayed a yellow onesie with pink bows all over the butt. "I'm not sure I care as long as it's healthy. Is it better to find out ahead of time?"

Bev folded the shirt and picked up another that declared Ain't no Auntie Like Mine. "It helps for showers and things like that. Some people will want to do the pink girly girl stuff or the sporty blue boy stuff. You might want something more neutral for your nursery. I had Disney for all my kids. What better way to go than the happiest place on earth?"

I thumbed through a pile of boys' outfits on the same table. One sported camouflage and said Mama's New Man on the front. *So cute! Wait? Nursery?* I dropped the shirt back on the table. My condo only had one bedroom. It was huge, but still only one. Where in the hell did I put a crib? Did I need a changing table? I looked at the other baby items staring at me from the shelves. Rocking slider chair. Baby bathtub. Stroller. Bassinet. Swing. Bouncer. Something called a diaper genie. Toys. A box to put the toys. Where did I put this stuff and all the other paraphernalia that came with a baby?

Fuck me, I had to move.

Bev noticed the expression of alarm on my face. "You don't have to decide everything today, sweetie. You do have time."

Yes, I have time. Not a lot, but enough if I'm careful and don't put off planning. "I'm good, Bevvie. I just realized my place won't cut it. I'm gonna have to look for a bigger condo, or better yet, a house."

Her brow wrinkled as both eyebrows rose. "A

house is a lot of upkeep for one person. I have first-hand knowledge about that."

Visions of swing sets, plastic pools, and running through puddles in the backyard after a rainstorm swam through my head. A real Christmas tree with homemade macaroni decorations. Linoleum on the kitchen floor, perfect to surf across in sock feet. I made up my mind. "A house. I want a house. It's not like I can't afford it. My place is nice, but it's only that. A place. I need something I can make into a home. A real one like yours. I like my condo, but actually, I feel at home when I'm over hanging with the kids at your house."

Bev's eyes softened, and her mouth curled upward. Of all the people in the world, she knew me the best. We bonded as freshman teachers years ago. When she looked at me, she didn't see a rich bitch with her nose in the air. She saw a fellow teaching crusader whose goal was to develop young minds and enrich their lives. One night of drunken confessions, I opened up and talked to her about my life and my family. Money doesn't mean happiness. Her experiences with her ex-husband proved that, and stories of my childhood years sealed it.

"There's lots of houses in my neighborhood for sale, but every one of them is a fixer-upper. If you want to look at them, I'm sure Connor and Owen can help you, but I expect you'd rather get something move-in ready."

"Owen's still here?"

"Yeah, and it looks like he may stick around for a while. Connor took him to help with a deck build this week and let Owen do the designing. He must be pretty good, 'cause the homeowner's neighbors saw it and wanted one. You've seen those big domino sculptures, right? You knock over just one and that leads to a bazillion more falling. That's what's been happening with these renovation jobs. Connor booked two more after this new one and has consultations on four more. Owen is staying to do those jobs and maybe longer. If this keeps up, they'll have work all summer. Connor plans on letting Owen do the majority of designing and building. Supervision too if there needs to be a work crew hired. He really needs to get back to his woodshop and get the backorders filled."

I knew about Connor's custom furniture business. He had a workshop in the back of their house that he recently expanded. I peeked inside once while he worked. Custom tables, boxes, beds, dressers, all in various stages of completion and with more orders coming.

"Owen doesn't seem the type to lead a work crew.

He's rather quiet."

"He does most of the work himself, and yeah, he doesn't say much, but his designs are brilliant. You should go by the one he's working on now and take a look."

"Maybe I will."

I didn't quite know what to think about the news that Owen would be sticking around for a while. There was something disturbing about him. Not creepy or scary—I didn't feel unsafe around him. Quite the contrary, I was more comfortable around him than my own family, but there was still something about him that drew my focus more and more. Perhaps we bonded when he held my hair back for me while I vomited my guts out at Bev's. Not many people could say they had that dubious honor.

Not something I needed to think about now. Back to the house idea. At least three, perhaps four bedrooms. A yard. I need a yard with a fence for safety and in case I wanted to get a dog for my kid. A patio for cute patio furniture. Maybe some of Connor's stuff. I'd better make an order now if I expected my own set before next summer. Shit, how long did it take to buy a house?

I slapped the last of the clothes over as my thoughts kept circling. I had to call the family lawyer about my trust, then a real estate agent, check bank qualifications. Fuck, I was still a teacher with a shit salary. I needed to just buy a house outright and skip the mortgage. Was there a tax advantage? Damn, I'd have a dependent from now on.

The beginnings of a headache bloomed in my left temple as the ideas and thoughts played through my head like a merry-go-round.

Bevvie took pity on me. "You don't have to solve every problem now, Mellie. Tell you what. Come to dinner at my place tonight, and we'll get a plan together along with a timeline. I know that will keep you a lot calmer, having something outlined and on paper, right?"

My BFF was the biggest godsend. The difference between her support and the attitude of my family had no comparison. The buzz of tears started in my sinuses. Fuck, I was getting to be a weepy Wendy! "Thanks, Bevvie. You mean the world to me."

Her face softened. "Back atcha. Now what do you think of this?" She held up a long-sleeved T-shirt that read You're Kickin' me, Smalls.

Both of us laughed. I hadn't realized how much I needed that.

Owen's phone buzzed, and he stood up from his crouch near the newly finished deck benches to slip it from his back pocket. Connor's voice came to him.

"Just got confirmation on the Herndon job. Whatever you showed them, they liked. That books up two more weeks next month, and I'm getting way behind in the wood shop. When does Garrett get finished with his job?"

"Two months. Maybe three."

"Jesus, Mary, and Joseph, I could use his help. If this workload keeps up, I might even have to call Patrick and Angus."

Owen grunted but said nothing. Patrick and Angus were the youngest of the MacAteer men and were identical twins. Garrett and he were fraternal twins. They shared a womb and were very close but didn't look exactly the same and had distinctive personalities. Most people had trouble telling Patrick and Angus apart, and the two brothers functioned so close to a unit, it was rare that they spent any time away from each other. They were also the biggest party people in the family. Constantly playing jokes, cutting up, starting fights, and getting into whatever trouble they found. Still, they were brothers and would have Connor's back if he needed them.

"Hard workers."

The truck door closed with a bang as Connor answered. "Yeah, they do work hard and know their jobs, but they bring trouble wherever they go. They helped a lot when we remodeled the duplex into the house, and I appreciated them coming for that. They also tag-teamed a couple of women into thinking they were the other. That woman, who came to the jobsite? Angelique, I think her name? She wanted to see Patrick, but it was Angus she slept with. Christ Almighty, what a mess."

Owen imagined Connor shaking his head as he swore. "I get it. I'll stay for the summer and through the fall. Might stick around longer if the work stays steady."

"We're already booked for the next two months, just the two of us. Remind me to text Garrett this weekend and check his schedule."

"Need to set up my camper."

"You're welcome to stay in the guest room as long as you want."

Owen shrugged even though his brother couldn't see it. "Need my own space. Kids need theirs. You got a new wife."

"Alright. You can hook up to the woodshop. The bathroom in there is usable, but the shower is small. You can still come in the house for that if you want."

Owen grunted again, not seeing a need to respond with words. Connor took the noise as an affirmative answer.

"As Mattie would say, coolio. I gotta run. I'm over at Home Depot picking up a load of decking boards and taking them to the Maggini place. You on for tomorrow morning?"

Owen glanced at the finished Harris job. Jerry had more work for him to do inside the house, however that hadn't been scheduled yet. "Yeah. Just cleanup left."

"Great. Mind running by the grocery store for burger buns on the way home? Melanie's coming by tonight."

Owen couldn't connect the need for bread and Melanie's visit. Visit was a loose word anyway, as she seemed to spend just as much time at Connor and Bev's as she did her own place. Every time he saw her red sports car pull up in the driveway, a thrill ran down his spine that he would see her.

"Pick up some black bean burgers too while you're at it, and check the label before you buy. Abby won't touch the beef patties and will only eat the bean things if it says organic. Jesus, Mary, and Joseph, I hope this is just a phase for her. She inspected the fridge this morning and told us we were murderers for cooking eggs. I love her, but I wish someone took the time to write a raising-a-teenage-girl survival manual."

Owen chuckled. He knew Connor would give his stepdaughter his last working kidney if she needed it.

"See you at home."

Home. The sound and taste of the word sat on Owen's tongue. Home. His camper fit his needs, but much like his older brother, he had the desire to find a place. His own place. Wife. Kids. Family. He'd spent most of his childhood and adult life moving from job to job with no permanence. He liked where he landed, here with Connor and family, and so far, there was no shortage for work. Maybe now was the right time to think about it. He missed his twin, as they'd worked side by side for years, but Garrett's on-again/off-again girlfriend had rejoined the picture, and Owen couldn't make plans around his brother's life.

He stretched his arms overhead and felt the tight muscles of his back loosen up. He'd kept the site mess to a minimum, and most of the tools already sat in their places on the back of his truck. Black bean burgers? They didn't sound appealing in the least, but if they kept the peace at Connor and Bev's place, he'd get them. Trader Joe's wasn't too far and not a big deal for him to stop by. The tailgate of the truck slammed shut with a loud bang.

CHAPTER SEVEN

The stately columns of the sprawling white mansion gleamed white in the sun as I drove up to my parents' house in Arden. This rich neighborhood sported multimillion-dollar houses with every lavish comfort anyone ever thought of or wanted. My mother's closet was big enough to house a family, and my father's custom wine cellar had its own temperature-control system separate from the house. If the power dared to go out, his precious collection of bottles wouldn't be affected.

The large stone fountain burbled away as I parked in the cobblestone circular driveway in front. I grew up here with my older brother, in the lap of luxury and with a silver spoon. Yes, I was spoiled, but I'd like to think I outgrew at least part of it. My brother didn't.

The midday sun was high and bright in the clear blue sky. My dad should have finished his golf game by now and be at home. My mother spent her Sunday mornings in bed after a night of wine indulgence but should be up and awake. It was rare they were in the house at the same time, which was why I'd timed it to catch them now. Still, it took me several minutes of deep breathing and forced relaxing before I approached the front door. I hated this place. I hated it with a deep passion.

Bedelia, their housekeeper, opened the door and smiled. "Miss Melanie, so goot to see you." The ancient Czechoslovakian woman wore the same plain blue uniform and flat work shoes she had for years.

I grinned back at her. She was the one person I looked forward to seeing. "Bee-Dee, it's good to see you too. Are they here?"

She kept the same expression, but her eyes dimmed. "Yes, on the veranda enjoying a light lunch. Will you be joining them?"

"Bee-Dee, it's me. You don't have to be so formal."

She didn't move. This sent off warning bells.

"Dr. Magnus is with them."

Shit, my brother. I hadn't rehearsed telling him too. I

was hoping to make the announcement to my parents and let them have the pleasure of telling Magnus my news. That way, they could all sit around the dinner table and trash me to their hearts' content. But it was for the best this way. I could get it all done at once and then leave before the bashing conversation got started.

I nodded and took a deep breath. Outside of this house, I exuded strength, intelligence, and confidence. An alpha female warrior. This house reduced me to the insignificant little girl from my childhood. Bedelia understood and gave me a sympathetic look and took my hand in her old gnarled one.

"Don't let them get to you, *moje dítě*. You found yourself a long time ago."

Yes, I did. I could do this. My shoulders lifted up and pulled back. The bright floral print pencil dress I chose this morning made a statement of its own. I will not be cowed.

My heels clicked on the polished wood floors as I walked through the cavernous main floor rooms to get to the back of the house. I saw the trio of people through the floor-to-ceiling windows. Dread focused in my stomach as I approached them. They sat around a glass-topped table under a covered pergola. My mother wore a wide-brimmed garden hat and large sunglasses, probably trying to cover up a hangover.

My father still wore his golfing shorts and shirt. I did my best not to look at my brother.

"Mother. Father," I greeted them. Mom and Dad were not in their vocabulary nor mine. "Mags."

The heat of his glare bounced off my cheek at the hated nickname, however, he remained silent, reminding me I was beneath his regard. My palms grew moist, and I swiped them against my dress.

"My word, Melanie, I wasn't expecting your company today. What brings you out here, darling?" My mother's sweet southern accent sounded like those of the big plantation southern belles she emulated.

I noticed no one invited me to sit, so I stood and tried not to shift from foot to foot. The morning sickness had already come and gone for the day. I hoped.

"Yes, dear, pleasant surprise." My father picked up his fine china mug and sipped at the dark custom-blended coffee. He ordered several types of beans to be carefully measured and ground. I knew this because I heard him once instruct how he wanted his morning cup of joe prepared and how if his coffee didn't meet his exacting standards, the cook would look for a new job. He didn't ask if I wanted one.

Magnus still didn't say a word as he picked up a similar cup.

My mouth dried up, and I bit my tongue to get some juices flowing. *Fuck, Mellie, just say you're pregnant. Two words. I'm pregnant. That's all!*

"I need... I have to..." I dry swallowed and kept going. *Just pull it off quick like a Band-Aid, Mel.* "Guess what you're gonna get for Christmas?" I paused for a moment and took a huge breath. "A grandson or granddaughter."

At first, the three faces looked at me in confusion, trying to figure out the joke. My mother was the first to comprehend, and the look of horror on her face was just as bad as a slap across mine. "*A grandchild?* Oh my stars! You're having a baby? Out of wedlock? Oh!" She put down her cup of tea and started fanning herself with a white linen napkin.

"Take it easy, Deloris. It's not the end of the world." My father's reaction, or lack of it, surprised me. I'd imagined him to be the first one to throw stones.

"Congratulations, little sister. You fucked up again."

Not shocked by my brother's attitude.

Mother continued to fan and pant. "Oh, what are we to do? I can't show my face in public. A fallen daughter. Oh, my nerves!"

Yeah, mine too. Overreacting much? "Plenty of women have children and raise them as single parents, Mother." I couldn't quite keep the sarcasm out of my voice as she kept up her drama. My mother had had a brief stint as an actress in the local theater scene. She'd had a few parts, but no lead roles when she met and married my father. From then on, she treated her life as one big play. Her dramatics were common enough that I didn't pay much attention to them anymore.

The chair made a creaking noise as Magnus leaned back and lifted his own cup. "Still a fuckup, but I guess we can't expect anything else from her. I bet she doesn't know who the father is."

I hated the way he spoke about me like I wasn't there. To him, I was nothing more than an inconvenient embarrassment. My father had retired a few years ago from his surgical practice. Dr. Martin Miser had inherited a successful physician's private care office from my grandfather and continued his practice to become a successful maxillofacial reconstruction surgeon. Magnus followed in the family footsteps and now partnered in the office as an orthopedic surgeon. Me? I was supposed to follow one of two career paths: either marry a doctor in the practice or become one. Instead, I taught math in a public school. None of them had ever forgotten their disappointment in my choices.

"I know who the father is, asshole. He doesn't want anything to do with us."

"Melanie! Your language!"

Ironic that my mom will get upset if I use the word asshole, but Magnus can get away with saying fuck.

Magnus just smirked. He knew he won when he got under my skin. "So when are you getting rid of it?"

"Check your hearing. Didn't I just say the G word?"

He waved an imperious hand in the air. "Adoption? You can't possibly be a mother. How can you expect to support a child on what you make?"

He had no idea he echoed Peter's words. My head was filling with pressure, ready to explode. "I'm not broke. My bank accounts are fine. My insurance is fine. There's nothing wrong with me financially."

"Oh, you're talking about the play money you get from your little job. Christ, you'd go through your trust fund in a heartbeat if we didn't regulate it for you."

"No one 'regulates' my accounts but me."

"Please, dear sister, grow the fuck up. Your allowance was set a long time ago."

"Trust dividends, not allowance. And I got control of it years ago when I turned twenty-five. Same as you."

"And if it weren't for me, you'd be getting nothing."

"That's not how trusts work. Why are you so concerned? It's no secret you don't give a shit about me. I don't expect you to give a shit about my baby either."

He put his cup down, folded his arms, and looked me in the face. I stared back, wishing my eyes had laser beams. "No, I don't give a shit about you or the bastard you have inside you. I do give a shit about you bringing down our family name."

Really? I put my hand up, thumb next to my ear and pinky extended to my mouth. "Uh, ring, ring! The twenty-first century is calling. Big news! Women don't get pregnant by themselves. Who knew? No one blinks an eye anymore when unmarried women have babies. You know what? We even get to vote now!"

"Stop." The single word from my father had Magnus biting back anything else he planned on saying. Martin cut into his circular fried egg and spread the liquid yolk over the white. I'd seen him do this for years. Every morning, the same ritual. "You've shared your news, Melanie." He doubled up a strip of the coated egg white on his fork and lifted it to his mouth. Not once did he look at me.

With nothing else to be said, I turned and left. My feelings were numb. I didn't expect roses and balloons, but the cold dismissal hurt more than I thought it would. I got in my car and fought the tears while I scrambled for my phone. Fuck, it was dead, and I didn't have my car charger. Banging the steering wheel and screaming sounded like a great idea for a second or two. Instead, I started my car and spun out of the driveway, not caring if I left marks.

"It's okay, it's okay, it's okay." I repeated my litany over and over again as I drove on autopilot to Bevvie's house. I'd said these words to myself over and over, but I'd stopped believing them a long time ago. Uttering them out loud was just a habit at this point in my life. Memories crowded my mind as the familiar roads flew by.

The yellow van from the private school dropped me off in front of my house, and I skipped through the foyer in my new pink dress. My kindergarten teacher had told me she like my shiny black Mary Jane shoes and white socks with the lacy cuffs. I loved it when she called me pretty and liked my clothes. I had my colored pictures in my hand of the new numbers we learned. All the way up to one hundred! That was a lot. The other kids counted on their fingers, but I didn't need to use them. I could count to one hundred all by myself.

Mommy liked being told she was pretty too. She went to the spa every day to be pretty, and sometimes, I didn't get to see her until dinnertime. I had to go upstairs to change clothes, and Bee-Dee would make me lunch. Then I could play or watch TV for the rest of the day. At least until

Magnus came home from school. I stayed in my room when he did, 'cause he liked to yell at me and call me names until I cried.

My room had pink walls and matching lacy pillows on the bed. Mommy's and Daddy's rooms were side by side across the big space. I had to walk all the way around the inside balcony to get to them. When I got to the top of the stairs, lots of noises came from Daddy's room. Happiness made my heart jump, 'cause Daddy was home. I wanted to show him my numbers, but the noises were scary. It sounded like a monster panting. Bee-Dee told me there were no such thing as monsters, but I thought there were. My friend at school told me if you yelled at a monster and pointed your finger at it and told it to go away, it left you alone. I was sure Daddy didn't want them in his room, so I pulled down on the latch real quiet and opened the door.

Mommy had the biggest room in the house, but Daddy's room was big too. He had a big bed, and it looked like he was jumping on it like I did sometimes to my princess bed. Then I saw his bare butt, and I had to put my hand on my mouth so I didn't laugh. It would be so funny tomorrow if I told my friends about seeing my Daddy's butt. He was bouncing on top of the new maid. I didn't know her name, but she was naked like him. Her big boobies moved round and round, and they were both making pig oinks, and it sounded like it hurt.

My tummy suddenly felt bad. It was funny at first watching my Daddy and the maid, but deep down, I understood that it wasn't funny. I wasn't supposed to see this. I wasn't supposed to see my daddy's bare butt. I wasn't supposed to hear him grunt and bounce on the maid. This was wrong, but I couldn't stop staring. The maid spotted me and screamed at my daddy while she tried to push him off. He turned and looked at me and kept bouncing. I wanted to run away so bad, but my feet were stuck to the floor. My daddy saw me watch him, then he looked at the maid and told her to shut up. He kept bouncing.

When he turned away from me, I had my feet back again. I ran downstairs to the kitchen. Bedelia had made my cheese sandwich and soup.

"Come on. Eat your food while it's hot."

"Thank you, Bee-Dee."

She looked at me with concern. "You didn't change your clothes. What's the matter, moje dítě? School no goot today?"

I shook my head and kept my eyes on my princess plate. I didn't think she wanted me to tell her about my daddy's butt and the bouncing and how I didn't like it and how it bothered me. Her gaze rose to the ceiling, and she scrunched her lips into her teeth. She did this when a pot boiled over or something spilled on the floor.

Just then, my mommy walked in from the spa.

"Bedelia, some tea. Oh, you're home already." She sat down on the other side of the round table as Bee-Dee pulled out one of the china teacups with the flowers and gold rim. "Chamomile with lemon this time. I have such a headache."

I sat staring at my sandwich with my hands folded in my lap.

Mommy sighed. She was mad at me. "Why are you still in your school clothes? I've told you dozens of times, you're supposed to change into play clothes immediately after school. What if you drop something on your dress and it stains? People will say you look like a ragamuffin and your mother doesn't dress you appropriately."

I kept my eyes on the hard brown crust of my sandwich, thinking about how I liked the soft white part better.

"Impossible child," she huffed. "I never have any trouble at all from Magnus. He's always perfectly well behaved. I cannot understand why my second child is such a hooligan."

"She hasn't had a chance to go upstairs yet, ma'am." Bedelia placed the teacup on the table, and my attention was drawn to the tiny wisps of rising steam.

Mommy huffed again. "You shouldn't have given her food until she changed her clothes."

I looked up at Bedelia, and she shook her head at me in warning as she answered. Her lips were still curled inward. "Yes, ma'am. It won't happen again."

The cup clinked against the saucer when Mommy lifted

it and blew on the hot liquid. My eyes returned to my sand-wich. Fear of what she would say next kept me from picking it up and biting into it.

"Bedelia, I noticed Martin's Mercedes is back in the garage. Where is he?"

I held my breath to suck back any noise as I started to cry. If I stayed real quiet, she wouldn't see and I wouldn't get into more trouble.

"He's... he's busy, ma'am."

Mommy put the cup back on the saucer without taking a sip. "I see."

I tried not to make a sound, but a hiccup escaped.

"Oh, for heaven's sake, stop crying! I said I have a terrible headache, and you sit there caterwauling, making it worse. Such a selfish little girl! No consideration for anyone else. If you can't control yourself, you may leave the table and go to your room. Insufferable child. I don't want to see you until dinner!"

I twisted my fingers together as I got up and left the room. I wanted to run, but I'd probably get yelled at again. Running in the house was forbidden. I climbed up the stairs, my steps heavier with each tread. When I got to the top, I saw Mommy had come up the stairs too, but on the other side. I looked at her back through the carved rails as she stood outside Daddy's room. Her hands balled up into fists, and she tucked her arms tight against her hips. I still heard the bouncy sounds and the monster grunts. I pressed the back of my hand against my mouth to keep real quiet and held my breath. Mommy's back stood really straight, and she didn't move. She looked like one of the statues in the big garden. I didn't move either. If she saw me watching her, she'd get madder and yell at me again.

She stood there for a long time. So long, I thought my air would burst out. I opened my mouth and let out my breath real slow and tried to take in air without making a sound. My knees shook so much, I thought I might fall down if I took one step. My head got all wonky and my eyes got fuzzy. I still didn't dare move, I was so scared.

Mommy finally walked to her room. Once she closed her door, I took a big breath. My head cleared up, and I ran on tippy toes to my room. I pulled down on the shiny handle real careful to keep it from clicking. When I got inside, I closed my door and slowly let the handle slip back up for the same reason.

Once I entered my own space, I was safe. I got on my bed and pushed my face tight into my pillow. I cried then. Big crying. Mommy would get mad at me if she saw me, but as long as she didn't hear me, I could cry.

A hand touched my back, and I jerked up to see Bedelia. I flung myself into her generous arms and used her shoulder instead of my pillow.

"It's okay, moje dítě. It's okay."

CHAPTER EIGHT

"Cut to the left. Sharp. Sharper. Okay now back up straight. Oy, where did you find this heap? Shoulda got Eva to draw up a tiny house plan for you."

Owen eased his camper into the spot next to the woodshop as Connor coached him. It barely fit, but it was the best place to have water and electric hookup. After he made the decision to stick around for the summer, he'd wanted to set up a spot separate from Connor's family. They were his family too, but he needed his own space, and the ancient holiday rambler fit that need.

Eva, his younger sister, had designed and built her own tiny house as a teenager and kept it for years until it met with an unfortunate accident at a job site in Wilmington. A mislaid cigar by their father had burned the beautiful mobile structure to the ground and caused a rift in the family that hadn't healed. To this day, Fergus MacAteer had not spoken to his daughter, nor had he met his grandchildren or step-grandchildren. Pity. The old man's stubbornness kept him from reaching out, and he'd missed a lot. Kids only stayed young for so long, and after those childhood years disappeared, the man he called father might end up grieving that lost time.

It may not have been a tiny house, but Owen had put his own personal stamp on the camper. The inside had been gutted to make room for a bed big enough to accommodate Owen's size. There was still the small kitchen area that wasn't good for any serious cooking, but adequate for his needs. The shower was expanded just enough to fit, and since the woodshop had a bathroom installed, Owen planned on taking out the camper's toilet for the near future. Not that it made much difference. He'd seen both of Connor's young stepsons whizzing off the back deck and getting yelled at by their older sister.

Beverly and the kids had gone to their church services earlier this morning. She worked as the pianist there, and Owen marveled at both her talent and her weekly workload. She had invited him and Connor to come along, however they both declined in favor of getting the camper situated while the kids were occupied.

He shut off the engine to his big black truck when he saw the red Audi jerk to a stop in the driveway. Melanie got out and hurried toward them.

"Hi, MacAteer male type people. Is Beverly around?"

Her light tone and bright fake smile didn't fool Owen. Something was wrong.

Connor wasn't fooled either. "She texted after the services finished that she was gonna do a grocery store and Arby's run on her way back. Should be here soon. What's the matter?"

"Oh, nothing. I'm fine. Just peachy." The dark streaks under her eyes didn't support her lie at all. "I was just in the neighborhood and thought I'd come see everyone for a bit."

"You don't look fine, Mellie. Come in the house and sit down. I'll call Bev and see if she's getting close."

"No, no, don't bother her. Really, Con-man, I'm good. I'm totally good. I'm so good, there is no limit to the goodness."

Tears tracked down her face, and she brushed at them impatiently. "Don't mind this shit. I'm good. I swear I am."

Owen watched her for a moment. She crossed her

arms in front of her middle, fighting to keep herself contained. It didn't take a genius to see she was losing. He tucked his keys into his pocket and moved to take her in his arms. As he enfolded her in the cocoon of his body, she leaned into him. The morning had been long and hot and the afternoon not much different. Owen knew his sleeveless T-shirt was soaked with sweat from working outside, but she snuggled her face into his shoulder, not seeming to care.

"Dad bay?" *Shit! Maybe she didn't catch the reversed words.*

"You guys already heard about my condition, right? My hormones are all outta whack. That's all."

Connor spoke. Owen kept his silence. "Yeah, we had a family meeting about it. Sarah has been looking up baby names, and Abby is hoping you'll go for natural childbirth so you don't start the baby's life with what she calls toxic chemicals. Personally, I'd go for the drugs."

She gave a light laugh, and more tears flowed down her cheeks. "I think this is in my top ten of bad days. Make that the top five." She pulled away from Owen and swiped at her eyes. Two perfect black rings circled her eyes, with matching ones on his shirt. "Well, shit, Owen. Looks like I marked you."

He shook his head. "No dig beal." *Fuck, he did it again!*

Melanie didn't say anything. She swiped again at her eyes, licked a finger, and smeared the black smudges more. "I bet I look like a rabid raccoon on crack. Mind if I take a trip to the bathroom and get this shit cleaned up a bit?"

Connor pointed to the back door. "Take all the time you need, *mo rún.*"

Owen watched as she made her way to the house. The floral dress showed off her gentle curves and long legs. She looked like she was strutting on a runway rather than stumbling through a backyard. Somehow she managed not to sink her spiky heels into the dirt.

"Put your eyes back in your head, boy-o. Bev may not take kindly to you staring at her best friend's ass."

Owen broke his gaze away from the retreating back. "Not staring. Worried."

Connor sighed as he moved to unhook the camper from the truck and finish the set up. "I think we're all worried for her. She's a strong, smart lady, but her life is about to change. Big time."

Owen's triceps burned as he cranked down the camper's ground braces. "You got your kids all at once. No babies."

Connor pulled the cotter pin and unlocked the

connecting ball joint. "No babies of my own, but I raised our sister, Eva, and those two hooligans, Patrick and Angus. Biology doesn't make you a parent."

Owen grunted a response but didn't say anything. Connor's assertion about parenting was spot-on, as he had spent his life taking care of his family and had now stepped into taking care of another one. The kids still spent time with their bio dad, but the visits were getting more and more rare.

Melanie's bio baby daddy, Peter, had taken himself out of the picture, and Melanie hadn't brought up his name since the night she came to the house and got sick. If he hadn't had overheard that name, he wouldn't have known it. He couldn't wrap his brain around how anyone would consider abandoning their child, but that's exactly what this Peter person had done.

Connor had pulled the thick power cord from the camper's side when a flurry of noise came from the house. Mattie, followed by Jacob and Muttface, ran into the backyard.

"Tag!"

"No, you tag!"

"I was here first."

"Nuh-unh, I was."

"Yuh-huh, me."

"No, me!"

"Connor!"

Muttface ran around in circles, barking his head off, while Connor laughed. "I don't think it matters who's first in tag. Just the one that's it."

This set off another word barrage.

"You're it!"

"No, you're it."

"No, you!"

"You!"

Connor reached down to scratch the ears of the excited dog. "You're both wrong."

The boys stopped their arguing and looked at Connor in question. Owen guessed what came next.

"The truth of the matter, boys..." Connor spoke quietly, making the two kids approach closer to hear. "The truth of the matter is..."

They came within arm's reach.

"What I mean to say is... I'M IT! Aha!"

Mattie squealed in delight as Connor grabbed him and tossed him over one shoulder. He still managed to catch Jacob under his arm in a football hold. There weren't too many more years Connor would be able to do that, as the older boy was growing into a lanky, tall man-child. "Oy, Owen! Go get the bin. Need to clean up the yard."

Mattie laughed and squirmed. "Nooo! Don't throw me away! I'll fart on you!"

"Then I'll definitely put you in the bin."

Owen watched them play. His heart swelled with happiness for his older brother. After a lifetime of hard work and sacrificing for his family, he had something special in Beverly and the kids.

"Arby's had their five for five sale today. Guess what Mom brought home for lunch?" Sarah made the announcement from the back deck. Owen looked up to see Melanie had returned and had her eyes on the antics. The black smudges were gone, but she swiped at her eyes. Owen wondered what she thought while she gazed at the play between stepfather and sons.

"Oy, last one in is a rotten egg!" Jacob yelled as he made a dash for the steps. Owen chuckled at the speech pattern the boy had picked up from Connor. Mattie scrambled behind with Muttface nearly tripping him.

"Wash up first and don't hog all the horsey sauce!" Connor clapped Owen on the shoulder. "Ah, it's a good life, boy-o. We'll finish the job in a bit. I need to go help my lovely wife get groceries in and put away."

Both men climbed the steps, and Connor disappeared inside. Melanie swiped her eyes again and shifted them to meet Owen's.

"You good?"

She smiled a watery smile and brushed at his shirt as if knocking off a piece of dirt. "Yeah, O-man. I'm always good when I'm here."

Jesus, Mary, and Joseph, she was beautiful! Owen focused on her parted lips and had the urge to taste them. Would they be as sweet as he imagined?

A conversation between Abby and Beverly drifted from the open back door.

"Arby's fries their potato cakes in pure organic vegetable oil and no animal fats, right?"

"I don't know, Abby."

"Did you get my salad?"

"Yes, it's in a separate bag."

"I wanted Ranch dressing."

"Ranch dressing isn't vegan."

"There's a non-dairy kind."

"Not at Arby's."

"Mom!"

Melanie groaned and leaned into Owen's body, face planting in his wide chest. "Please tell me there's an alternative to teenagers?"

His arms came up automatically to rest lightly around her back. "Send them to Bevvie."

She laughed against his shirt, and a spark shot

through his shoulders to his groin. What he wouldn't give to hear that sound over and over again.

"Thank you for being such a good friend."

Friend. A sharp needle pierced his chest at that single word, and his good mood deflated.

Beverly poked her head outside. "You two better get in here before the boys scarf all the mozzarella sticks."

Melanie straightened herself. "Mattie will save some for his favorite Auntie M."

"No, I won't!" came a faint call through the screen door.

"Little booger!" She ran after the imp.

Owen stood a moment on the empty deck. Friends. She saw them as friends and nothing more. He moved to enter the house. It could be worse, he supposed. She could regard him as an acquaintance through the family or even worse, not regard him at all. From what he observed, her relationship with Beverly had lasted longer and was more solid than with any boyfriend she'd ever had. If her friendship meant he had a place in her life, he could be happy with it. At least he told himself that. Maybe someday he would believe it.

CHAPTER NINE

WHO EVER THOUGHT A TEENY TINY LITTLE BUNDLE OF cells would become my entire focus? My life had changed. Weekend trips to the beach, wine tastings, parties, and clubbing held no appeal to me anymore. Instead, I stayed home, looked up recipes, and clicked through shows on streaming cable channels I never watched until now. I thought about how every bite I put in my mouth affected the life form inside me. I thought about the security of my finances and the future that I needed to plan. I thought about what labor would feel like. I thought about all the complicated issues of raising a child. What if my kids turned out to be special needs? Could I handle that? What if they got sick? What if they got cancer? What if I couldn't raise them right? What if I failed as a mom and ruined their life? What if? What if? What if?

Fuck me sideways, it was enough to give me headaches. If Bevvie ever had any doubts about her ability to parent, I couldn't tell. She was good at it. Her astounding patience for Abby's quirks, support for Jacob's science and inventing passions, understanding of Sarah's penchant for debate and her more recent political obsession, the stamina to keep up with Mattie's constant energy, keeping up with a household and cooking on a nightly basis, plus working full-time, all of these things made me think of her as super mom. The kids thrived in school, bringing home good grades and excellent behavior reports. They looked happy and secure in their family, knowing they were loved and would always be.

How the hell was I supposed to do all that when I couldn't even bake a decent pan of brownies? Even from a premade mix?

The blackened bricks mocked me from the counter where I threw them after I burned my wrist on the edge of the oven.

"Son of a bitch!" The acrid smell of burnt chocolate filled the air as I ran my wrist under cold water. I could count the times on one hand that I'd turned on the oven since I bought my condo eight years ago. It had been perfectly clean and pristine until I got it in my head I needed to learn to cook. Now it resembled a war zone of crispy drippings from countless over-spills. I could scramble a decent egg, but that about summed up my culinary skills.

I tried brownies for my Fourth of July contribution. The obligatory invitation came from my parents to the country club party, and I made my obligatory decline. My mother made her complaints about me not visiting enough, and how disappointing I was to my father. She made mention about their upcoming Labor Day gala and how much I needed to be there for appearances' sake. I heard nothing from Martin nor Magnus. No surprise.

I'd opted for several years to join Bevvie and her family for the big all-day festival in Pack Square Park. There were kids' games, crafts vendors, music from local bands, food trucks, the works. I would rather spend the day watching Mattie stuff himself silly with cotton candy and go full-blown Tasmanian Devil cartoon than with the stuffy formal luncheon and afternoon drinking group of women my mother wanted me to join.

I picked up a knife and stuck it under the corner of one brownie to see if it could be salvaged. The corner broke off with a crack and flew across my living area. A sigh escaped my lips. Nope, not happening. I dumped the ruined pan into the trash can and made plans to visit the Trader Joe's bakery on the way to the house. No need to poison anyone today.

The plan today was for me to go to Bevvie's place, then all of us would cram into the two huge trucks and park on the top floor of the Hilton hotel garage deck. We would spend the day at the festival, then enjoy the fireworks with blankets spread out in the truck beds. That event started after sundown, and the view from the deck would put the sparkling show directly overhead.

As per usual, the chaos at Bev's house was in full swing when I got there.

"Mom, did you pack my organic granola bars?"

"Top shelf in the pantry."

"Mom, where are my shoes?"

"Where you left them last time you took them off."

"Mom, can I have some fried Oreos later?"

"If you can find them, but only two."

"Mom, I only found one shoe."

"Too bad you have two feet."

"Mom, I'm hungry."

Connor came down the stairs carrying a load of blankets. "Oy, Jacob. Your other shoe is in the hall closet. Abby, can you take these to my truck, please? Morning, Mel."

Mattie skimmed across the kitchen floor in socks. "Hi, Auntie M! Mom says I get *two* fried Oreos today!"

My stomach twisted a little at the thought of the grease-dripping, sticky, sweet treat. The morning sickness had cleared up for the most part, but every once in a while it would make an appearance. "Awesome sauce, kiddo. Morning to you too, Connor."

Sarah sat at the table munching a bowl of cereal. Owen sat next to her, drinking a gargantuan cup of coffee. The gentle giant raised his eyes over the white rim and nodded in my direction. I tilted my head up with a smile and winked at him in greeting. Yeah, it was a flirty move, but I felt really good.

I should have known better.

The weather burned sunny and hot. I had on loose white shorts and a sleeveless cotton blouse. My clothes still fit okay at this point, even though I'd started my second trimester. Only seven extra pounds gained so far, making me a little rounder, but no significant baby bump yet. My bag held water bottles, extra sunscreen spray, sunglasses, and ponytail ties. On my feet were padded sandals. I could wear heels all day long with no trouble, but the look didn't fit with the casual family outing vibe I wanted.

Somehow, we got ourselves to the festival by midmorning. Abby walked off to find her friends and ignore everyone for the day. Jacob, Sarah, and Mattie went for the rides and games with Connor and Owen. That left Bevvie and me by ourselves to wander through the displays. God, how I loved festivals! Handmade jewelry, handbags, pottery, artwork—this place was crack to a shopaholic like me. In no time at all, I had several bags hanging from my wrist.

Bevvie picked up a soap bar from a table and inhaled the scent with her eyes closed. "Oh, this is nice. I should get some of these, 'cause I know who made them."

I blinked. "You know someone who makes soap?"

She picked up another colorful bar. "Well, kinda." She put down the bar and ticked off her fingers one by one. "Connor's sister's husband's MC brother's wife has a shop in Bryson City called Soap-n-stuff. I recognized the name on the label. Eva gave me some last year for Christmas along with matching bath bombs. Unbelievable! If I could've moved into the tub for a week, I would have."

We picked through the soaps, oohing over the luscious scents and color patterns. Bevvie had three in her hand and I had twelve when a loud voice behind me cut through our marveling.

"Well, well, well, if it isn't little Melanie Miser."

Fuck. My stomach twisted on itself, and icy fingers traced over my spine as I snapped up straight. I locked my knees to keep them from shaking, and every muscle contracted to wire tight rigidness. I raised my chin a few degrees and turned to face the man I hated most in the world.

Robert, my brother's best friend and my biggest enemy, stood right behind me. He had become a big-time investment banker and moved to Charlotte years ago. Our two cities were separated by a two-hour drive, and I would love to see that distance tripled. Quadrupled. Hell, the bastard could move all the way to California, and it still wouldn't be far enough away.

"You look beautiful as ever. How's life been treating you?"

His face smiled, and his tone sounded curious and friendly, but his eyes fixed on my breasts, and I had to tamp down the impulse to cover them with my arms.

"I'm good, Robert. Real good. Why are you here?"

He shrugged and picked up a bar of soap and sniffed at it. "I moved back to Asheville last month. I'm taking over for my dad at First and Trust Bank as president and CEO. Magnus didn't tell you?"

"Magnus and I don't speak any more than we have to."

He wrinkled his nose at the scent and put the bar back down. "Ugh, Lavender. Kiki loves this smell. I think it's revolting."

He poked at another one but didn't pick it up. "Personally, I'd rather be on the links, but the bank has a booth, and Dad thought it was a good idea to meet and greet the locals since I haven't lived here in a long time. You know. Get reacquainted with old friends?"

"Who's Kiki?"

"My wife for now."

"For now?"

"Yeah. She's my third so far. We got married last summer, and since then she's put on a ton of weight. Fat women aren't my thing."

"Prick," Bevvie muttered under her breath.

He didn't bother to acknowledge her presence. "Love to get together for drinks sometime and catch up."

"I'm not drinking these days."

"Coffee then."

"I'm not doing much coffee either."

His pretty blue eyes and all-American charm faded as his irritation showed. "I'm sure you can find the time to spend with an old friend. We have a past together, in case you don't remember."

My throat closed up, choking off any words I had.

He took my silence as a sign of acquiescence and smiled like he'd just won the lottery. "We'll talk soon, yeah?" He leaned into my personal space and kissed me on my cheek. Blood roared in my ears, and I became a cold marble statue as I watched his back moving away.

"Good-looking and great body, but those asshole remarks about his wife? What and who the hell does he think he is?"

Pain in my forearms made me realize my hands were clenched in tight fists. I relaxed my fingers and threw back my shoulders. The noise in my head had disappeared, and I flipped my hair back to throw off the black mood that had come over me. "The who part is Magnus's friend, and the what part, you nailed already. He's an asshole who doesn't matter. Not anymore."

I turned to the vendor sitting under the canopy. "How much for all the lavender-scented items you have here?"

The woman's eyes rounded. "All of them?"

"Yes, all of them."

She sputtered and counted the remaining soaps, lotions, bath bombs, oil infusers, and body sprays. The total came up to just over five hundred dollars. She inserted the register device in her phone as I handed her my credit card.

"Holy shit, Melanie. Are you buying all this stuff just because he doesn't like lavender?"

"Yup. I knew you were smart."

"Damn, Mellie, that's a lot of money. You'll be smelling like lavender for years with this much stuff."

I smirked at her. "That's the plan. If I run into his ass again, I want a fucking cloud of lavender around me at all times."

She rolled her lips between her teeth. "I don't know whether to laugh at your sense of justice or cringe at the amount of money you just spent."

She was right. This was an expensive impulse buy and the chances of me running into him on a regular basis were pretty low. Perhaps I didn't need this much lavender-scented stuff, but I had to have it. I just had to, and I couldn't explain to her why. "Let me put it this way. I'd spend almost any amount for a chance to fuck up that man's day."

The vendor bagged everything while Beverly's typed rapidly on her phone.

"What are you doing?"

She looked up at me. "With this many bags, we're going to need help getting them to the truck. I'm texting Connor to see if he and Owen are close."

"To borrow from Mattie's vocabulary, coolio."

I pulled one of the spray bottles from a bag and spritzed my wrists and neck. The floral smell surrounded me, and I inhaled it deep into my lungs. "Mmm. Just in case I have the displeasure of running into him again. I hope they come soon. After they get our stuff to the trucks, I'm gonna want some junk food. Has Mattie already had his allotment of fried Oreos?"

CHAPTER TEN

A warm male body cushioned my head as I brushed my hand over his stomach. His breathing increased under my ear, and a tingle started between my legs. My hand moved lower, unzipping his pants and slipping under his clothes to find his dick already hard. Saliva flooded over my tongue at the thought of his taste, and I swallowed. If I moved just a few inches down, I could have him in my mouth. I stroked him with my fingertips, caressing his shaft from balls to head, and he swelled even more. He squirmed under me, pushing into my palm, and I wrapped it around him, stroking firmly. His hand grabbed my wrist and held it still. "Mel, wake up. Please."

Holy Fuck! I was lying across Owen's chest with his dick in my hand. I let go immediately and watched it slap on his stomach, pointing north toward me. A drop of clear fluid appeared at the tip. I had to stop myself from sticking out my tongue to lick it off. I'd done enough damage already.

"Oh my God, Owen! I'm so sorry. I didn't mean to grab you. Fuck, where are we?"

Pieces of memory came to me. After my encounter with Robert, the men took our purchases to the trucks, and we spent some time stuffing ourselves silly at the food trucks. I tried a bunch of different tacos, barbecue, roasted corn cobs, and whatever else struck my fancy. I had two fried Oreos alongside Mattie, both of us scarfing down the gooey, messy treats. All that greasy food made my stomach churn in rebellion, and I got the bright idea to get a hotel room to nap for a bit. Owen came to check on me, and I asked him to stay with me. He curled up in the bed with me to watch some TV, and apparently, we both crashed and missed the fireworks.

Now the early morning light peeked into the room, and my hand had rubbed all over Owen's junk. *Why does this shit happen to me?* I sat up and figured out quick I wore only my underwear and one of the T-shirts I bought yesterday. "Damn, O-man. I am so sorry. I was having a fantastic dream and… I didn't realize… I didn't mean to… fuck, this is embarrassing."

He lay on his back, statue still and breathing deeply

as if fighting for control. His dick remained pointing due north and hard as a rock. He still wore his jeans, but I had expertly opened them to put him on display in all his glory. As far as dicks went, his was very pretty. It had a nice shape with an extra wide purplish head and long, thick shaft. His erection still hadn't gone down. Should I finish him off? A few veins stood out along the length, just begging for me to trace with my tongue. How would he react if I stripped off my panties and mounted him? My pussy was already wet from the dream, and it had been months since it saw any real action. My vibrator didn't count.

Nope. Don't go there, Melanie. Owen is more than just a quick fuck, so don't treat him like one.

As if he read my thoughts, the big man next to me took a deep breath and heaved himself out of the bed. "It's okay. Stay here. I'll be back."

His jeans remained open as he walked awkwardly into the bathroom. The giant back tattoo surprised me. A sword pommel sat between his shoulders, and the blade extended down his spine with a phrase on it I couldn't make out. The design was simple, with no extra curlicues, shadings, or colors. A moment later, the shower came on. No doubt it was a cold one.

I relaxed back on the rumpled bed and sighed while I stared at the ceiling. How would Bevvie and Connor react to me and Owen spending the night together? Should I even worry about it? So far, Bevvie had never said a word to me about my lifestyle or life choices, even though I knew she worried about them. She was the least judgmental person I'd ever met and the most supportive, but would a one-night stand with her brother-in-law be too much for her? Too much for me? We hadn't had sex, so would this situation be considered a one-night stand? Owen never struck me as a one and done kind of man, but this wasn't the start of something, was it? I had never had a long-term boyfriend, and the thought of it terrified me. The idea of putting my heart out there to get stomped on? Not happening.

I pulled on my shorts and managed to find my bra before Owen came out of the bathroom. He had refastened his pants, but I got a good look at his bare upper body. Damn, he looked good! He didn't have the carefully developed, cut muscles of a body-building weight lifter, but he still had a lot of definition in his pecs and arms. His stomach was lean and flat with long lines on either side that tapered into his jeans. No other way to put it. Owen was *hawt*!

Still, I couldn't go there. I didn't do long-term and if Owen was anything like his brother, that's what he would expect. I'd admit the thought intrigued me and didn't scare me as much as with other men, but still the risk existed. If I screwed it up, I could hurt a lot of people, including me.

How did I handle a scene where I just woke up in a hotel room bed with my hand gripping Owen's dick? Simple. I ignored it like it didn't happen.

"So, what big plans do you have today?" I fluffed out my hair and kept my tone nonchalant.

"Yard work. Woodshop. Watch a game or play with the kids. You?"

"Probably go shop at the mall for a while and scroll through Netflix for a movie tonight. Wanna join me later?" *Shit, Mel! That's not how to tone it down!*

He smiled and shook his head. "Kids tonight. Connor and Bev are out."

"Date night?"

"Yeah." He pulled the shirt he wore yesterday over his wet hair and smoothed it over his body.

"That's nice of you to help them out. I've done that a few times to give them a break. Abby give you trouble?"

"No. Texts all night."

I laughed. "Yes, that's Abby's *modus operandi* on a nightly basis. Think you'll need help? I can come over?" *Fuck, why did I say that?*

"Depends." He looked up at me and grinned. "You gonna manually override me again?"

I turned beet red. "Look, Owen… I… uh… that is to say… um…" *Holy shit, I'm sputtering. Me. The woman who prides herself on being bold and in control at all times.*

Thankfully, Owen showed me some mercy. "Don't worry about it. Nothing happened. I'm okay. You're okay."

"I really am sorry." *Lame, Mel. Really fucking lame.*

"Let it go. I'm not mad."

"You're sure?"

One side of his mouth curled up. "Can't be mad. I woke up to a beautiful woman."

Ooooh, lots of tummy flutters. "So what's the sword on your back all about?"

"*Freagarthach,* or Fragarach. Sword of Irish mythology. Called The Whisperer or The Answerer or The Retaliator. Legend is only men who stand above the stone of destiny can wield it. The stone shouts, and the sword whispers back."

"And the writing?

"*Is iad na muca ciúine a itheann an mhín.* 'It's the quiet pigs that eat the grain.' Means quiet people are strong people and will win in the end."

I pondered as I slipped on my sandals. "Does that have a lot of meaning for you?"

He waggled his hand up and down. "Got drunk with Patrick and Angus one night and got it. Fits me."

"Did they get tattoos of swords too?"

"Nah. Something else."

His relaxed manner helped quell my worries. If he truly had no problems with this morning, then perhaps I shouldn't either. "You know, I think this is the most you've ever talked to me. Whole sentences and everything."

He sat on the only chair in the room to put on his socks and shoes. "I'm learning more about you. You snore."

"I do not."

His hand came up, and he waggled it up and down again.

"You're teasing me, right?"

"Maybe. Maybe not."

"O-man, I do *not* snore."

"Just little ones. Kitty snores."

OMG, did he just say the word kitty? Argh! If I pay no attention to it, it will go away.

"You hungry?"

I grabbed the change of subject like a drowning woman grabs a float. "Starving. You going to feed me?"

"Yeah." He picked up his wallet and watch from the nightstand. "Gotta get your car first. Still at the house."

Shit, he was right. Bevvie and Connor would see it and not say a word, but the kids might. "Think it's still early enough they won't notice?"

"If we leave now, yeah."

"Fine. Let me go pee, and I'll be ready."

I took a little more time in the bathroom to wash my face of makeup remnants and finger comb my hair. A dab of the complimentary lotion got smeared under my eyes. I didn't have anything else, but at this point, Owen had seen enough of me that being barefaced shouldn't be a shock.

I looked at my reflection. "Well, Mel, it could have been worse. At least you weren't humping him like a dog in heat or sucking him awake. He's cool. You're cool. Get over yourself."

I walked out of the bathroom, prepared to be my usual lighthearted smartass. One look at Owen's gentle face sent that right out the door. God knows why! My sinuses filled as the urge to cry hit me. "Oh, fuck. Stupid hormones!"

Owen came over to me at the first sniff and opened his arms in invitation. I didn't hesitate to put myself there. His masculine musk surrounded me as he wrapped me up and pressed me close. He gave the best hugs. "Thank you, O-man."

He kissed the side of my head. "I got you."

Those three words echoed in my head. Yes. He did. He had me.

I pulled back and sniffed again. "Fuck, I need some food. Quit wasting time and feed me. I'm in the mood for a big stack at IHOP."

"WHAT'CHA MAKING, UNCLE OWEN?" MATTIE SKIMMED through the kitchen and rounded the counter to watch his uncle peel and chop.

"Boxty and sausage."

"What's boxty?"

"Potato pancakes."

"Are we having breakfast for dinner?"

"Sort of."

Muttface joined them and sat at Owen's feet. The dog stared with intensity at each hand movement, ready to pounce on the first dropped crumb.

"What's that stuff in the pot?" The boy pointed to the stove.

"Boiled cabbage."

"Doesn't that make you fart a lot?"

Owen chuckled. Lately, Mattie had become fascinated by the sounds his butt made. "It can."

"Coolio! Hey, Sarah, want to have a fart contest later?"

Sarah looked up from her book. "No, and don't feed Muttface any of that stuff. He'll stink up the whole house."

"Who's farting?" Jacob came down from his room.

"No one yet. Gotta eat some cabbage to load up." Mattie ran into the den area and executed a perfect dive roll over the back of the couch, missed the seat, and fell to the floor with a thud.

"You hurt, boy-o?"

"Nah. Don't tell Mom."

Owen didn't know whether to laugh at the boy's words, caution him about his gymnastics, or take the cabbage outside and dump it for the squirrels so Mattie's fart contest got delayed. Visions of little gas clouds floating from behind fluffy gray tails teased his brain. Did squirrels fart? *Don't say that out loud. Jacob will want to make that into an experiment.*

It had been just a month since the Fourth of July Festival, and his workload had increased to the point he and Connor were booked solid through until early

November. As long as the weather stayed sunny and warm, everyone and his cousin wanted a custom-designed deck, porch, pergola, or shed of some sort built in their backyard. Currently, Connor had talked to several people about kitchen updates in the winter months, and Jerry Harris had already called about the design of his wife's hobby she shed in their basement. Owen couldn't complain. His living expenses were minimal, and his bank account grew fatter. Maybe the time had come to put down some roots at last. He liked Asheville, and obviously he could make a nice life at doing what he loved.

"You boys are disgusting." Abby made an appearance and plopped down on the couch next to Sarah. "God, I'm soooo bored."

"Too bad Autumn had a date tonight."

"Shut up, Sarah."

"You're not supposed to say that."

"I'll say it again. Shut *up*, Sarah."

"I'll tell Mom."

"God, you're such a brat!"

Owen glanced at his phone on the counter and debated on calling Melanie to come run interference with the girls. He couldn't pick it up, as his hands were in the potato, flour, and buttermilk mixture.

"You're just mad 'cause you gotta stay home while Uncle Owen babysits us."

That set Abby off.

"I don't need a babysitter. Jacob doesn't even need a babysitter. Uncle Owen is only here for you and Mattie! You're the only babies in this house."

"I'm not a baby!"

"No, you're a childish brat!"

Owen rinsed his hands and picked up his phone. His still wet thumbs flew over the letters.

Owen: Help.

Melanie: What's wrong?

Owen: The girls are fighting.

Melanie: Any hair pulling or blood?

Owen: Not yet.

Melanie: Does big, strong Uncle Owen need help from little Auntie M? ;-)

Owen: Yes.

Melanie: LMAO on my way. Need anything?

Owen: No.

Melanie: Not even ice cream?

Owen hesitated. She knew his weakness for ice cream.

Owen: Okay but hurry.

Melanie: ;-)

The past weeks had settled into a routine. After the Fourth of July weekend, without fail, Melanie came to the house on Saturday night to play games, watch movies, do girly stuff with Abby and Sarah, and just be a part of the family. If it got too late, she crashed in the guest bedroom. This weekend, Beverly had a rare day off from her Sunday morning church service gig, and Connor had asked if he would take the kids for the weekend so they could have a date night somewhere besides home. They left this morning for a bed-and-breakfast place up in Hot Springs and planned on spending the evening soaking in one of the outdoor hot tubs.

Owen got to be the adult in charge, and Melanie had said she would help. He realized he needed it. Refereeing the kids' squabbles turned out to be more than he thought. He hoped a trip to the emergency room for Mattie wouldn't be necessary.

He pulled the golden brown boxty cakes from the pan when Sarah yelled through the house. "Auntie M is here!" One glance at her clean bare face and pink satchel told him what the evening's activities included.

"Facials!" Both girls squealed and forgot their snit at each other.

"Are we doing nails, too?"

"Did you bring the natural clay mask or the oatmeal one?"

"Can I have another loofah? Mine fell apart."

"How 'bout the hair mask stuff? Can we do that too?"

Melanie laughed. "Yes, all of it. I brought the organic natural stuff just for you, Abby." She sniffed the air. "Oh, what is that heavenly smell?"

"Mosskey!" Mattie dove over the couch again, this time coming to a perfect sitting position. He bounced on the cushions in his excitement.

"Boxty," Owen corrected.

"It's potatoes made into pancakes. Uncle Owen made farty cabbage too."

"Oh, really? Are you going to try to fart the alphabet tonight?"

Mattie stopped bouncing and looked at Melanie with wide, surprised eyes. "You can do that?"

Her laugh rang out. "Not me, monkey-butt. You. I've heard it's possible, but you have to concentrate and practice a lot. I bet there's a YouTube how-to video. When you try it later, point that weapon of mass destruction away from me, yeah?"

Owen shook his head and groaned. "You just gave the boy a life goal."

She shrugged and moved to put two tubs of ice cream in the freezer. "Look at it this way, O-man. He'll eat what you serve him tonight, and it will give him something to do that doesn't involve swinging from the ceiling or sliding down the banisters."

Owen turned off the burner and pulled the sausages from the oven where he'd kept them warm. "Oy, wash up. Food is ready."

Dinner progressed without incident. All four kids ate plenty, and very little food was leftover. Even the cabbage disappeared. The boys took their turn in kitchen cleanup, while the girls set up for their night of girly pampering upstairs in Connor and Bevvie's spacious room. Owen heard them argue over what movie to watch.

"*Princess Bride?*"

"We've seen that a hundred times. *Pride and Prejudice?*"

"That one is old."

"So is *Princess Bride*. How 'bout *Beauty and the Beast?*"

"Animated or live version?"

"Live, of course."

Owen's respect for his sister-in-law and her patience grew with every sentence. How did she ever do this as a single parent?

The boys settled for video games. Owen sat and watched them play for a while, but the constant jerking movements of the screen made him dizzy. He climbed the stairs to check on the female population of the house and got a glimpse of three heads wrapped in towels and three faces covered in grayish, lumpy gunk. Abby shrieked when she spotted him looking in and slammed the door in his face.

Jesus, Mary, and Joseph, if he ever had children of his own, he hoped God would spare him the complexities of raising teenage girls.

He spent the rest of the evening with a book until the boys called it a night and scampered upstairs to bed. "Don't forget to brush your teeth."

"We know, Uncle Owen."

He leaned against the banister and listened to flushing toilets and running faucets. Connor had done a great job in designing the second floor. The kids' bedrooms might be small, but each kid got their own space and shared a bathroom in between rooms. The master bedroom and guest room also shared a more spacious and adult-friendly bathroom. Beverly had remarked more than once how much she loved the jetted tub Connor had put in for her. He wondered if Melanie had a jetted tub in her condo and used it much.

The object of his musings came down the steps with Muttface right behind her. She wore dark purple lounge pants and a loose T-shirt that read "I'm a

Teacher. What's your Superpower?" Her full breasts swayed heavily under the cloth, and his groin tightened.

"Muttface needs to go out. You want anything from the kitchen?"

"Another bowl of ice cream. You pick the flavor."

She grinned, and he watched as she walked away. She had grown a little rounder in her hips, and there was a fullness to her face, otherwise, he couldn't really see her pregnancy. She still got queasy, but he hadn't noticed any more significant morning sickness.

The back door opened and closed, and Owen pictured her standing on the deck in the moist night air waiting for the dog to finish its business. The moonlight shone in her hair, turning it the color of burnished gold, and she had her hands on her hips, telling the canine to "hurry the fuck up." Christ, what he wouldn't pay to have that scene for real on a nightly basis. His dick swelled uncomfortably against the zipper of his jeans, and he shifted back on the sofa, splaying out his legs for some relief. He laid his head back against the high cushion and recited the Gaelic alphabet in his head to distract himself.

"This is rather domestic. Sleeping already?" Her soft voice came to him along with the click of canine nails on the wood floor. Two bowls of cookies-and-cream were in her hands.

"No, just resting my eyes."

Muttface sniffed at his knee and then thumped up the stairs, presumably to sleep with one of the kids. The sofa moved as Melanie settled next to him. The clean scent of lavender wafted to his nostrils as she leaned over him to pick up the remote, and he silently ran through the alphabet again.

"Mind if I put on an action movie? There's only so much fairy tale romance crap I can take." She clicked on the TV and lowered the volume. Gunfire and shouts emanated from the flat screen speakers.

"You don't like *Princess Bride* and Cinderella stories?"

"Not particularly. They're okay for kids, but adults know better. The ball doesn't last forever, and after the big-ass sparkling wedding, Cinderella still has to take off her pretty dress and start a normal everyday life. There's no such thing as a happily ever after."

"Bite me." Owen cringed when the words left his mouth. "C-came out wrong. Might. Be. Not bite me."

Melanie stayed silent for a few seconds and then let out a huge laugh. "Oh, shit, O-man! That was classic."

He relaxed when she kept laughing. "Normal life has happy endings. Look at Connor and Beverly."

She wiped at her eyes. "You have a point, though I think they're more the exception than the rule."

The movie had gotten to a long, complicated chase montage when Melanie conked out and snuggled into Owen's side. Her arm flopped across his lap with her wrist just over his crotch. He froze in place as she sighed and started lightly snoring. His arm came over her back and she curled in tighter. He contemplated the top of her blonde head. Natural. No dark roots. Cut in a simple style for a rather complicated woman. Friends, she'd labeled the two of them, but did friends fall asleep on each other? Did they touch with such casualness? Confusion ruled in Owen's mind as he tried to reconcile the idea of "just friends" with a woman whose hand rested on top of his dick for the second time. He knew it was unconsciously done, but the fact she was comfortable with him and sure enough of her welcome to nestle into his body spoke volumes.

This woman had the capability to hurt him, whether she wanted to or not, and the last thing he wanted was to be just another man in a long line of men.

How should he handle it? Did he need to handle it, or did he only need to protect his heart?

Melanie made a muffled noise against his chest.

She was probably down for the night. Owen contemplated waking her up to get her to the guest room upstairs, but when he tried to move her, she gripped his hip and wouldn't budge. He leaned his head back against the sofa and closed his eyes. Just a few minutes, then he'd try again.

CHAPTER TWELVE

THE DISMISSAL BELL RANG OUT, AND THE BODIES MOVED in one massive unit, unfolding from the small desks, jamming books into backpacks, and scrambling for the classroom door. I called out assignments as they left.

"Homework is on page twenty-three. Test next Thursday. Everything is posted on the class calendar page. Tag me there if you have a question over the weekend, and I'll do my best to get you answers as quickly as possible."

I wasn't sure how many kids actually listened to me, but I'd started the class off with the same information. Hopefully those teenage minds remembered one of the two reminders. The school year started two weeks ago, the first one for teachers in preparation, and the second for students. I had six classes this year, including one for calculus. I hadn't planned on teaching the higher math course, but the normal calculus teacher took a tumble off his roof and spent his first week of planning in the hospital in traction for a shattered pelvis and broken back. Finding long-term subs turned out to be just as hard as finding higher math teachers, and our esteemed principal decided to split up the advanced classes between the remaining instructors.

I also moved up as head coach of the mathletes team. This didn't bother me, however it did add even more to my work day and work schedule. The last few years, I'd been the head of the math department, mainly because no one else wanted it. Ever since I accepted that responsibility, more and more duties were piled on my back. Homecoming advisor? Ask Ms. Miser. School club sponsor? Ask Ms. Miser. Need an academic liaison? Don't ask. *Tell* Ms. Miser. It seemed like the answer to any problem dealing with numbers or student activities was *oh, Melanie Miser can do it. She's single and doesn't really have a life.*

Gah! I needed to get my shit together about next semester. The January due date meant I would need a long-term sub for the second half of the school year. Fuck, I hoped I could find one! I might decide to take the entire semester off, which would drastically impact everything I did at the school. Was there anyone who could take my place? Probably not. Teacher burnout was a real thing and made a lot of people in my profession leave after a few years. Most of the veteran teachers in my department had settled into a comfortable zone and were coasting into retirement. They wanted no more work than what was necessary for their classes, and even then, only the minimum. My days during the school year extended far beyond hours in the classroom, simply because work had to be done, and as the top dog, I had to do it. At last the weekend had arrived.

Labor Day weekend, that was. Historically, it was supposed to be a remembrance of the labor movement. It was about the dedication, economic contributions, and achievements of American workers. For some, it was a three-day weekend of sales, cookouts, and firing off any leftover Fourth of July fireworks. For teachers, it was one last summer hurrah before the super tight school calendar gets started. Meetings, classes, planning sessions, after school study groups, football games, club activities, homecoming parade, senior recognitions... the list was endless. The next real break won't be until the end of November, and afterward, the big end of the semester exam push starts. Fuck, I'm tired just thinking of it.

I'm also tired just thinking of what I have to face this weekend.

Bevvie popped her head into my class. "I see you're still standing. New class gonna work out okay?"

I sighed and opened the bottom drawer to my desk. "Like I have a choice in the matter. I swear the troll is out to get me."

"Troll?"

"My new nickname for Principal Bradshaw."

"I thought that's what you called my ex-husband?"

"He's a troll too. Anyway, Bradshaw asked if I could add the debate team onto my club sponsorships. The debate team? Really? I'm a math teacher, for fuck's sake. What the hell do I know about debate?"

"Maybe he likes the way you argue."

"Maybe he needs to kiss my ass."

"That's an all-day job."

"You can kiss my ass, too."

She laughed. I'm so lucky to have her as my BFF. Our banter might sound mean to other people, but I had no doubt she would always have my back. One distressed phone call would bring her and her family to stand with me no matter what.

I pulled out an unopened box of Little Debbie

Swiss Rolls. I had another one of Zebra Cakes and Oatmeal Creme Pies in there as well. Her eyes lit up.

"You gonna share? If I buy those things for the kids, the most I get is a sniff before they're devoured by the voracious mob."

I ripped open the box, tearing off the lock tab in the process. They wouldn't last long here either between the two of us horking them down. Besides that, there remained the potential of a juvenile or two in the hallway getting the scent and bringing the whole herd. "Knock yourself out."

I tossed her one double pack and tore open another for myself. Oooooh, yeah baby! Rich over-sweet creamy chocolate goodness!

"You coming to the game tonight?"

"Probably not. I'm really beat, and I have the summons to deal with on Saturday." I shoved an entire roll in my mouth and chomped down. The decadent flavor burst on my tongue, and I groaned with appreciation. The morning sickness had gone away and left me in a perpetual state of hunger. I alternated cravings between sweet and salty. Mostly sweet. I even kept a stash of snack cakes in my kitchen and on the night-stand in my bedroom. I wasn't usually a dessert-eating person, but these days I couldn't resist those uber-sugary sweet treats. Mattie and I had a lot in common for the time being.

Beverly tore open her own pack. "Do you *have* to go to that vipers' den?"

I shifted the massive bite to one cheek before answering. "It's easier to give in than argue. I tried skipping out before, and it took them years to get over it. I still hear about that one missed party even now. I'll make my rounds to keep my mother happy, glad-hand a few people, avoid Magnus like the plague, and get the hell outta there. I figure two hours should do it, then I'm not obligated again until next year." My words were garbled with the masticated wad I had in my mouth, but manners be damned. This was Little Debbie!

"After the shitstorm last time you went there, I don't want you to go by yourself."

I grinned at Bevvie's mama bear face. "You wanna come with me? Maybe I'll take Mattie and let him swim in the fountain. That would make Magnus's head explode."

She rolled her eyes at me. "Mellie-Jellie, you are such a PITA."

I blew out a crumb-filled raspberry at her. "You love me."

"Yes, I do, but you're still a big, fat PITA. I was thinking more on the lines of Owen."

"Owen? Why?"

She dropped the wrapper in the trash can and ticked off her points finger by finger. "One, he's big. Big enough no one will mess with him. Two, his quiet nature is intimidating when he wants it to be, and I'm sure he will want it to be at this shindig. Three, he's protective of you. Four, it will make me feel a lot better knowing someone like him has your back for those two hours."

I swallowed the mass in my mouth, and my throat worked to get it down in one go. "So you're saying Owen needs to be my plus one because it makes *you* feel good?"

"Yes."

I wanted to laugh. I really did, but the sincerity on Bevvie's face had me thinking. It wasn't such a bad idea to have someone I liked go with me. I thought about it for a hot minute. Owen did look intimidating. He might not scare Magnus, but I bet he would keep the other vultures off me. She was also right in that he seemed protective of me. After my last disastrous family gathering, he'd given me a long hug when I showed up at the MacAteer house. He kept our hotel night secret between us, and I'd been around him enough times to be comfortable with him. In fact, when I was with him, I felt safe. More than that. I felt… I felt… fuck, I couldn't examine that right now.

I picked up my second roll, this time only biting half off so I could talk without looking like a chipmunk with packed cheeks. Still not great manners, but who cares? This was Little Debbie, after all. "I suppose I could ask him, but do you really think he'd go? It's a lot to ask for someone to face my family. Maybe he's putting up with me only because I'm the super cool godmother to your children."

She eyed the open box of remaining Swiss Rolls. "No, he really does like you. He's just shy and uh… well…."

Her hesitation put my Spidey senses on guard. I handed her another pack of the snack cakes. "Something wrong with him?"

She waved off the second treat, even though I knew she wanted it. "No, nothing is wrong with him." She sighed and propped a round hip on my desk. "It's not a secret, per se, but he's kinda sensitive about it. Owen has a speech problem that didn't get fixed when he was younger. You might have noticed he communicates more in words, not sentences? Sometimes reversing sounds? The occasional stammer? He's an extremely intelligent man, he just has a speaking issue with some people."

I blinked. "Me in particular?"

"Not you in particular. He used to have that problem with me and the kids until he got to know us. I think once he gets relaxed and in a comfortable situation, the speech problem goes away or at least doesn't happen as much."

I swallowed the last of the cake and licked the chocolate scraps from the cardboard. "Well, he's been talking to me in complete sentences for some time now."

Surprise showed on Bevvie's face. "He's been talking to you?"

"Yes, and with a fair amount of articulation. Whole sentences and everything." I gave in and opened another package of sugary bliss and handed one of the two rolls to a drooling Bevvie. *It's not so bad if we split a package. Right?* "We teachers are trained on how to work with anyone. Speech problem? Puh. I noticed a few odd words, but there's nothing off-putting about it. Certainly nothing hard to handle."

She bit off the end of the roll. "I'm glad you two are getting along. He's a hard nut to crack, but he will eventually. I hope you do take him with you this weekend. You'll never find another man to have your back like a MacAteer man. I swear it's in their DNA."

"Ewww, gross, Mom!" Abby walked into my classroom in a long skirt and T-shirt that sported a giant tie-dyed peace symbol. "Do you realize how many chemicals and toxins are in that thing?"

Bevvie popped the rest of the cake in her mouth and chewed with overzealous relish. "Yes, and they're sooooo yummylicious!"

"Ugh! You're eating poison."

"Says the girl with a secret stash of Twinkies under her bed."

"Mom!"

"Don't deny it. I found the wrappers in the trash."

"Those aren't mine…, they're… um… they're Jake's, and he's just hiding them from Mattie."

"Sure. Whatever you say."

"MOM!"

I laughed out loud. I couldn't help it. This family was the best thing to ever happen to me. They meant the world. "I love you, Abby-pie. Don't ever change."

I turned to Bevvie and tossed the second wrapper into the trash. "I'll text Owen tonight and ask if he'll go with me this weekend. You're right. I'll probably need the backup."

This would be more than hanging with the family

at a festival or sitting with the kids. This would be a date with Owen MacAteer. I liked the idea. I liked it a lot.

"Miss Miser? A word, if you please."

Ugh, nothing like seeing your boss, all stern and serious, standing in your doorway. Beverly took her cue from the foreboding face of Mr. Bradshaw the troll. "I'll talk to you later. Let's go home, Abby-pie."

"Mom, I said not to call me that anymore. I'm Star-glow now."

I nearly burst into laughter as Bevvie muttered, "Trolls and spacey teenagers, God help me," as she passed me on her way out. If it wasn't for the frowning hound dog face of my principal, I think I would have enjoyed the moment more.

"Yes, Mr. Bradshaw, what can I do for you?"

"I received some very disturbing news this morning."

The budget for the math team has been cut. The school bus routes have been changed. The grocery store ran out of bran cereal. Different scenarios crowded my mind.

"I received your request for parental leave for next semester."

The back of my head buzzed. I could already tell where this conversation would go. Nonetheless, I played it off. "Is that all? Gosh, Mr. Bradshaw, I thought something terrible had happened, like the school board decided to bring back blackboards and chalk to replace our whiteboards and markers."

My sarcasm sank like a boat anchor. "Miss Miser, am I to think you're pregnant?"

I gave him my brightest smile while gritting my teeth. "Why yes, Mr. Bradshaw, I am. I am pregnant, and my baby is due in late December or early January. Thank you for asking."

He shuffled a bit. "You're an unwed woman."

OMG, open a dictionary and find some new terms, preferably in this century. "Yes, I'm aware."

"This is highly inappropriate, Miss Miser."

I kept the fake smile on my face but began to bristle. "According to the state policies, any parent or guardian is allowed up to twelve weeks of leave for parental bonding without danger of losing his or her job. That same policy says I only need to give you forty-eight hours of written notice before taking that type of leave. I've given you an entire semester to get a long-term sub for my classes. I'm not sure what you find so disturbing about it."

"You're pregnant."

"Yes."

"And you're not married."

Moron! "We've already established that, sir, and

there's nothing in this policy about being married or unmarried." I supposed being deliberately obtuse didn't help my situation, but truthfully, I got a kick out of needling the old bastard. "What exactly is the problem?"

"I don't think the parents will be very happy to have you teaching the girls in your classroom."

More like he will not be happy to have me teaching the girls in my classroom. Old goat!

I crossed my arms over my chest and stood up straight, towering over the man, and prepared for battle. "Three years ago, the chemistry teacher, Dillon Rathbone, got caught boinking a student in the lab after school. You let him stay in his classroom until the board hearing for permanent dismissal. That same year, Randy Barnett, a history teacher, had three, *three* DUI arrests, including one during a school trip he chaperoned and drove the bus. He's still working here and still keeps a bottle of vodka locked in his file cabinet. The rumor of Coach Blake Perdue giving steroids to his football players made the rounds last year, but no charges were ever filed. To this day, he's still in question, however when pressed, you defend him and puff up with pride at the team's winning record."

The man started melting into a puddle of weak goo. "Um... do you have a point, Miss Miser?"

"My point, Mr. Bradshaw, is you're a chauvinist. Yes, I'm a single pregnant woman. This does *not* affect the safety of my students nor the integrity of my class-room. I'm not going to parade around the school with a scarlet letter printed on my chest, especially when so many of my male colleagues have been granted pardons by you personally. I've given you a more than generous amount of time to find a long-term sub capable of teaching my classes. Anything else is nun-ya."

His face turned red, and he sputtered. "I don't understand."

"Nun-ya business."

I have to give him credit for trying. He pushed his horn rims up and mustered the stern look back on his face. "Miss Miser, this is not the same thing as having a bottle of bourbon locked up in a file cabinet."

"Vodka."

"No, it's bourbon. I... uh...."

Jackpot! His face drained of color when he realized what he'd just confessed. "I'm... uh... that is... well... um... good day to you, Miss Miser."

After he slunk off with his tail between his legs, I had to sit down, as my knees jellified and wouldn't hold me up any longer. He was right. Some people existed who would look down on me in judgement.

My mother and brother had already declared me to be an embarrassment. My father didn't have enough regard for me to be on his radar. A hiccup caught me by surprise. *Fuck, don't cry, Mel. Not here. Not worth it.*

The clock read four thirty before I left my classroom and walked to my car. I sat at the steering wheel and stared into nothing for several minutes, then my stomach shifted.

Not nausea. Not sickness. Just a little twist. I held my breath. It happened again, but this time it felt like a little poke. My baby moved around inside me, and I pictured him or her rolling over. I had a sonogram scheduled for Monday morning, since schools were closed, and Beverly had volunteered to go with me. I covered the spot with my hand and received another light kick.

"I don't give a shit what other people think. They can say or do whatever they want. It's you and me, kid, and we're gonna rule the world." I wiped my eyes. "By the way, if you hear mommy say shit or fuck or damn, that doesn't mean you get to say it. Rules and all."

I pulled out my phone and scrolled to Owen's number.

Me: Hey, what are you doing tomorrow afternoon?

The dots waved up and down for a moment.

Owen: No real plans. Probably work in the woodshop with Connor or laundry.

Me: Wanna come with me to a party?

Owen: Not much of a party guy. Where is it?

Me: My parents' annual Labor Day bash.

Owen: I thought you were on the outs with them.

Me: It's complicated. Yes, I'm on the outs but if I don't go, I'll never hear the end of it. Only an hour or two, and there's usually a pretty nice buffet spread. We can make an appearance and leave. You'd be doing me a huge favor.

The dots danced and stopped several times before I got a response.

Owen: What do I have to wear?

I sighed in relief. A weight came off my shoulders. I knew Owen wouldn't let me down.

Me: Casual business if you can. Khakis and a polo shirt is fine if you have it. If not, whatever you have that's clean.

Owen: I have some clothes that will work. Time?

Me: Around one-ish will work.

Owen: I'll drive my truck if you don't mind. Your car is nice but too small for me.

Me: Deal. Pick me up at twelve thirty?

Owen: Yes.

Me: It's a date. BTW, I just felt the baby move.

The dots stopped moving. Uh-oh. TMI? Should I have not used the word date?

They jumped a few times.

Owen: Happy for you, Melanie.

I couldn't help the grin that burst out of me.

Me: Thanks! ;-)

I closed the app and buckled my seat belt. Junior flipped again. "Yeah, I'm hungry too, kumquat. What do you say you and me go get a chicken gyro from Nick's Grill and binge on Netflix tonight? I'll tell Bevvie about the troll on Monday. Good plan?"

My kid wiggled in affirmation. "Okay, biscuit. Okay."

CHAPTER THIRTEEN

STICKY-HOT HUMIDITY LAYERED ON TOP OF ME AS I opened the door of the black hulk that was Owen's heavy work truck. He came around the side and offered me a hand. I accepted as the ground looked like it was far away from my perch in the oversized vehicle. Cars were lined up at the portico, waiting for the valet parking attendants to find space for everyone. Owen had found a spot close to the driveway exit instead of waiting in the line. That way we didn't have to wait for someone to bring us the vehicle when we wanted to leave. The grass would be flat there for a day or two, but the rest of the lawn would also have some damage from all the guests my family invited for their annual Labor Day gala.

Why the fuck did I come here today?

Because if I didn't make an appearance, my mother would drop into a hysterical fit and guilt trip me for life. My father would sniff his disapproval and tell me in his own way how disappointed he was in me. Magnus didn't count. I already knew he would prefer I go far, far away and never return. As much as we hated each other, it amazed me that we shared a blood tie.

I smoothed the blue and white floral maxi dress over my ripening body. At five months, I was starting to show a little, and the loose-fitting dress hid my slightly rounded stomach. Did I look pregnant? Maybe a little, but there was enough material swinging around my body that it was hard to tell. No doubt the gossip was making the rounds, but I didn't need to add any fuel to the fire. Let them keep guessing.

Owen folded my hand into his as we approached the house. The strains of a string quartet wafted past my ears, and the smell of smoky barbecue mixed with lilac floated in the air. Strange combination, but I was noticing more and more strange combinations these days. It seemed all my senses had become super acute. Food tasted richer, colors were intensified, and odors had strengthened. Touch was also affected, in that I was more aware than ever of the man standing next to me. Despite the heat of the day, his presence burned.

He turned to me with those incredible green eyes of his. "Okay?"

I was sure most of his talking today would be in one- and two-word sentences and mostly to me. No big secret that social settings weren't his favorite way of spending an afternoon. I couldn't really blame him either, as the one we faced today, I thought of more as a gauntlet than a party. I fake smiled at him. "Yeah, I'm good. Let's get this shit show over with."

I could tell he wasn't fooled by my false bravado, but he kept moving.

The back of the house held a few hundred people or so. Some were friends, but the majority were work acquaintances of either my father or Magnus. It was limited space, so the privilege of being one of the select few to attend was a big deal. I'd questioned for years why they didn't hold this party of theirs at the country club. More of their people could come with less mess and disturbance to the house. I had the feeling it was more to do with showing off the family wealth than spending time with friends and colleagues.

Wait staff hired for the day wandered around carrying trays of miniscule hors d'oeuvres. Pregnancy was hard work, and my appetite had increased significantly. These tiny bites of nothing wouldn't cut it for long. Owen picked up a star-shaped cucumber slice topped with a dot of cream cheese and a tiny roll of smoked salmon. He eyed it for a moment before he popped it into his mouth and crunched down with a frown. The waiter scurried away before he could pick up another one.

"Fake food," he commented.

I had to agree. "It's a fake day, O-man. Let's get through it, then make like birds and get the flock out."

Piper Long, one of my mother's cronies and the biggest gossip at the country club, approached me. "Melanie, darling. How are you?" She air-kissed both of my cheeks and gave Owen a dismissive glance before looking down at my hidden middle. "You're looking just lovely these days."

Bitch. I know what you're looking for. "I'm well, Piper, I hope you are. This is Owen MacAteer."

She twisted the ruby drop pendant hanging from her surgically tightened neck. "My, he's certainly a big one!"

Jeez, why does she always have to titter like that when she talks? Oh my God, did she just crotch shoot him?

Yup, she did. Her eyes darted again to Owen's lower half. WTF?

I thought Owen looked good on a daily basis— even more so that time I saw him shirtless at the hotel

—but today, he was exceptional in tan pants that hugged his tight ass and a pale green polo shirt that fit tight across his broad shoulders. The logo of his family company was stitched on the breast rather than a fashion one. Irish Pub Builders sat on top of a small shamrock. His hair had been freshly buzzed and his short beard trimmed neatly. He looked hot, or should I say *hawt*? Piper thought the same, judging by the hungry, speculative expression on her face. Owen shifted toward me and seemed uncomfortable under the older woman's scrutiny. Time to shut this shit down.

"Yes, he is a big one, Piper." I turned and fitted myself to Owen's side. His arm came up and automatically wrapped around my waist, drawing me closer. I almost tittered myself at the thought he was using me as protection from the geriatric cougar. My hand came up to rest against his hard chest, and a nipple tightened under my palm.

I didn't know why I did it. Maybe because Piper was watching. Maybe because I spotted Peter on the other side of the pool with Prudence Mayfield. Maybe because Magnus stood next to them, and the trio's attention was squarely on us. Maybe I just wanted to. I put two fingers to Owen's jaw and directed his mouth to mine. The kiss was a light one, closed mouth and entirely casual. I wasn't expecting the spark that jumped between us. His body jerked as it hit him too.

Piper waved to a group of her cronies and made some lame excuse to move off and go talk to them. I nodded and smiled at her, but my focus was completely on the man standing beside me. Every movement he made landed in my gut. His palm dropped from my waist and brushed lightly over my ass as he reached to clasp my hand firmly in his. He stuck his other hand in his pocket and simply waited for me to decide what to do next.

"I guess I need to make sure my parents see me so I won't get the third degree next week. We don't have to stay long. Just enough to keep them satisfied and off my back. I really appreciate you doing this for me."

"Always."

A thrill zinged through me at his simple one-word answer. A wealth of meaning sat behind that word. Bevvie was right. I'd never find another man to have my back like a MacAteer man. Like Owen MacAteer.

Out of the corner of my eye, I saw Piper point at me and Owen and then circle a finger around her stomach. It didn't take a genius to figure out what her gesture meant. The other ladies reacted with looks of indignant shock or disapproving frowns. One woman pressed her fingers against her mouth as if stifling a laugh. My hand crept up to cover my lower stomach. *Fuck you, bitch! Say all you want about me, but say anything about my kid and it's on.*

Owen squeezed my hand. He'd seen the old biddies as well and didn't like it.

I spotted my father and mother standing together in front of the fountain, greeting their guests. Magnus had left his spot near the pool and lurked somewhere in the crowd. I hoped to avoid running into him. That would make the day a bit more bearable.

Owen plucked another cucumber star from a passing tray as we walked over to my parents. I guessed it would take three or four of those trays to fill him up. Maybe more. My mother had dressed up to the nines today in a dusky pink floral dress that came to just above her knees. One shoulder was covered and the other bare. I wasn't sure it was a good look for her, as it showed the thin and wrinkled skin across her collarbone. It was designer and cost at least four figures, which made it okay. My father wore a suit and tie. How the hell could he stand that in this heat? In his hand sat a crystal tumbler of amber liquid and ice cubes. No doubt it was his favorite bourbon.

"Melanie, darling, how good of you to come." Deloris's sugar-sweet southern came through gritted teeth. I could hear the underlying message, *don't embarrass me,* in her words. I leaned over as she air-kissed me on either cheek. My height was always an issue for her, and her eyes darted to the kitten-heeled sandals I wore. Nine West instead of Jimmy Choos, but I doubted she could tell the difference. "My, what a handsome fellow you have here."

"Mom, this is Owen MacAteer. Owen, this is Deloris Miser, my mother."

He stuck out a hand, and Deloris looked at it in fright before gingerly taking it. "Nice to meet you, Mr. MacAteer."

Martin kept silent as his attention wandered through the crowd, it being beneath him to acknowledge my presence. *Nope, not dealing with this shit!*

"Daddy, this is Owen MacAteer. Owen, this is my daddy, Dr. Martin Miser."

I watched him cringe when I called him "daddy." He never liked it when I was a child and liked it even less now. Owen repeated the handshake extension.

"What line of work are you in?" No greeting, no reciprocal hand. He didn't even bother looking Owen in the eye. Just a cold question, and he couldn't care less about the answer.

"Construction. Own a company."

Deloris *oh my-ed* and *how nice-ed* while Martin grunted, sipped at his drink, and pointedly turned his head away. *Fuck me sideways. Seriously, why did I come here today?* My mother insisted on this, but it was obvious my father wanted nothing to do with me. Nothing new there. An awkward silence settled between us, and I froze. What did I do about my father's rudeness and my mother's nervousness? Nothing. Nada. Anyone else, I wouldn't have hesitated to tell them off or walk away. With my parents, I'd never been able to stand up to them. An icy sick feeling crept up the back of my throat, and I flashed both hot and cold over my body. My breath shortened, and my heart raced. In my world, I had control of myself and my life. In this house, I was nothing. Less than nothing and would always remain in that position.

I think Owen sensed the panic attack battle that brewed inside me, because he took over. He jerked a nod at my parents and took my arm. "Food."

That was enough to break me out of the downward spiral. I smiled up at him. *God, it's so nice to have someone taller than me!* "Okay, O-man. Buffet is right over there. Gotta feed my big man and my little one."

Deloris gasped at the pregnancy reminder and plastered a big smile across her pained face to cover up her slip. My father didn't react. Too far beneath him.

The buffet contained lots of artfully prepared food bits that were more show than substance. More cucumber stars, stuffed olives, cubes of different cheeses, tiny rounds of mini quiches, triangles of stuffed spanakopita, everything light and pretty, and no bigger than a bite. Owen eyed the offerings and said nothing. He handed me one of the small party plates and started filling one for himself.

"We can go for burgers later if you want. My treat."

He shrugged and popped a quiche in his mouth. "Won't starve."

His short answers bothered me some. He'd been talking more and more to me in the last weeks but hadn't said much since we got here. I hoped it was only his nerves from being at the party and not nerves from being at the party with *me*.

"What the fuck are you doing here?" The loud, cutting voice startled me enough that I dropped the bite I'd picked up. Shit, Magnus had decided to make an appearance.

"I'm here at Mother's request. She left me four messages just yesterday telling me I had to be here today, so I came."

"Yeah, right. Any excuse to embarrass the family further, eh, Melanie?"

"I'm not embarrassing anyone. She won't let up

when she wants something. It's better to be here than deal with the fallout next week. You know that."

"All I know is you have no business showing your face. I talked to Peter, and he filled me in."

That panicky feeling came racing back up my spine. "I haven't seen Peter in months. He has nothing to do with anything."

A waiter came up with a tumbler similar to my father's. Magnus grabbed it without looking at or thanking the man and took a long drink. From the glazed look in his eyes, this wasn't the first one. "He told me about your bitch fit in a public place and how you tried to pawn your bastard off on him."

"You weren't there and didn't see what happened. He insulted me enough to deserve a face-full of coffee."

"Insulted you? You're the one who got knocked up."

"I didn't do it by myself."

"That's your problem, Melanie. You always blame someone else for your shortcomings. You never take responsibility for anything. You were a burden as a child and a burden now." He took a big sip of his drink. "Christ, when I think about the trouble you've caused this family, I want to vomit. You're nothing but a goddamn slut. Makes me sick you're such a waste of space."

My gut churned, making me want to vomit myself. My older brother had considered me the ruin of his life since my birth. I couldn't recall one happy brother-sister moment, only memories of his constant criticism and abuse. Not pretty enough. Not smart enough. Not talented or special. Too tall. Too skinny. Too emotional. Waste of space. Waste of space. Waste of fucking space!

A memory flashed before my eyes. One I'd rather forget.

I floated in the pool on one of the air-filled lounge chairs, my eyes covered in Oakley Wayfarer sunglasses, and a cold glass of iced tea in the cup holder. The sun beat down on my dozing twelve-year-old body. This year there had been many changes in me, both physical and mental, and they happened fast. My height shot up five inches, making me clumsy when I moved. I bumped into doors or rails, spilled glasses at the dinner table, and knocked over things while trying to control my longer legs and arms. Magnus sneered at me with disgust most of the time at my awkwardness, which made me more self-conscious. I grew breasts almost overnight, two big fleshy balls that hurt a lot and were still getting bigger. Bee-Dee helped me get bras that fit and kept them contained, but I still had other kids at school stare and make fun of me. Worst of all, I had my first period. Thank God that started here at home one weekend with no one at home but Bee-Dee and me. The bloody mess and pain had me thinking I was dying, but Bee-Dee explained what was going on with my body and showed me what I needed. Mom shrugged when I told her about my experience. I didn't really expect any other reaction.

School had ended for the year, and I had all summer to lounge in the pool, work on my tan, and go shopping. Mom might not want me around, but I had friends that did. More than likely because of my rich girl status and because they had crushes on Magnus. Whatever the reason, at last I found myself in a group. I'd also found Ms. Blessing, my math teacher. Most seventh graders hated math with a passion, but I loved numbers. Simple, exact, and structured. Two and two always equaled four. We studied pre-algebra in preparation for next year, and I couldn't wait until fall for that class. English and social studies? Nah. Give me more math.

My half-asleep mind floated along with my body, thinking about clothes and what the new fall trends would be, when a loud voice startled me, almost sending me into the water. I froze instead.

"Damn, Magnus. When did your sister grow that rack? Bet you could shelve books on those things."

I kept still, hoping they thought I slept on, but opened my eyes to see Robert Corrigan, Archie Mayhew, and

Magnus standing at the edge of the pool. The black of my sunglasses kept them from noticing I was awake.

All three were dressed in golf clothes, and I guessed they were coming back from a game at the country club. Magnus got a brand-new car for his birthday, and he and his friends spent hours driving around in the gorgeous red Saab convertible. I never asked him to take me for a ride. I already knew the answer he would give.

Robert spoke again. "She got hair on her pussy yet?"

Magnus frowned at him. "How the fuck should I know? I try not to be around her any more than I have to."

"Just wondering how ripe that cherry is."

Robert laughed. The look in his eyes made me uncomfortably aware of my near-naked state. I wore my favorite pink bikini that showed a lot of skin to get as much of me tanned as possible. Now I wished I had donned my frumpy one-piece suit. I wasn't stupid. Bee-Dee had explained to me about sex and boys and more changes that would be coming. I knew what pussy, rack, fuck, cherry, cunt, ass, dick, and cock meant from older kids at school. Lying there on the raft in the middle of the pool, I was conscious of my body being displayed. Hearing Robert use those dirty words in reference to me scared me. Fear bloomed in my bare stomach, and I had to concentrate hard to keep still and not tremble. I didn't know what else to do. Go away, go away, go away, I chanted over and over in my head.

Archie answered my silent prayer. "Fuck, Rob, she's only twelve. Give her a few years before you go after that fruit. Let's drive over to my place and play video games. My parents aren't home from their cruise, and the liquor cabinet is full."

The raft started to spin away from them in the current. I held my breath as they faded from my sight. If I couldn't see them, they couldn't see me, right?

Robert laughed again as they moved off. "What do you think, Magnus, old buddy? Mind if I bang your little sister sometime?"

"I don't give a shit what you do. She's useless as it is. Fucking waste of space."

Right then, the universe decided to fuck with me some more. My head swiveled as if controlled by something else, and my eyes locked onto a figure on the other side of the fountain. Robert stood there with a model-thin blonde next to him glittering in a white sheath dress and heels more suited to a formal evening than an afternoon party. If this was Kiki, his third wife, whatever weight he claimed she had gained at the July festival certainly didn't show much to me. *Prick!* Maybe I'd mail her one of my bottles of lavender body spray.

Robert paid no attention to his wife or the man who spoke to him. His eyes were on me. Watching. He lifted his glass in salute and stared at me over the rim. He had the same smug look on his face he'd perfected years ago. One I wanted to tear off with my nails. The man speaking noticed Robert's distraction and turned to see what held his interest. I barely recognized Archie. The years had not been so good to him. His round stomach stuck out, straining the buttons on his shirt and forcing his jacket to stay open. Somewhere along the way, he'd lost his neck and now sported a long sag of flesh that hung from his chin. The wispy hair left on his head attempted to cover his pink scalp with an artful combover. The effort was wasted.

I tore my eyes away and clutched at Owen's arm like a lifeline. "How 'bout not airing my private business in public, Mags."

"How 'bout keeping your legs closed for a change."

Direct hit. The world saw me as a kick-ass, take no prisoners, tough wonder woman. Within these walls, I turned back into that scared, vulnerable, tongue-tied twelve-year-old. My heart rate doubled as my head filled with a silent roar of white noise. The world condensed into a pinprick, and I broke out in a cold sweat. *Fuck, Melanie, where are your fucking balls?*

I didn't have to find them. Owen brought his to the party. The plate he held dropped and shattered on the decking, and my grip broke as both his arms shot out.

One hand grabbed Magnus's shirt in a tight fist and the other his throat. Owen was both taller and wider than Magnus and had no trouble body-slamming my brother onto the buffet table. Food trays flew everywhere, splattering the surrounding people. Gasps and screams erupted from the crowd, and the quartet stopped playing. Neither Robert nor Archie moved to help their friend, perhaps too stunned that anyone would dare call him out on his actions.

Magnus choked and pulled at the iron-band arms that held him down. Owen didn't seem fazed at all by the struggling man beneath him.

"Stop." The word exploded from Owen, even startling me. I'd never heard this gentle giant raise his voice or even get annoyed. The volume of that single word showed the amount of anger in the man. Magnus stilled and waited under Owen's grip.

"Apologize."

A red-faced, food-covered Magnus tried to brazen it out. He thrashed again on the table and sent more plates, canapes, and garnishes to the littered floor. "You fucking bastard," he garbled, "I'll fucking have you arrested for assault. I'll sue you for every penny you have and will ever earn!"

Owen smiled. "Bring it."

My parents showed up. Mother stood there crying

and ringing her hands. "Oh my, how could you, Melanie? Why do you bring such destruction everywhere you go?"

"Let go of him, or I'll call the police." Why did my father's threat seem so empty?

Owen's grip around Magnus's throat strengthened, and my brother stopped fighting. He stilled and glared at Owen with pure hatred. Owen didn't move. "Apologize. Now."

"I'm sorry."

Fuck me, Magnus gave in. My brother, who never in his life got held accountable for his words or actions, apologized to *me*. Yes, it was under duress and he probably didn't mean it, but the fact he did it shocked me. A weight lifted from my shoulders, and I straightened my back. I couldn't remember another time in my life someone stood up for me against my family. Bee-Dee tried to protect me as best she could, but no one had ever taken on my brother and won.

Owen let go of Magnus and moved back as my brother rolled off the table. His immaculate designer suit was covered in colorful bits of food. He coughed and staggered upright, stumbling and slipping in the mess as he tried to regain his composure. "You're gonna regret this."

Somehow Owen had remained clean throughout the drama. "Useless prick."

He took my hand and started walking away, leading me gently. As he approached my parents, he paused. Mother whimpered in fear and hid behind my father. He stood stock-still with his usual stone face. I had no idea what emotions flowed behind that rigid mask of his.

Owen looked him in the eye with barely a glance at my mother. His hand came up and a finger pointed at my father. "Your *daughter*. Shame on you."

The only reaction from my father was a slight tightening of his lips. Deloris gasped and clutched at her neck. Drama queen all the way.

The weight of a hundred eyes rested on me in silent judgement as Owen led me from that place. Some pain infused my heart, but for years, I'd taking verbal abuse from my brother. My mother never had been the classroom participation mom, so there was no maternal closeness between us. My father? I might as well not have one. The numbness in my brain flowed through my nerves. No thoughts. No anger. No regrets even. That lack of emotion brought me resolution. I. Was. Done.

We got to the truck. Owen still vibrated with fury as he lifted me into the cab. Rage poured off him in waves, and his face stayed taut. He climbed in on his side and slammed the door shut. His hands grabbed the steering wheel with a white-knuckled grip.

"Owen?"

"Need a minute."

Silence filled the cab of the truck. I fidgeted for a few moments before trying again.

"Owen? O-man?"

He brought his eyes to mine, and I would swear I heard the crack of the lightning that zapped between us. His body leaned toward me, but he didn't have to go far, as I met him halfway, my mouth slamming on his with sheer need. Our positions in the cab made the kiss awkward as hell, but the passion behind it eclipsed any difficulty. I sucked at his lips, and his tongue plunged between mine, licking and taking over. My heart raced, and I grabbed at his shirt, fighting the pull of the seat belt. Fuck, if we were anywhere else, I would have mounted him right then and there.

"Take me home." I managed to pant. His eyes were shining with his own need, and his breath labored heavily. He pulled back and, without a word, started the truck.

CHAPTER FOURTEEN

Owen watched as Melanie fumbled at the lock. His breath sawed in and out of his chest, making it ache. On the drive from her parents' place to her home, she'd scooted as close to him as possible on the bench seat of his truck, her hand on his crotch keeping his dick at rigid attention. He'd thought she would crawl in his lap if there had been enough room. When she pulled down his zipper to free him, he'd almost driven off the road.

"Easy, Mel."

"I don't want easy." Her throaty voice had sent his body into overdrive.

She finally got the door to her condo open, and both of them stumbled inside. Owen barely got the door closed before she launched herself at him. Her hand hiked the long skirt up around her hips, and she wrapped her legs around him. He caught her with his hands under her ass, and she leaned in for a long kiss.

"Mel, slow down."

"I don't want slow."

She wants this. She wants me.

He got them over to the granite counter and planted her on it. She pulled at his shoulders and tightened her thighs to keep him from moving away. As if he wanted to. He focused solely on the woman pressed against him, hyperaware of everything. Her stiff nipples, her writhing body, her stroking hands on his back. She was turned on big-time and not afraid to show it to him.

She bit his lower lip and drew it into her mouth, and he groaned at the electric line that shot straight to his dick. Her hand came up and yanked down one dress and bra strap, baring herself to him. The rosy nipple beckoned. He took the hint and lowered his head, drawing that tight peak into his mouth and pressing it with his tongue. He heard her gasp and felt her arch as she leaned back, pushing her breast further between his lips. She bared her other breast, and he switched sides. His hand came up to pull and play with one nipple while he sucked and stroked the other. His dick was so hard it hurt.

I need to taste her. I need to go down on her and feel her come.

"Fuck me, Owen. Just fuck me." Her breathy demand sounded in his ear. She reached down to cup him in her hand, and he almost came in his pants.

He pulled back from her grip and pushed his hand between her legs, feeling the wet crotch of her panties. His thumb pressed against her distended clit, and she cried out at the contact. She writhed against him like a cat in heat, demanding his attention. He took her wrists, pulled them away from his hard dick, and gently pushed them behind her back. This made her arch backward, presenting her bared breasts higher. Her whimpers of need shot straight to his dick. He didn't know how much more he could take.

He leaned back in so their mouths were just inches apart, and his eyes locked with hers. She panted as the heat between them ramped up. There were words he wanted to say, wanted to ask, but the intensity of the moment was too much, and he couldn't find the right ones. He wouldn't do it. He wouldn't fuck her. Not like this. Maybe tonight was his one shot, but he wanted to be more than a scratch to her itch.

"Do it, Owen. I need this. I need you, baby. Don't leave me hanging."

He transferred her wrists to one hand, and the

other hand moved back between her legs. A finger hooked in her panties and pulled the material away, exposing her hot core. This time when he touched her, nothing sat between his skin and hers. He stroked between the drenched folds and found the hard nub of her clit.

"Yes! Fuck, yes!" She arched further, leaning back and granting him open access.

He slid a blunt finger inside her channel, and she shuddered as his thumb circled her clit again. Her knees spread farther apart, and he looked down to watch his digit enter her body. Her hips flexed, and she ground against his hand as he brought her higher. He pushed in as deep as he could and felt the waves of her orgasm as she came. Christ, what he wouldn't give to feel this around his dick. He imagined what it would be like. To be in a bed, their bed, making love as many times as they could. Then taking a break for food or something and going back for more.

He released her wrists and stepped back. The hard outline in his pants wasn't going away and the soft look of satisfaction on her face made it worse. He mumbled, "Excuse me," and walked to her bedroom in search of the bathroom, hampered by his heavy erection. Once he found the bathroom, he closed the door and opened his zipper, letting his dick spring out in relief. Déjà vu struck him as once again he stroked himself to release. Blood rushed from his head, and he gulped in huge amounts of air as his balls tightened up and his spine tingled. It didn't take long for him to come, spraying into a wad of toilet paper.

He stood there a few minutes, catching his breath and letting his head stop spinning. He knew he played with fire and fully expected he would be the one to burn. Today gave him more insight into the woman he loved. Yes, loved. He knew she didn't love him back and probably never would, but after seeing that shit today, he wanted even more to be there for her. The MacAteer family was far from perfect, and the brothers had had many arguments over the years. Even did some scrapping between them that left black eyes and bloody split lips, but that only lasted until one of them got into real trouble. Then it was all hands on deck. He'd stood by Garrett during their younger escapades and bailed out Patrick and Angus on more than one occasion. One thing anyone could say about the MacAteer brothers? When the chips were down, they bonded together, and nothing could come between them.

Melanie's family? Nowhere near that kind of support. He still couldn't fathom a brother calling his sister a slut and dragging her through a public humiliation. Drunk or not, you didn't do that. Ever.

He flushed the toilet and washed his hands. One last deep breath, and he open the door to face whatever was coming.

"Why won't you fuck me?" She sounded calm, but underneath Owen heard a note of uncertainty.

He knew many men would have taken her offer and not looked back. That would make him just another mark on a measuring line. He wanted her, but he couldn't be that kind of man. "Not like this. Not when you're vulnerable. Not when I can't tell if you want me or just want to fuck."

His words sounded wrong when they came out of his mouth, but like all words, once said, they couldn't be unsaid.

She changed from turned-on wanton to angry wench in a flash. "You have a problem with wanting to fuck?"

He shook his head and tried to find the right way to say what he needed her to hear. "Today I can't. I won't. Rough day on both of us. Too easy to fall in bed to work out frustrations. I've done that with other women in the past. Not fair. Made me feel like shit. Not gonna use you to make me feel better. Not gonna let you use me for the same reason."

She paused, and the snapping fire in her eyes faded. The fight went out of her, and she seemed unsure and scared. "So it was okay for you to make me come by other means? Just not your dick?"

Owen dropped his eyes to the floor. "I'm sorry if I took it t-too far."

Her mood changed again, and Owen recognized it as a mask. She jumped down from the granite counter and smoothed over her skirt as if nothing happened. "No, you didn't do anything bad. I wanted to come, and you made that happen. Frankly, I don't think you went far enough, but I get what you're saying. My parents are hard to deal with, and my brother is worse. He makes me crazy when I'm around him, and sometimes I need to blow off steam. I'm sorry if you think I used you for that."

Her sudden indifference disturbed him, but he followed her lead. "Don't worry about it. I'm good. He's an asshole like-ke all the rest. All mouth. No bam dalls." He took a breath and blew it out. "Damn balls."

She smiled big and wandered over to a cabinet to pull down a water glass. "One thing is for sure. Everyone will remember that party. I'm sure there were phones out taking pics and videos of Magnus getting his ass covered by cucumber mush and paté. I hope he doesn't decide to press assault charges. I'm so sorry. I shouldn't have put you in that position."

"If he d-does, I'll deal. Not your fault." His voice sounded harsh even to him. "Parents. Brother. Those are toxic people. You know it. I know it. Don't need that shit. Don't dwell on it."

She filled the glass at the refrigerator dispenser, keeping her back to him. He swore he could see the wall she was building. "This is the second time I've put my hand around your dick and you didn't try to take it further. You could have fucked me tonight, all night. Probably in the morning too. Why did you stop?"

"Taking advantage. Not right."

"Don't you want me?"

She kept facing away from him when she asked that question. Those four words sent a shard through his gut. It didn't matter how dispassionate she tried to seem, or how blasé she tried to appear. She had cracks in her walls. Ones that exposed her tender heart, leaving it open and unprotected. Owen suspected other men might not notice or wouldn't care and simply walk away. He couldn't do it.

He moved behind her, letting her keep her guarded stance. His arms rose and surrounded her body, pulling her against him gently. He pressed his lips against her temple and felt her trembling. The ball was in his court, and it wouldn't take much for him to shred her to pieces. He wondered if she knew she had that same power over him.

He tightened his arms, hoping his words conveyed the message he desperately wanted her to receive. "If the time comes when you invite me to your bed, I'll be there not because you opened your legs to me. I'll be there because you opened your heart to me."

She made a noise in her throat while he held her. He noticed the white knuckles of her hand as she held the water glass in a death grip. When she relaxed that hard hold, he let her go.

"Always got your back, Mel."

He left the condo, his emotions in turmoil and second-guessing himself. *Should I have just had sex with her? Should I have said something different? Done something different? Should I have told her I love her?*

Owen got in his truck and looked up in the direction of Melanie's condo. She was a beautiful and broken woman. Her family be damned. If the police showed up to take him into custody for assaulting her asshole brother, so be it. He had bail money. He smiled. If given the chance to drive a fist into Magnus's smirking mouth, he'd take it in a heartbeat.

I COUNTED TO TEN AFTER I HEARD THE CLICK OF THE door closing. Then I counted to ten again, forcing my breathing to be deep and even. It didn't help. My heart continued to pound as if trying to burst through my chest. I expected the glass in my hand to have shattered by now with the fierceness of my grip. Water sloshed around inside it when I placed it on the counter. My shaking got worse as I moved to sit on my sofa. I raised my legs to curl my body into a tight little pod and covered myself with one of the folded throws I owned.

"You have a problem with wanting to fuck?"

"Today I can't. I won't. Rough day on both of us. Too easy to fall in bed to work out frustrations. I've done that with other women in the past. Not fair. Made me feel like shit. Not gonna use you to make me feel better. Not gonna let you use me for the same reason."

His words played in my head. Was he right? Was I looking for any port in a storm, and would any man with a functioning dick work at this moment? I supposed I could stay angry at him for suggesting I was simply looking to get laid, but truthfully, I had done this before with other men. Used sex to make myself feel better. More often than not, any relief I got was temporary, and I spent days afterwards justifying or running away.

"You could have fucked me tonight, all night. Probably in the morning too. Why did you stop?"

"Taking advantage. Not right."

I closed my eyes and let the tears fall down my cheeks unchecked. Twice I had thrown myself at Owen, practically begging him to fuck me, and twice he had refused. Perhaps he didn't want me after all. He could be disgusted by my preferred lifestyle and only have helped me because of my friendship with Beverly.

Deep down, I knew that wasn't true. If it were, he wouldn't have gone to this party with me. He wouldn't have taken on Magnus and demanded an apology from him. He wouldn't have pointed a finger in my father's face and said, "Shame on you."

"Don't you want me?"

"If the time comes when you invite me to your bed, I'll be there not because you opened your legs to me. I'll be there because you opened your heart to me."

Oh. My. God. *Please don't let me fall in love with this man. I couldn't bear it if it didn't last.*

Who the fuck am I kidding? I might already be there.

CHAPTER FIFTEEN

NORTH CAROLINA FALL WEATHER WAS A FICKLE BITCH. One week, the temperature could be so hot, eggs would fry on the sidewalk, and the very following week, the weatherman would be announcing blizzard conditions.

My school uniform for the time being centered on staying cool in loose and blousy dresses with long boxy jackets. Not exactly fashionable, but I didn't think I needed to advertise my condition any more than necessary. I probably should give my students more credit, as they didn't blink an eye at my burgeoning belly. As predicted, a few disapproving looks came from some of the older, more conservative teachers, but other than that, no one made a big deal.

For several weeks, the school year took up all my

free time. That, and the new class I had to teach. People had no idea how much work it took to be a teacher. Preparing an entire semester of lesson plans, finding materials, making tests appropriate to the state's standards, setting up the bulletin boards in the classroom, calendaring all the events for sports, field trip absences so as not to disrupt routines any more than needed, figuring how best to teach students with IEP's, helping prepare for the frickin' SATs, and of course the never-ending task of grading papers. My classes held from twenty-seven to thirty students each, and there were seven of them now. It didn't take a mathematician to figure out that meant every assignment could potentially put me at grading well over two hundred papers at a time. And then there were the emails. Holy fuck, the emails! Parents complaining about said grades, too much homework, could their kid get extra credit, and why did it take so long for me to answer?

Still, I loved my job. I loved when my students got the concepts. I loved the positive atmosphere in my classroom. I loved it when kids asked me about being on the math team. I loved the study groups that formed with some of my mathletes as tutors. Even during my brief planning time, all twenty minutes of it, kids would come and hang out with me between classes, ask questions, and sometimes just stop by to say hi.

I loved being a teacher.

I also loved Friday night football and went to every game, home or away. Bevvie and I sat together, and she always brought her brood with her. Abby had considered trying out for cheerleading last year. Apparently this had changed since her vegan phase started. Jacob would be at this school next year and had already gotten established in a group of science kids. He won the state science fair in his division last year, and his reputation had spread among the science geek squad as a potential player for the robotics team. Sarah stayed by me most of the time, treating me like the cool auntie I was, and Mattie acted like Mattie. I tag-teamed with Bevvie in watching him to make sure he didn't climb the fence rails or the announcer's booth.

A drop in temperature had me donning an extra layer. The weather prediction had rain coming, but not 'til way after the game. My favorite Dolce and Gabbana jacket wouldn't fit right now, so I'd opted for my fluffy Gorski cashmere poncho. Both pieces were actually knock-offs. Yes, I had enough money to buy a two-thousand-dollar piece of clothing, however, I saw no need to spend that kind of green on a label no one ever saw. My mother would die of embarrassment if she knew I had Vera Wang and J. Lo on my back instead of Saint Laurent and Chanel.

The pale gray wool brushed softly against my neck as I unfolded my stadium chair and plopped down next to Bevvie.

"Hey, trouble," my hoodie-clad BFF greeted. "Did you hear about the Collins boy? Confirmed case of mono. I've got an extra economy-sized bottle of hand sanitizer in my room if you need it."

I nodded. "Yes, I heard. He dated Amelie Grace last year, and I think he's with Tracie Edwards now. I don't know if the girls have it yet, but I bet it's coming. Knowing his reputation, I wouldn't be surprised if a few more girls came down with it."

Bev chuckled and pulled out her phone. "Connor has the kids over at the concession stand. You want something?"

"They have razzy-ritas yet?"

"Ha ha, very funny." She assumed what I called her radio announcer voice. "You have the choice between the delightful sparkling taste of a variety of carbonated beverages, the creamy confection of hot chocolate with marshmallows, or the slightly bitter notes of dark, rich coffee. Decaf, of course, with thick cream and a touch of sugar."

"So the usual. Coke, Sprite, Swiss Miss powder packs, or Costco-brand Keurig pods."

"You're messing up my presentation."

"You'll get over it. Hot chocolate sounds good. Decaf is a sin."

"And one you have to indulge in right now."

I sighed. "Yes. As soon as junior gets here, I'm moving into Starbucks for a month."

Her thumbs tapped at the screen of her phone. I spotted Abby and did a double take. She wore jeans with perfectly symmetrical rips at the thighs, black boots, and an off the shoulder oversized pink sweater. Her hair was styled, and she had on full makeup.

"I take it the hippie phase is over?"

Bevvie rolled her eyes. "Yes, thank God. Samuel finally went too far out for her. I could handle the vegan part, but then he declared all vegetables should be eaten raw. Not because it's healthier, but because it's cruel to cook them. He told Abby that she should only eat apples that have fallen to the ground and not pick any from the tree. I got a lecture from him about how inhumane it was to grind wheat into flour. He claims he's heard potatoes cry out in agony when someone chops them up or peels them and broccoli screams in pain when in the steamer. Don't get me started on what he says about cooking rice. Not even for love is Abby going to subsist on only cucumbers and arugula."

I pondered for a moment. "If plants had cognitive thinking brains and nervous systems, then would he consider harvesting murder? The act of chewing would also be a form of veggie mistreatment, right?"

Bevvie gave me a look of horror. "Don't go there. There's a big crock-pot of beef stew on my kitchen counter right now with the mangled bodies of all sort of veggies in it. You're welcome to come by after the game."

I smiled. "Carrot killer."

"Yep. I'm the notorious squash strangler."

"Lima bean basher."

"Hash-slinging slasher."

"Onion annihilator."

"Tomato terror."

"Pea... uh... picker? Okay, you win." I laughed.

"Torturing more produce, love?" Connor came up with his hands full of steaming Styrofoam cups. Sarah walked sedately next to him carrying two more cups, while Mattie skipped and circled them. I wasn't really surprised to see Owen behind them, his large hands wrapped round the delicate white foam. He silently handed me one of the cups. Dehydrated mini marsh-mallows slowly disintegrated on top. I took a cautious sip. Hot chocolate? How 'bout barely lukewarm.

"I'm sure the police have already issued an APB on me." Bevvie grimaced at her own drink.

Owen sat next to me, his hand dwarfing the small white cup. He raised it to his lips and swallowed the entire contents in one go. His face scrunched up, probably at the barely there chocolate flavor. I met his eyes and gave him my best sympathetic look. We hadn't talked much since last weekend when we almost ended up in bed together. I'd typed a dozen texts and deleted every one of them instead of sending. Sharing my feelings didn't come easy to me, and even though texting was safer, I still chickened out. Owen must have sensed that, and he backed off. A lot.

The band marched onto the field to the roars of the crowd, and the tinny sound of the announcer crackled over the outdated loudspeaker. Ugh! Someday, I really wished the school would finally spend some money on new equipment. It would be nice to join the twenty-first century before it became the twenty-second century. Retro might be in as far as teenage fashion, but the teachers needed up-to-date computers, smartboards, and tablets. The clunky monitors from the early nineties just didn't cut it.

"We need a fundraiser."

Bevvie glanced up at my random statement. "We do fundraisers all the time. Every department, 'cause the budget is lopsided. Better money management would go further. You remember the shit with the band when Bradshaw said they had to pay to use the field for practice? He said it was because the band caused too much damage to the grass for the football team to play. Coach Vann said that was bull because the team practices on that same field every day. Bradshaw also told all the teams that they would have to fund their own transportation to off-campus events. School functions not supported by school money? Something's fishy in the office."

"Bradshaw's cologne."

Beverly snorted and choked. "Don't do that when I'm enjoying my fancy gourmet *chock-oh-lah!*"

"Stick with singing, sweetheart. Your Italian is way off."

"That was French."

"I rest my case."

"PITA."

I made kissy noises at her. Connor grinned, and Owen grunted out a laugh. Junior decided to get in on the action and started turning flips. Visions of a tiny alien body using my liver and bladder for punching and kicking bags flashed through my mind. I had to pee. Again. "Excuse me for a minute. Anyone need something while I'm up?"

Owen stood. "A bigger cup."

OMG, Owen made a joke!

I laughed. "I agree, but you don't have to come with me. I can go to the bathroom all by myself now and get you another hot chocolate on the way back."

Mattie hopped up and down the bleacher steps on one foot, bumping into several people in the process. "Sorry. Excuse me. Hey, Mom? Can Uncle Owen get me a hot dog? I'm hungry."

Sarah and Jacob chimed in.

"I want one too."

"I don't want a hot dog. Those things are nasty. I want a pretzel."

"They don't have pretzels here. Those are at the baseball field."

"They do too have pretzels."

"Do not."

"Do too!"

"Do not!"

"Mom!"

Beverly looked at the clouded sky and appeared to be saying a prayer either for patience or deliverance. "Owen, would you mind?"

Owen grinned and stood up. "Come, bunkee-mutts."

I turned to Bev with a questioning look on my face. She shrugged. "He heard you call them that some time ago and he started calling them that too. He reversed monkey-butts into bunkee-mutts once, and the kids liked it so much it stuck."

We made a noisy entourage to the concession stand and bathrooms. Sarah took her uncle's hand on one side while I stood on the other. Jacob led the way, turning around to walk backward and talk about anything and everything that hit his head. Mattie jumped and gamboled around us like a baby goat. How the hell did Beverly manage four children, all with such different personalities and characteristics?

The short line at the concession stand meant I went to the restroom while Owen got to deal with all three juveniles at the same time.

"See? They have pretzels."

"Yeah, those are in a snack bag. Not the big soft ones you get at the baseball games."

"They're still pretzels."

I laughed as I left the small group. "Can't argue with her logic, now can you? Sarah, you'll make a great prosecuting attorney someday."

She lifted her chin at me. "I don't want to be the attorney. I'm going to be the judge."

I had no doubt this little adult-in-middle-school-form would be just that.

I'd turned to make my way to the restrooms when I heard someone call Owen's name. Jerry Harris walked up to the stand. I knew him from high school way back. He'd been a year ahead of me and always seemed to be on the outside looking in. I remembered him as being what me and my posse of girls called "high school furniture." Not a popular guy, not really that attractive nor unattractive either. Came from a poor family and had to work at the car dealership as a janitor at night. Never into sports or any school activities. He was just there, going to classes, making adequate grades. Average. Totally average.

High school furniture. Not exactly a nice moniker, but high school kids aren't known for their kindness towards each other. I had to admit, he'd done very well for himself. He now managed that car dealership, lived in an upscale house, had married a beautiful woman he met in college, and had two children. A real success story, when I thought about it.

I sighed. I loved my cute sporty Audi, but putting an infant car seat in my vehicle? Nope, it wouldn't look right. Time to go car shopping.

Junior started playing jumping jacks on my bladder, and I almost pissed myself. "All right, all right, I get it. I'm going. Jeez, kid, you're gonna have to learn some patience."

"Hey, Owen MacAteer!"

Owen looked up to spot Jerry Harris coming toward him, his two kids in tow. His wife must be on the bleachers somewhere enjoying a respite.

"Jodie loved the design for her she shed. She's all excited about getting it done before Christmas. Think you can book us in?"

Owen ran through his mental calendar. Connor hadn't been joking when he said he had more jobs coming in than time to do them. Now that Owen had done so much work in the community, his name was more and more popular as the go-to guy for outdoor deck construction and custom home remodeling. "Got time in October. Halloween." His comfort level with Jerry had grown to where he could talk more around the man.

"Great news! I'll tell Jodie to get it scheduled. You know how she is about her day-to-day timeline. Hey, you know, Bertie closed on her new property a few days ago and is moving in soon. Guess you'll be around for a while so maybe you can meet her after all. She really is a nice woman. I think you'd get along great."

"Look, Uncle Owen! They have nacho bowls tonight. Can I have one plus a hot dog?" Mattie spun in circles, grinding the toe of his shoe into the fine gravel. "And a Coke? And a brownie from the bake sale?"

"No Cokes or brownies, doofus. Mom would kill Uncle Owen for buying you that much."

"No, she wouldn't. She loves me and Uncle Owen, too."

"Yeah, she loves all of us, but she still won't let you eat that much junk food."

"Nachos ain't junk food."

"Are too."

"Are not."

"Are too!"

"Are not!"

"Uncle Owen!"

Jerry laughed out loud at Owen's pained face. "I can see you have your hands full. Please keep Bertie in mind. Jodie is pushing me hard to find people for her to meet. You know how it is."

Owen nodded even though he didn't know. Not

really.

The junk food debate raged on with Jerry's two kids joining in the cacophony.

"The nachos they make use fake cheese that comes out of a can."

"What's fake cheese?"

"It's made of chemicals. Not real milk, and they have to dye it orange to make it look real."

"That's why it tastes so good."

"Yeah, it tastes good, but it's not good for you. It causes cancer."

Mattie stopped spinning and gaped. "Nachos give you cancer?"

"Not the nachos. It's the chemicals they put in the nachos to make them taste good."

"Why is stuff that tastes good bad for you, and stuff that tastes bad good for you?"

"I don't know."

"Uncle Owen?"

Owen looked down at Mattie's dusty face and answered in the only way possible. "Ask your mom."

A burst of laughter sounded behind him. Melanie walked up and put her arm through his. "Spoken like a true male." She turned her attention to the other man. "Hey, Jerry, long time no see. How are you?"

Jerry's jovial mood dropped a bit, but he recovered

quick, as a professional salesman should. "I'm good, thanks. Nice to see you, Melanie. I hope you're well, too."

"Fantastic. I need to come see you soon for a new car. Something more sedan-like and roomier than my Audi. Got time next week?"

"Sure, sure. I'm there every day. Just come in and ask for me. I'll be glad to help you out. Are you two… uh… dating?"

Owen felt Melanie stiffen next to him, and she dropped her arm from his. "No, we're just friends. That's all. Just friends."

The food debate got louder.

"I think broccoli tastes good, and it's good for you."

"Ewww. Broccoli is nasty."

"No, it's not."

"I kinda like broccoli, but I hate brussels sprouts. My dad said they look like turtle heads. Who wants to eat those?"

"Blech. I don't think I can ever eat a turtle's head."

"It's not really a turtle's head. It just looks like one."

"That's so gross."

Owen pulled out his wallet, handed the kids five dollars each, and pointed at the concession line. "Go."

"Yeah! I can get a hot dog *and* nachos!"

"What about the chemical cheese?"

"I'll eat some broccoli tomorrow."

Jerry grinned. "Perfect save, Owen. Absolutely perfect. Nice seeing you here, and I'll catch you next week, Melanie." He moved to take his kids to the line.

Owen stood alone with Melanie, his head and heart full of conflict. Her words firmly put him in the friend zone, and she'd sounded fearful that anyone would wonder about their relationship status. This bothered him. He wasn't the most educated man in the world, but he still made a good living. He had difficulty talking to people, but it got easier the more he knew and trusted someone, as he was beginning to trust Melanie. Then there was the encounter after the party fiasco at her parents' house. He had had his fingers and mouth on the woman now standing beside him. He knew her taste and the sounds she made when she came. Friend zone? That hurt. Maybe it shouldn't, but it did.

"Well, O-man, that was interesting. You do a lot of work for Jerry?" Her nonchalant tone bugged him.

"Yeah."

"We went to high school together. Did you know that?"

"No."

"I remember he always worked at something. His family didn't have money, and he had to get a job in high school just as soon as he turned sixteen. I think he swept floors at the dealership at night, and now he manages the place. I admire that."

Owen grunted that he heard her but didn't respond otherwise.

"I'm thinking about house hunting in the next few weeks. My condo is okay for now, but I know it's not going to be big enough. Want to come with me? I could use your expertise on houses and construction and stuff like that."

Several emotions flashed through Owen. Resentment topped them. Just moments ago, she'd held his arm like they were a couple. She'd fallen asleep on top of him several times during movie nights at Bevvie's house. He'd come to her defense against her brother and family, risking the chance of assault charges. She intimately touched him more than once, and he had reciprocated. Yet he was just a friend who could be relied on for errands and house advice.

Guilt followed the resentment. He had no right to be angry, as he had yet to tell her directly how he felt about her.

"If the time comes when you invite me to your bed, I'll be there not because you opened your legs to me. I'll be there because you opened your heart to me."

He'd dropped hints from time to time, but never

come straight out and admitted his feelings. How he would trade the world for the chance to be at her side as her man and not as her convenient friend.

She poked at him with a finger and teased him without any clue of the conflict surging inside him. "Back to caveman style communication, eh? You okay?"

"Fine."

"You don't sound fine."

Another grunt.

"Seriously, O-man, what's wrong? Jerry say something bad?"

"No."

"Then what is it?"

Owen lifted his eyes to hers and for a moment, he just stared, hoping she would get it. He didn't have the words. Those blue orbs of hers held genuine question and then widened. Her lips parted and her jaw dropped.

Yeah, she got it.

"Look, Uncle Owen! I put my nachos on my hot dog. That way I can eat it all at once."

Sarah opened her bag of pretzels and shook out a few. "That's so gross."

"No, it's not."

"Yes, it is."

"No, it's not."

"You're gonna make a big mess."

Mattie gave an impish grin. "Yup. An' I'm gonna enjoy doing it."

The group made their way through the crowd back to the bleacher seats. The kids devoured their food, the adults chatted, and everyone cheered and stood when the team scored. If anyone noticed the sudden coolness between Owen and Melanie, no one remarked on it.

CHAPTER SIXTEEN

"Show us your tits."

"I don't want to."

"Come on, Melanie. It's not like you're shy."

"I just don't want to."

Robert and Archie had me trapped behind the bleachers on the other side of the stadium. Magnus stood close by, visibly mad his sister had crashed his party. Archie had said they had booze and invited me to come over. I knew Magnus had swiped a bottle from Daddy's liquor cabinet. He's been doing it for years and either had never been caught or Daddy didn't care. I also knew the last thing he wanted was to have me around him and his friends, but Archie asked me if I wanted to hang out during the "lame ass" football game. A chance to be seen with the most popular upperclassmen? Social score!

Robert tipped the bottle back and took a swallow of the amber liquid. "You're mature enough to drink, aren't you? Not a little girl like Kelly Barlow?"

I stuck my nose in the air and tried not to show my fear. Kelly was younger than me even though we were both freshmen. "Of course I'm mature enough. Hand me the bottle."

I took as small a sip of the booze as I could manage. It took all I had in me not to gag at the fire that burned down my throat.

Archie reached for the bottle. "What did you do with Kelly?"

Robert shrugged. "I took her out last week, and she cried when I felt up her tits. Pretty damn small. Not even a good mouthful yet."

"Did you suck 'em?"

"Nah. She bawled like a fucking baby so much I didn't even try to get her shirt off. Waste of fucking time. I bet she has old granny bras, anyway. How 'bout you, Mel? You got pretty bras?"

The liquor settled in my rebelling stomach. Every instinct I had screamed I should run, but I had to brazen it out. No way did I want Robert spreading around I was immature or too squeamish to date. "Yes, I have pretty bras, and no, you don't get to see them."

He laughed. "What? You're not telling me you're one of those gotta-put-a-ring-on-it girls, are you? Fuck that."

He grabbed the bottle and took another healthy swallow. "I ain't buyin' 'til I tried it."

My head swam. I glanced over at Magnus. He had his hand in his pocket and pulled out a weird-looking cigarette.

"Is that pot?" I blurted out.

He didn't answer. His other hand produced a lighter, and he fired up the joint, sucking deep and holding his breath. He handed the cigarette to Robert, who did the same. The air smelled like sweet hay and dirty burning grass. I really wanted to run. But what would they say at school on Monday? They were seniors and practically ran the place. They could ruin the rest of my days with one well-placed sentence.

"Come on, Melanie. Don't be a baby. Show us your tits."

I stuck my nose even higher while locking my legs together to keep them from trembling. "You've seen tits before. You don't need to see mine."

"Is it Magsie that's got you so frigid? He doesn't care, do you, Mags?"

"Shut up, asshole, and quit calling me that!"

Robert laughed, and chills went down my spine at his tone. The atmosphere thickened with anticipation. Archie and I shared a glance, and I braced myself for whatever came next.

"You develop some brotherly love all of a sudden? Does it

bother you we want to see your sister's big, beautiful, bouncing breasts?"

Magnus took back the blunt and sucked another lungful. "I don't give a shit about her or her breasts. She's still my sister, and much as I loathe her, I don't want to see any part of her." He handed the smoldering cigarette to Archie. "Here. I'm leaving. Do what you want."

Archie took the offering. "You really don't care?"

"Not in the slightest."

My brother turned and walked away, leaving me with his two best friends, one of whom weaved back and forth, drunk and high. Pain lanced my heart, stiletto sharp, with a quick stab. I had no words as he rounded the corner and disappeared.

"Alright, big brother is gone. Let's see those beauties."

I turned back to Robert. His glazed eyes fixed on my chest, and I had the urge to cover myself. "No."

I took a step back and hit the cement block wall. Archie crowded me on one side, and Robert moved in front.

"Take off your shirt."

"No."

"Do it."

"No!"

Robert moved in closer, and I pressed against the wall, scared stiff. Two against one, and they were bigger and stronger. "Archie, hold her hands."

I tried to make a break and run, but Archie caught me and held my arms back. I had no control. No choice but begging. Tears filled my eyes. "Please don't do this."

Robert reached out and undid the buttons on my blouse, revealing my favorite pale pink Victoria's Secret bra. His eyes bugged out at the sheer cups that showed the shadow of my nipples. "Damn, those are some fine tits."

I could feel Archie's breath near my neck. "Come on, man. You've seen 'em. Let's get out of here before someone comes."

Robert ignored him. He reached out and palmed me, his thumbs sweeping across my nipples before digging into the tops of the cups. His breathing increased as he started dragging them down.

"What's going on here?"

A new voice interrupted Robert, and he jumped back. "C-Coach Dan. Um. Nothing. Just playing around is all."

Archie released my arms, and I jerked my blouse closed. Relief flooded me as I moved to put some distance between them and me.

"Just playing around, huh? Booze and blunt? You know how I feel about my players using drugs. Two-game suspension."

Robert sobered up. "What? You can't do that!"

"I just did."

"My dad will hear about this."

"I'm sure he will, and he'll also hear about his kid smoking dope and drinking on campus. How well do you think that will go over during the next election?"

That shut Robert up faster than anything else would. He glowered at his coach but remained silent.

"Sorry, sir. Won't happen again." Archie grasped the situation and turned into a placating jellyfish.

"Suck-up."

I guessed the friendship between the two of them had a few cracks.

Coach Dan turned to me with a pointed finger. "And you, you little cocktease. Stay away from my players."

I didn't expect that from someone who just rescued me. "I didn't... I don't...."

"I don't care what you did or didn't do. I've seen girls like you for years. Flashing your boobs at boys and expecting them not to look or touch. Keep those things covered and get the fuck outta here."

I stood there, gaping in incredulity until the coach roared "Go!" at me. What else could I do? I walked away. I didn't run. I didn't cry. I didn't falter or stumble. I buttoned my shirt and found the steel in my spine that I had developed over a lifetime. Magnus had disappeared altogether. No help there, and I wasn't foolish enough to expect any. I made my way through the crowd and found Matilda at our *normal spot near the top of the student section of the bleachers.*

She frowned at me when I sat down next to her. "Where've you been? Game's almost over."

There was no way I'd tell her what occurred with Robert or the coach. "Magnus ditched me. Mind if I bum a ride home?"

Matilda's nose crinkled. "OMG, he's such a douche. Sure thing."

For the rest of the quarter, I smiled a lot, laughed a lot, chatted a lot, made comments about the game, clothes people wore, the cheerleaders, and anything else that my brain produced. I came home to a dark house. My father was more than likely out catting around, while my mother lay passed out drunk in her room.

I walked stiffly into my own room and shut the door with a soft click. I started undressing and that one act turned frantic. A whimper escaped my throat as I tore the clothes from my body and threw them on the floor. No. I'm not going to cry. I'm not going to cry. It's okay. It's okay. It's okay.

My favorite bra sat on top of the pile. I looked at it for a long moment, my mind going blank, before I picked it up and tossed it in the trash.

A cry burst from my throat, and my eyes popped

open as I ripped out of the dream. More like night-mare memory. I told no one about the incident, thinking I wouldn't be believed. My word against theirs? Yeah, right. Other girls who had talked of being cornered and touched by Robert had been ridiculed and labeled as psycho bitches. Hindsight being 20/20, it would have been a small price to pay for keeping my dignity. Instead, I kept my mouth shut and dealt with it like everyone else: by ignoring it.

I uncurled my hands from the tight fists I'd made. Rigid with tension, I lay flat on my bed. Wet from my eyes dripped down my temples, and I swallowed the huge lump in my throat.

The two-game suspension didn't happen. Robert played lacrosse, and I stayed silent. Now, years later, I still kept silent. Some things in life you shared with your people to get them off your chest and find a peaceful resolution and relief. Others, you took to your grave for fear of what other people would think. I wondered if that ever killed anyone.

Junior distracted me from my musings by doing a morning stretch with all four limbs in all directions. "Oh, jeez, kid. You're gonna make me pee myself."

I had to pee a lot these days. My bladder had become Junior's trampoline, and his antics had become very visible. I could be standing in conversation with someone with the alien noticeably moving around in my belly. My breath would catch at the flips, kicks, and pushes. His ginormous four-way stretches made me fear for the classic sci-fi movie scene. The real kicker? I still had three months to go.

I got up to take care of immediate business and get my day started. We were entering the phase of the school calendar that some teachers loved and some dreaded. The holidays. Hallowgivingmas to be exact. Witches and ghosts sat across from cornucopias and Santa's helpers on store shelves. People were making treks to the mountains to see the green foliage turn into the colorful shades of fall, and of course there was pumpkin-spice-flavored everything.

Exam and SAT prep had started up, and my tutoring schedule filled quickly. Some of my students had to be helped through late-evening Skype sessions, as their after-school activities and my tutoring hours didn't always mesh. I always made sure the parents knew about the online meetings, and I tried to put two or three students in at the same time. Even with whatever streamlining I could manage, my days were still incredibly long. Somehow, I still had to fit in doctor visits, start birthing classes, and sign up for the breast-feeding seminar. OMG, babies were a lot of work, and the little booger hadn't even arrived yet.

Still, I managed to snag a real estate agent and get a list of properties to see. I had paid for my condo outright years ago, and with the housing market on the rise, I should turn a profit when I sell it. Or should I rent it out? Owen still lived in his camper thingy in the back of Bevvie's house. Maybe he would be interested in my condo?

I hadn't seen him much in the last two weeks since the football game when we ran into Jerry. I texted him about coming with me to see some houses and he texted back an affirmative, but not much more than that. I got the impression he was mad at me, but I had no idea why. I didn't have the time or patience to deal with it, anyway.

I moved sluggishly through my morning routine. Jeez, I was so fucking tired! Crazy-ass dreams, memories, or whatever had kept me from any serious REM sleep, and it showed. I considered calling in for a sub and taking the day off, but I needed to keep my sick time for the upcoming maternity leave. Besides that, my calculus class had been struggling, and any lost class time would put them even more behind.

"You look like shit, Mellie." Bevvie poured herself a huge cup of coffee in the teachers' lounge.

"Thanks. I feel like it, too. How the hell did you do this four times?"

"I'm talented like that." She sipped at the oily brew and frowned. "Blech. I think John made this pot. It's strong enough to grow hair from your ears. Watch out for grains at the bottom."

"I could use a serious caffeine jolt, but not a good idea for Junior." I grabbed a bottle of water from the fridge and popped a prenatal vitamin in my mouth. "Why do they have to make these things the size of horse pills?"

"Damn, you're in a pissy mood. You sure you need to be here?"

The missile moved down my esophagus and landed with a thud in my stomach. "Nope, I shouldn't be here. I should be home in bed catching up on all the sleep I didn't get last night, but that's not going to happen. I figure this is practice for after Junior arrives and sleepless nights become the norm."

Beverly laughed as she added more creamer. "Yeah, it's the norm all right. I haven't had a decent eight hours since Abby's birth. You worry about them being born, then about hunger, wetness, cleanliness, boo-boos, sickness, stitches, grades, team sports, circles of friends, college years, drugs, drinking...."

I held up my hand. "Stop. You're not helping."

My BFF had the gall to laugh at me.

"I'm serious, Bevvie. How am I going to handle this by myself?"

Her face dropped its comedic look and grew thoughtful. She pulled the water bottle out of my hand and put both that and her cup down. She took both of my hands in hers and held them tight while giving me the deepest, most heartfelt look she'd ever given me. "Because you're not alone and never will be."

Tears burned, threatening to fall, and I had to swallow hard. My smartass self had no words, so I just nodded.

She shrugged and turned back to her coffee. "Abby is planning on a European trip from the babysitting money she plans to get from you. Sarah says she's ready to move in with you to help you cook so neither you nor the baby will starve."

Solemn moment over. I laughed and dashed at my wet eyes.

"You still on for the Lamaze thing tonight?"

She took another sip of the freshly doctored coffee, made a face, and dumped it in the sink. She pulled the glass carafe and dumped it as well. "Yes, I'll be there. Seven, right?"

"Yes."

"Miss Miser, I'd like a word with you."

Mr. Bradshaw's voice made me jump. I hadn't heard him sneak in the lounge, and I resisted the urge to roll my eyes at Bevvie. She pressed her lips inward, probably reading my mind.

"I have a few minutes before my class starts. What can I do for you?"

"There's been a complaint against you."

I blinked. Formal complaints were supposed to be handled in private, not the teachers' lounge with people coming in and out. "What kind of complaint?"

"Mary Pembroke is concerned about her son being on the mathletes team. She doesn't want Terrence exposed to any licentious behaviors, and she's afraid you'll have a bad influence because of… of… uh… your condition."

Heat flashed through me, both from anger and embarrassment. I caught Bevvie's frown from the corner of my eye. She filled the pot from the sink and started making fresh coffee, but kept her mouth shut. "I'm not sure what you're implying, Mr. Bradshaw. Does being pregnant make me a bad person?"

He pushed his glasses up on his nose and looked up at me. "Miss Miser being an unwed mother sends a bad message."

"What bad message?"

"That this behavior is acceptable."

"What behavior are you referring to?"

His face scrunched up with the frustration of being questioned. "The behavior that got you in this condition in the first place."

Bevvie turned and I'm sure would have thrown down for me, but I beat her to it. "I'm here every day, all day, Mr. Bradshaw. I've taken on extra classes with no complaints. My students get free tutoring from me, whereas the going rate for that service is fifty bucks an hour. My teaching evaluations are outstanding, and my colleagues have made no objections as to how I run the department. My personal life does not enter my professional one. All my doctor appointments are made outside of school hours. I do not talk about my baby to any student in this building. Yes, I am pregnant. Yes, I'm having this baby, and I'm not married. I'm not sure what it is you think I can change about this situation to make Mrs. Pembroke happy."

"You shouldn't be coaching the math team."

A stab through the heart would have been less painful. Then my anger flared. "You want me to drop the mathletes so that Mrs. Pembroke will let Terrence be on the team?"

He drew up to his full height, which barely reached my shoulders. "Yes, Miss Miser, I do."

"Mr. Bradshaw, what students qualify for this team?"

He sputtered and shrunk at my question. "I… uh… I'm not sure exactly."

"The department discussed this issue last year and decided the students had to maintain a 90 percent average in all math classes and attend all weekly practices. What competitive divisions do we have?"

"There's more than one?"

God, I wish I could slap the confusion off his face! "Yes, there are. Algebra One and Two, Geometry, Statistics, and Calculus are the ones we have at this school. How many kids do we have in each division?"

"I don't know."

"Depends on the competition. Some are teams of two, some are four, and some are eight. Which divisions do we currently have teams for?"

"Uh…"

"We have three. Algebra One, Algebra Two, and Calculus. Wanna know why?"

The man's face got redder and redder, but I barreled on.

"I'm happy to tell you, Mr. Bradshaw. It's because the other three divisions do not have students with consistently high enough grades. The closest is Alex Askew in Geometry. Wanna know who else is in Geometry? Terrence Pembroke. He has a low C average, did not do well on the preliminary tests, and cannot make the practice sessions because he's on the cross-country team, the swim team, and his church basketball league."

"Mr. Pembroke is not on the math team at all?"

"No, he is not." *You pompous, arrogant, ignorant asshole!*

"I had not realized—"

"Furthermore," I interrupted, "I resent your implications and your judgmental attitude toward me and my child. For the last year, you have undermined me as a teacher, accused me of cheating, taken me to task for issues that have nothing to do with my professional life, and now just tried to embarrass the snot out of me for something that is none of your business or concern. I think you're trying to find an excuse, any excuse, to fire me. One more time, Mr. Bradshaw. One more time, and I'll sue you personally for defamation and harassment."

He huffed and puffed as he fidgeted with his glasses. "Now, Miss Miser, there is no need to take it that far."

"Try me."

His mouth opened and closed a few times. He glanced around the room at the few other occupants, but no one met his eye. He cleared his throat. "I suppose it's best if you stay on as the mathletes coach."

Not a pin dropped as he retreated from the room, but after he left, the place exploded with applause.

"I've been wanting to tell that man off for years."

"Way to go, Mel!"

"Outstanding!"

Bevvie showed a bit more concern. "Damn, Mellie. If that man didn't have it out for you before, he does now. Watch your back."

"He best watch his. I finished the online coursework a year ago for education administration. I qualify for his job now, and he should have retired long ago." I said jokingly, but her face told me my attempt at levity fell flat.

"I mean it. He may be an anachronism, but he's still got connections and power in this city."

"We'll see, Bev. Meanwhile, I'm late for my class. See you tonight?"

"Sure."

THE HAMMER FELL WITH A CRACK, DRIVING A NAIL INTO place. Owen stood up stiffly from his cramped position, and his back popped and cracked as he stretched. Jodie's remodeled basement space was almost done. Shelves and racks lined two walls; a counter and workbench ran along another. A changing booth sat in one corner. Jodie said she wanted to paint the space herself but had made some noises about having him do it for her because of her lack of free time. She'd started a business selling athletic leggings online and wanted the remodel for her storage and work area. Jerry called it her she shed, but the woman had more going on than just a hobby. She'd mentioned last time she came through the job site that her online store had tripled sales in the last month and she'd considered quitting her day job.

Jerry's praises had turned into four more remodels and custom design jobs. Two for kitchens, one for a kids' playroom, and one for a bathroom. Word of mouth, it seemed, did enough to keep him busy. Connor had backorders for his original handmade furniture, and whenever Owen got a break, he spent a few hours in the woodshop helping his brother. Work and money poured in at a steady pace, making his professional life solid.

Not so much the personal side.

Friends. He couldn't get the word out of his head and it repeated itself over and over again like a music earworm. Friends. Just friends. Friends only. He'd fallen in love with Melanie Miser, and it killed him to be around her as he didn't think she felt the same way. He had no idea if she'd even be receptive to more than friendship. Words were his biggest enemy, and he could see himself flubbing them spectacularly if he attempted to talk about it to her.

"This looks fantastic, Owen. Jodie will be so happy to have this finished. Her leggings stock is scattered all over the living and dining rooms. That's getting on her nerves, and mine as well." Jerry appeared in the doorway that led from the basement to the garage. "By the way, I gave your contact information to Bob Milhouse. He loved the deck pattern so much, he wants one at his place. Think you can work him in?"

"Try. Getting cold for outside."

Jerry ran his fingers over a shelf. "Yeah, I get that. Say, you know I mentioned Jodie's sister Bertie? She's in town now and working on her bed-and-breakfast place. Doesn't have a name for it yet, but she's thinking about Hideaway Inn. Cute, right? I think you'd like her once you met her."

Owen picked up his power drill and loaded a Philips bit in the chuck. He cursed silently and took it back out to load the extender first. Four drawer wheel tracks were next to be installed, and getting his arm in the back of the cabinet to screw in the back braces could be a challenge. The driver extender helped with that.

"Not sure. Busy with work."

"Bertie is really busy too. Maybe y'all can meet for coffee? It would go a long way to getting my wife off both our backs. Think about it, please?"

Owen sighed. He knew Jodie Harris was intense when it came to something she wanted. She was like that proverbial dog with a bone. He nodded at Jerry as he lifted the drill with the extender bit and reached to the back of the cabinet. The awkward movement pulled his back muscles as one hand held the brace and the other held the heavy drill.

"Think about it."

"Thanks, Owen. I 'preciate you."

The drill bit into the drywall and spun the screw into the brace. Owen put the tool down to recheck his measurements for the next brace. Jerry made noises and hesitated to leave.

"Um… say, Owen. Is it because I saw you with Melanie Miser a couple of weeks ago at the football game. She said you were friends, but it looked like you two were dating. Is it serious?"

Owen took his turn to hesitate. He wanted nothing more than to say yes, it was serious. That he and Melanie were in love and any other woman didn't have a shot at being with him. However, he couldn't. As much as he wanted to, he couldn't. Melanie's feelings toward him were ones of friendship only. She had made that clear.

Owen lifted the next brace and sighted the spot where it would go. "Not serious. Just friends." The words burned on his tongue as he uttered them.

Jerry sounded relieved. "Oh, good. Not that there's anything wrong with you dating Melanie Miser, but you don't seem her type. And there was some stuff back in high school."

Owen's focus jumped to high alert. The spot he'd picked for the second brace swam in front of his eyes. He looked back and forth between the first brace and the drywall to regain his bearings. "What stuff?"

Jerry let out a dismissive raspberry. "Oh, nothing against her. She was always really nice to me. Her brother always acted like an asswipe, but she was cool. It's… well… there were rumors about her and… stuff."

Owen closed his eyes and tried to clear his vision. Nope. No good. He unfurled from the cramped, uncomfortable position and stood up. He needed his tape measure and bubble level, two tools he owned but rarely needed. "What rumors?"

Jerry's silence made him look up from where he shuffled through his toolbox. The pudgy man, who usually exuded friendliness, wore a deep frown and kept his eyes to the floor. Fingers of unease crept down Owen's spine. He stood up to his full height and waited. He expected his towering body to prompt Jerry into answering. Jerry still hedged.

"Just some old rumors. No one pays any mind to them anymore. Long time ago. Just be careful is all."

As if a light switch flipped, Jerry changed from somber concern to car salesman. A big smile burst across his face, and his voice lightened up. "Not to worry, Owen. Not at all. I'll tell Jodie to get Bertie's schedule, and we'll get you two together. She'll be so happy. Yessiree, I think you'll like her. I do indeed."

Jerry left the room whistling an old country tune, leaving Owen to pull out his tools to finish the drawer rails. He measured the spot he thought would work for the second brace and discovered he was a half-inch off. This would have bound up the drawer at the halfway mark and screwed up the rest of them. Irritation flooded Owen's chest, and he wanted to throw down the tools and... and...

And do what?

Jesus, Mary, and Joseph! Confusion, hurt, frustration, and anger clouded his mind. Yes, anger. He acknowledged that he was angry at Melanie but angrier at himself for allowing it. He just gave the go ahead for Jerry to set him up on a blind date with another woman. That was on him and had nothing to do with Melanie's feelings toward him or lack thereof.

This was love? Falling in and out for convenience or on a whim? Was it that easy?

Air whistled in his nose as he took a huge breath and held it. He raised his face to the ceiling and blew out slowly, letting his irritation go with it. Working with tools when angry spelled disaster. Most of his jobsite injuries had happened when his focus drifted to anything other than the work in front of him. He stared at the white ceiling and sifted through his thoughts. Melanie was a player, no doubt, and had been for a long time. She probably didn't even realize her games with his feelings. Why? He'd never told her. Never admitted to her how much he cared about her. Never let her know the power she held over him. She might have an inkling of his love but had never acknowledged its existence. Based on what he knew about her, what he saw at her parents' party, what Jerry said to him, she would run far, far away if she knew the depth of his feelings.

Best if I keep it to myself and deal with it. I'd rather be her friend than nothing at all, even if it hurts like hell.

He noticed two cracks had formed in the smooth sheetrock above his head. He took one more big breath and turned to see if he had any spackling compound in his toolbox.

CHAPTER SEVENTEEN

C*ASSIE LAUGHED AND POINTED TO THE SHAPELY MANNEQUIN* *in the window.* "*I bet you would look so good in this dress. You should try it on and get it. Vincent Ziglar will stare at you all night at the game and not score one touchdown.*"

Matilda pulled me into the store. "*Oh my God, yes! You should totally try it on.*"

I laughed with my two best friends in all the world. Both of them knew I had a crush on the team quarterback. So what if he was a nineteen-year-old high school kid and dumb as a box of rocks? He was a senior to my sophomore, hot and popular, and that was all that mattered. Right?

The mall lights shone brightly as I pulled a size six from the rack. Damn, it was shorter than I'd thought. No big deal. I'll just have to be careful about bending over. *Make that* when *to bend over. If I flashed a little more skin* at Vincent, maybe he'd finally notice me. My friends giggled and pushed me to the dressing rooms in the back. I caught the store clerk watching us with a frown. Old biddy probably thinks I'm going to shoplift or something. Just wait till I pull out the credit card Daddy gave me. That'll wipe the smug look off her face.

The dress fit perfectly, showing off my breasts and legs. At sixteen, I had a woman's body. Lush, large perky and full double-ds, a high tight ass, and long legs that made me taller than most of my class. The silky slick fabric clung to my hips and flared into pleats that floated around me as I turned circles in front of the dressing room mirror.

"How much is it?" Cassie slipped a similar blue dress over her head, but it got caught on her wide shoulders and she ended up tearing it. "Fuck. I don't have enough money to pay for this. My mom's gonna kill me. Think the cashier lady will notice if I hang it back up myself instead of putting it on the reject rod?"

I shrugged. "I'll pay for it. Daddy doesn't care how much I spend."

"Won't he notice you don't have a navy blue dress with your red one?"

"Nope. He just pays the bill. I bought some stuff from Spencer's Gifts and he didn't blink an eye." My flippant answer fooled her. My parents seldom kept track of me, and my brother outright abhorred me. I spent a lot of time by *myself with little to no supervision. Most of my dinners were served in the kitchen with Bedelia. Been that way for years.*

Matilda's mouth formed a perfect O. Spencer's was the ultimate in the tantalizing adult world. The mall store had regular stuff like clothes, band posters, and stuff, but it also had lots of novelties too. Drinking games, gross gag gifts, and adult-themed party supplies were on the back shelves. Even better was the room cordoned off by a black curtain for people eighteen and over. One Saturday afternoon earlier that summer when I was alone at the mall and wasting time, I went behind that curtain. No one stopped me, and I found a treasure trove of the forbidden. Sex games, lubes, vibrators, anal plugs, dildos of every size, and other piles of sex paraphernalia. I spent a lot of time reading labels and looking at pictures until my middle quivered and burned.

"Oh my God! What did you get?"

I gave her my most I'm-so-worldly smile. "Anything I wanted."

The truth? I had no idea what half of that stuff was used for, and some of it was pretty scary. I still had to buy something, mostly to see if I could get away with it. I eenie-meenie-minee-moed on a big purple rabbit vibrator. It was currently sitting in the back of my closet in the hidden space behind my shoe rack. Still in the box. If the description showed up on the credit card statement, my dad never said a word.

"Damn, Melanie. You are so lucky to have parents like that. I can't go anywhere or do anything without my mom saying if it's okay. She always has to know what's happening in my life and what I'm doing every minute of the day. She's such a control freak!" Cassie slipped the torn dress back on the hanger. "My dad's favorite saying is 'my house, my rules.' He still sets a curfew for me, even though I turned eighteen last month. I can't wait for college next year. I'm gonna move out and not come back."

"Me too!" Matilda joined in as she fingered the silk blouse. "Being a sophomore sucks. Me and Mel have to wait two more years. That's so long!"

I made some sympathetic noises because I was supposed to. If only my friends knew how much I envied them. Controlling? Rules? Their parents gave a damn. Cassie's older brother had already graduated college and treated his sister like gold. Magnus would prefer I didn't exist.

I walked out of the dressing room area to get a better look at myself in the big three-way mirror. My two friends followed me. I twisted and turned, admiring the way my ass looked. "We'll keep shopping, but I'm getting this dress no matter what. Let's go get coffees and then go to that jewelry kiosk. I want some of those shiny rhinestone chandelier earrings to go with this."

My friends always agreed with what I wanted and planned. After all, I ruled the mall as its queen. My own little kingdom. Queendom?

"Oh my God, there's Vincent!" Matilda gasped and pointed outside the store. "Cory and David are with him. They are so hot!"

I bit my lip. Sometimes Matilda's over-the-top dramatics annoyed me, but she'd assessed the three boys accurately. They were the cutest and most popular in our school. Impulse hit me. "Watch this." I told my friends. I snapped off the price tag from the dress I wore and pulled a pair of high spiky heels from the display. They were too small, but I jammed them on my feet, anyway. As I tottered past the register desk, I slapped down the tags for the dresses and shoes and my credit card. "Here. Put everything on the card, and I'll be right back."

Matilda and Cassie watched as I squared my shoulders and sauntered up to the trio. "Hey, Vincent." I preened as his eyes locked onto my cleavage display. "Hey, Cory and David. Y'all did a great job at the game last night."

"Uh... thanks. You're Melanie Miser, right?"

I smiled at David, thrilled that he knew my name. "That's right. We have Algebra Two together for second period."

"Yeah, you sit in the front row and ace every test."

I let out a giggle. "Yeah, math is kinda my thing."

"Whatcha doin' today?" Vincent's growly voice sent a twist through my stomach. His gaze still sat on my chest, and that knowledge did a number on me. I might be a virgin, but I wasn't stupid.

"Shopping for the homecoming dance. You guys going?"

"Probably, but it's only a lame high school thing. The after-party at Colin's house is the real place to be."

I kept my disappointment contained. I hadn't even known about the after-party, let alone been invited.

"You got a date?" Vincent finally moved his attention from my breasts to my face. My stomach cartwheeled into my groin.

"You mean for the dance or the party?"

"Both."

"Not yet."

"You do now. I'll meet you at the gym after the game next Friday."

My stomach performed a triple back handspring. "Sure thing."

I turned before my knees gave way or I said something dumb. Did I just land the date of the year? Holy shit, I did! Homecoming with Vincent Ziglar!

"Hey, Melanie?"

I turned my head and looked over my shoulder. The man of my dreams was staring at my ass.

"I like the dress."

Shit, how did I respond? Should I say thank you? God, that's so lame. Should I wiggle my hips at him? No, too much. I decided to not say a word for fear of messing it up. I winked at him and went back in the store to collect my card, my openmouthed friends, and buy a different pair of shoes in the right size.

My eyes popped open as the last vestiges of the dream left me. Fuck, I'd been having weird dreams in full Technicolor all my life, but this one was more memory than dream. Homecoming for the high school was only a few days away, and of course my crazy hormone-laden brain had to go back to one of my own homecomings. That had to be it.

Fuck, I had too much going today. I didn't need to take the time to analyze a dream from an old memory. I was to meet Owen and my real estate agent after work to look at a house that fit my criteria and my budget. I liked the location and the pictures I'd seen online. Yep, I was getting excited at the potential move. New place. New life. New possibilities. What could go wrong?

I LEFT THE SCHOOL AFTER A LONG, ASS-DRAGGING DAY and drove to a development not too far from Bevvie's place. The neighborhood was newer than hers, but still in the middle-income bracket. Some houses sat on postage-stamp-sized lots, but the one I had picked was in a cul-de-sac and sat back from the road a good bit. The lot resembled a giant pie wedge with the house in the middle of it, leaving a long front yard and a wide backyard. A bunch of trees stood in front, which added a layer of privacy and shade to the house. The structure itself wasn't particularly attractive or ugly, and the layout of the house was pretty standard. The backyard sold it to me.

Whoever owned this house before loved the back-yard and spent a lot of time there. The covered back deck overlooked a wooded area that hid any other houses from sight. A burbling creek ran behind a chain-link fence, and I spotted a gate that opened to the water. Visions of me taking a child's hand and going through that gate to look for tadpoles and frogs in the mud crowded my thoughts. A concrete slab sat below with a built-in outdoor fire pit. I could see us roasting marshmallows and getting sticky fingers. Not just me and my kid. Bevvie and her family too. Since the yard was fenced in, Muttface could come, or perhaps I would get a dog. A young rescue that could grow up with my kid.

I turned back into the plain house with blank walls

the color of cream. No colors had ever been painted here, nor had any pictures adorned the walls, as evidenced by the lack of nail holes. The whole place appeared as a clean slate, waiting only for the touch of a family to make it a home. My home. Mine and my child's.

Owen had on a pair of reading glasses and was perusing a sheaf of papers about the house's statistics. I found it endearing that a big man such as he needed them. The young agent hovered close by, ready to answer any questions. She seemed slightly enamored of Owen by the way she watched him as he read. An unfamiliar heat flared in my chest, and I had a sudden need to make a point that he was here with me. Jealousy, perhaps? I walked over to stand next to him and threaded my arm through his. I expected him to wrap that arm around me. He didn't, and my heart crumbled a little. At least he didn't push me away. I couldn't have handled that.

"Water heater's old." His statement sounded a little terse. I heard warning bells and ignored them.

"New roof. Four years ago."

The short woman perked up. "Yes, the roof is new and is metal. I'm not sure exactly which type, but according to the company, it's seeded to last for about sixty to eighty years. It's the last roof this house will ever need." Her voice rang with the rehearsed sales pitch.

"Unless leaks."

Damn, Owen. Just dump a bucket of cold water on everyone, will ya? "I'm sure there's a warranty, right?"

"Yes, there is a warranty. I'm not sure of the details, but I can find out for you."

"Kitchen."

What the fuck? I expected Owen to speak in his truncated speech pattern since he didn't know the agent, but his clipped tone sounded rude. It grated on my nerves and made the agent visibly nervous. She gestured to the main part of the house. "Through here."

The open floor plan featured a living room, kitchen, and dining areas. The vaulted ceiling rose above an overlooking loft/den. Large windows and a skylight let in the evening natural sun and bathed the cavernous room in gold light. I loved it!

"Big windows. Lose heat in winter."

Another killjoy moment from Owen. I ignored him. "Does the gas fireplace work?"

The agent grasped that straw with a huge grin. "Yes, it does, and it has a blower too."

Owen grunted and pulled away from me to examine the kitchen. The plain black Formica against a white background looked unappealing, but with some nice tiles and backsplashes, this would be an ideal place to cook. That is, if I ever learned how.

"Bad outlets. Not code."

Huh? "What are you talking about?"

"Need breakers."

The agent became flustered. "Yes… well… the inspector mentioned that, and the owner is planning to update."

Another grunt from Owen. He ticked me off more and more as we moved through the house. He managed to find something wrong in every room. A ceiling fan wobbled, closet space was laid out strange, the way the vertical blinds had been installed, cracks in the bathtub caulking, wallpaper in the bathroom put on crooked… the faults kept coming and coming. Everywhere I looked, I saw the potential of what this place had for me and my kid. Owen's nitpicking got under my skin so much, I finally had it.

"What the fuck, Owen?" My voice rose in exasperation. "Everything you've cited so far is something that can be fixed or updated. What the hell is your problem?"

"Who?"

"Who? What do you mean, who? You, that's who.

You seem to have a problem with everything in this house."

He shook his head. "Who's gonna fix it? Me?"

I was taken aback. The thought never occurred to me that he wouldn't be helping me with this part of house maintenance. "Well, yes. I assumed you would."

He got quiet. Even for a man of few words, this quiet unsettled me. A sense of dread hit my belly that I'd made a big mistake somewhere along the way with Owen. I tried to tough it out and cover it up. I faked a big smile and tried to take his arm again. "Ahh, come on, O-man. I'm sorry I expected you and Connor to help me get this place whipped into shape. I just figured that was already understood that I'd be hiring you guys to do any work. I won't even ask for the friends and family discount."

It was the wrong thing to say. Owen stared at me, unblinking and unreadable. Then he handed the papers back to the fidgeting agent and walked out. I stood there in the awkward silence, the only sound Owen's heavy work boots clomping to the front door.

I smiled brightly at the agent. "I guess someone is in a mood, eh? I'll be right back."

Owen opened the door to his truck when I caught up with him. I was sure my anger showed as I grabbed his thick forearm to get his attention. "Again, O-man. What. The. Fuck?"

He whirled around and slammed the door closed. I took a step back. At first, I thought he was angry at me. His rudeness to the agent and general attitude of the last hour pointed in that direction, but his face showed something else.

"Wh-wh-at am I t-t-t-o you?"

His stutter amplified his question. He had to be seriously disturbed for his speech problem to come out this much.

"What do you mean?"

"Wh-what am-m-m I to you?"

"I don't understand."

He kept silent as we stared eye to eye. No anger reflected from those green orbs of his. Instead, he looked… he looked… well… he looked hurt. I sighed and let go of my own ire. "Owen, I don't know what you want me to say. You're my best friend's brother-in-law and the best uncle ever. The kids love you like crazy and I can see why."

He broke the stare and raised his eyes to fix his gaze at something over my head. Several long slow breaths went in and out of him. I saw his nostrils flare with each inhalation.

I kept speaking. "You're one of my closest friends,

and I've come to depend on you a lot. I'm sorry if I haven't thanked you enough for all you do for me. You need to know how much I appreciate you for everything. I really do."

I knew my words lacked what I really meant. I wasn't ready to admit to him or to myself where my heart stood. All the romance novels I've ever read say love is the most wonderful state and that when the right two people find each other, it's magical. Books were great, but I lived in the real world where love can be used as a weapon. Too many times in my life, love had either let me down or been fashioned into a sharp edge that cut me off at my ankles. I trusted Bevvie more than anyone else in the world, but she still didn't know everything about me. No one did. Owen came close. Real close to my heart, and I hovered on the edge of telling him, but I couldn't. I couldn't say the words. I wasn't ready to take that leap of faith and let someone in that far.

On impulse, I stepped in to hug him, and for the first time, he didn't hug me back.

"Buy it. Good one." He opened the truck door and climbed in, leaving me alone.

I watched as he backed into the cul-de-sac and drove off. He didn't look at me. Not once. A sense of abandonment hit my gut, followed by a succession of rage and resolve. *Fuck this, and fuck him. I'm not going to cry. I'm not!*

Junior chose that moment to wake up and play trampoline. The distraction of my kid jumping on my diaphragm broke me out of my unhappy state. I turned back to the house. The agent lingered around the front door, trying to be discreet. *Suck it up, Mel. You're doing just fine on your own.* "Well, kiddo, what do you think? We have a winner here?"

Junior executed a flip and punched my liver. "Cool. Let's go buy a house."

OWEN DROVE AWAY FROM THE SUBURB AND PAST THE streets that would take him back to his camper. Instead he went to the closest exit and pulled on the highway. He didn't have a particular destination, he just needed to leave before he unmanned himself any further in front of Melanie. He sniffed hard and resisted the urge to pound his hands against the steering wheel.

Stupid. Stupid. Stupid. Why had he ever let himself fantasize a woman like Melanie Miser would consider him for more? He'd thought he could let it go and be satisfied with friendship, but the house shopping got to him more than he wanted to admit. At first, he pictured her in the house, cozied up on her nice furniture in front of the gas fireplace. A baby sat in her arms, cooing and waving tiny fists in the air. He put himself in that image with her curled up and leaning against his side. Then the image changed. Someone else sat on that sofa taking her weight against his side as she smiled up into his face. The sudden thought struck him that the friendship card meant eventually she would find another man to be with on that sofa, watching the flames dance. There would be another man in the house he helped to pick out and fix up. There would be another man to hold her as she slept. There would be another man to be in her bed and in her life, leaving no room for him.

He ended up on the Blue Ridge Parkway and pulled over to the first overlook he came to. Night had descended, and the black sky sparkled with dots of light. He got out of the truck and walked to the stone wall that separated the road from the scenic vista. His breath puffed white in the cold air. No other vehicles passed by. No nighttime sounds of insects twittered. He was alone. If he wanted to let tears fall from his eyes, no one would see.

Most of his life, he'd sat unnoticed in the background. The workhorse. The quiet laborer. The one to call when there was a need for something to be fixed. All other times, he simply existed.

He leaned over the wall and looked down into the abyss. The outline of the rocky crags below him were hidden by the dark. He could make out a few shapes of the tops of trees, but the bottom stayed invisible. For long minutes he stood, marble in his frozen stillness while his heart cracked down the middle.

She only wants me as a friend.

She only wants my help as a handyman.

I mean nothing real to her.

She'll never care for me as I do for her.

His thoughts beat him up, circling around and around. Memories of past attempts at finding someone to love came to his mind, and his heart sank even lower. The time a high school girl made fun of his stutter. Another one when a woman said his body looked too big and bulky for her taste. Yet another date that ended early because she told him his education level would become a problem and she didn't think she would be happy with a man who did "manual labor" for a living.

Melanie didn't have a problem with his occupation. She never said a word about his size or shape, and never mentioned his speech issue. When he first moved to this area, the idea of being close to her thrilled him. Now, it hurt.

"*Amadán,*" he whispered. "Your own damn fault for letting it happen."

For months, he'd had almost constant contact with the woman he desired more than any other. He held her sleeping. He defended her to her asshole brother. He showed up when she called for help. He resisted the urge to fuck her when she was in a vulnerable state. He had kissed her, tasted her potent flavor, and made her come. Yet she still didn't see him as a man worthy enough to love.

A single tear fell from his face, and he watched it as it dropped to disappear into the deep black below him. The first time he'd cried had been at his mother's funeral. She spent his short life taking his back against the bullies who tormented him about his speech. She had been his support, his rock, his anchor, and he had loved her with a fierceness like he had no other. As her plain casket was lowered into a deep black hole in the ground, sheer loneliness had filled him. Even surrounded by his beloved brothers, he felt an acute sense of isolation. He stood silent and rigid as tears leaked from his eyes to make trails down his young face. Tonight was the second time he'd ever cried.

His phone buzzed in his back pocket, startling him.

He hadn't thought he had a signal up this far in the mountains. He pulled it out and saw it was Jerry calling.

Owen let out a sigh and tapped the green icon. "Yeah."

"Owen, buddy, been trying to reach you for a few days. I know it's late, but you remember Jodie's sister I mentioned?"

CHAPTER EIGHTEEN

I sat in the plush chair of the First and Trust bank in Woodfin. It was the furthest branch away from the main bank in downtown Asheville, as I had no intention of accidentally running into Robert. I decided to put a sizeable down payment on the house and go with a fifteen-year mortgage that I could handle on my teacher's salary. My accountant informed me of the tax advantages and how that would help my bottom line.

The small lobby looked as utilitarian and plain as any generic office space would. Beige carpet, beige walls, beige furniture. Even the tellers wore muted colors, as if in fear of standing out. I had no such problem. I wore black maternity slacks with a gold-patterned blouse and a bright red blazer. Red was supposed to be a power color, and I needed all the confidence I could muster. The certified check I was waiting to get was the biggest one I'd ever cashed from my account.

Junior punched my diaphragm with impatience, and I glanced at my watch to see how long I had before closing. The bank manager had said I needed to make this transfer in person because of the huge amount. I supposed that made sense, but I'd never had an issue before when I moved money around in my accounts. It figured this time I didn't have that option. I'd made an offer on the house, and it was accepted. Now I had to move quickly to get money in the right place before I closed on the deal. Excitement and dread hit me. It was a big move to own a house, but the anticipation of a great future for Junior and me thrilled me.

The manager put me in his private office to wait for a few minutes. I sat in an uncomfortable straight-backed chair and played a game on my phone. I was daydreaming of paint colors, blinds, and curtains when a pair of tasseled designer loafers came into my downward view. Crocodile made by Zelli, if I guessed correctly, and retailed at just over one thousand dollars. My palms started to sweat, and a slow-burning panic hit my stomach. *No, no, no, no, he can't be here. Not now.* Every muscle in my body tensed in readiness to fight or run. I swallowed the bile that raced up my throat, and I raised my eyes to meet Robert's grinning face. Handsome, stylish, worldly, smart, and the last man I ever wanted to be around.

"Hello, Melanie. Bill told me you'd be coming in for some paperwork. I'm surprised you came all the way out here. I would've been glad to help you at the main branch." He closed the door, and I jumped at the loud click of the lock.

Fucking control yourself, Melanie. You're a grown-ass woman. Act like it! "I like the customer service at this branch."

He smirked at the lie and moved to stand closer to the chair arm, his hips near my head as he looked down on me. Intimidation had always been his favorite game, and he enjoyed getting in my personal space, trying to play with me. "We're always ready to service our customers anyway they need it."

My gut clenched and rolled at his thinly veiled words and the invasion of my personal space. Robert's smug smile made me want to vomit and only sheer will power kept me from doing it. He reached out a finger to run over my shoulder. "The transfer you want is more than we can cover at this time. It will take several weeks to get it through. Might be tough for you to have it done before you buy this house of yours."

"That's bullshit."

He shrugged. "The bank president has to approve transfers of this much, and since I'm the bank president, I get to decide when it happens."

His finger traveled over my collarbone. It didn't take a genius to figure out where this was going. "If we came to some sort of arrangement, I can push the authorization forward. You make me happy; I'll make you happy."

I froze as the finger he touched me with moved over my neck and down between my cleavage. I prayed the bank manager would come through the door, papers in hand. Robert's hand started to slide under my shirt toward my breast, and I thawed in an instant. I leapt from the chair, almost knocking it over.

"Keep your hands off me!"

His smile turned predatory as he threw back his head and laughed. "Goddamn, you're still the same little spitfire from years ago. The ice princess, too good for anyone. Always kept her fucking nose in the air."

He pushed into me, and I had no choice but to move back until my spine hit the wall. My legs trembled and panic had my stomach twisting violently.

"Well then, princess, looks like you need my help to get what you want. You want that mortgage loan to go through, I need to get what I want. And I want a lot." He unbuckled his leather belt and unzipped his pants. I glanced down to see one of his hand holding and stroking his hard dick. He put his other hand on my shoulder and pushed down. "Let's start by you getting on your knees."

I panted. My control, my power, my iron will were no longer in me. My head buzzed with white noise, and I left my body. Melanie Miser disappeared, and only her shell remained. My knees started to bend.

A loud knock on the door startled both of us. "Excuse me, sir. I have those papers you wanted."

I came back into myself, and nearly puked on Robert's shoes. *Fuck this!* I grabbed the dick he waved at me and twisted it. Robert yelled in pain and shoved me back. I kept my grip on his favorite toy and cranked it harder. He got the message and stood still, gritting his teeth and seething with fury.

"Don't you ever touch me again, you slimy bastard. I remember everything."

"Fucking bitch!" he bit out as his face turned redder. "I'll get you for this!"

"No, you won't. You do anything to hold up my money, I'll be making an appointment with your daddy dearest. Former mayor and CEO might not appreciate his precious family honor smeared around. I'm not the same little girl you think you know. Don't try me."

"Sir? Is everything okay?" The timid voice at the door followed the rattling of the knob as the bank manager tried to open the door.

I let go of Robert's softened dick, and he gasped huge gulps of air. I turned to open the locked door, and he scrambled to get behind the desk, plopping himself in the fancy executive chair. The bank manager gaped at the sudden movement but kept his comments to himself. Probably a good thing, as I was sure Robert would fire him in an instant.

I reached out my hand for the sheaf of papers. "I'm not feeling very well right now. I'll take those home with me and look them over."

The confused man gave them to me without question, and I strode out of the bank, my head up, and my aura full of confidence.

That lasted only until I got outside, where I emptied my shaky stomach in the parking lot. My hands started shaking, and I barely kept my knees from collapsing. One of my hands rested on my pounding heart and the other on my belly. I could still smell Robert's expensive cologne mixed with the sick-

ening musk of his arousal. The impulse to call someone, anyone, flew through my brain. Owen, or Bevvie.
I fumbled for my phone, dropping it twice and
cracking the screen. Dead battery. Fuck.

I bleeped the locks on my car and crawled inside.
Once I locked myself in, the shakes started so bad, my
teeth rattled. *Stop this, Mel. Stop this right now.* I fought
for control. *Not gonna let him get to me. Not gonna let
him win.*

Gradually my panic attack subsided, and I calmed
enough to drive away. The urge to spend money and
lots of it hit me. My therapy. I needed to get my phone
fixed anyway, so I pointed my car in the direction of
the mall. My safe place.

CHAPTER NINETEEN

Owen pulled at the collar of his shirt. He owned only three polo shirts, all of them printed with the green shamrock Irish Pub Builders logo. The majority of his clothes were for work, with a few casual shirts and a pair of "nice" jeans and a pair of khakis. He sat at the mall coffee shop sipping a chai tea and wondering how he got into this mess. The woman he was supposed to meet had texted to say she was running late. Owen appreciated punctuality but realized circumstances didn't always make that possible.

Three kids screaming about Halloween costumes ran by, followed by a frazzled woman yelling for them to stop. He wondered if he should buy any candy in case some stray trick-or-treater made it to his camper doorstep on Tuesday night. Highly unlikely, as

Connor's bunch had made plans to participate in their church's trunk-or-treat event. Maybe he'd go. Maybe not. He knew the chances of running into Melanie were high, but he couldn't live his life avoiding her. It had been only four days since he saw her at her new house, and they hadn't spoken or texted.

"Owen MacAteer?" A pretty brunette came up to him, her deep brown eyes questioning. He nodded once as she sat down across from him.

She looked different from Jerry's wife. Jodie regulated every bite she put in her mouth and then spent hours on the treadmill working off any errant calories that might have made their evil way into her system. This woman was tall enough to make it to his shoulder and had a nice, robust build.

"Hi, I'm Bernadette, but everyone calls me Bertie. Thank you for dealing with my sister and brother-in-law. I know how pushy they can be."

She seemed very comfortable in her own skin. A waitress came by, and she asked for a plain coffee with cream and sugar. "I hope you've not been waiting long. I bought a farmhouse recently, and there's a lot of work to do on it. I'd hoped to do a lot of the work myself, but it's harder than I thought." Her easy, secure smile did a lot to dissipate Owen's anxiety in meeting her.

"Not long."

"Good. I hate being late, and I didn't anticipate the traffic here around the mall would be this thick. Do you come here often?"

Owen shook his head.

"I understand. I don't do a lot here either. I just moved back here recently, and there is so much work for me to do right now, I don't get out often."

Owen took a sip of his tea and tried to come up with something to say.

The waitress brought a steaming cup to the tiny round table. Owen had his wallet halfway out when Bertie thanked the woman and handed her some cash. "Keep the change." He didn't expect the move and tucked his wallet back into his pocket, waiting for her to speak.

"I'm sure you don't have time to waste, and I don't either, so if you don't mind, I'll get right to the point. My sister Jodie is a wonderful person, and I love her to death, but she's been pushing for months for me to get out and meet new men. She's been nagging Jerry to set me up with every available single man he knows, and I'm afraid you're the latest victim."

Her face showed the same serenity as her words. Owen relaxed and smiled. "No problem."

She let out an easy breath. "Thanks. My divorce

is finally official, and it's a good thing, but I still need time to heal and be just me for a while, you know?" She took a sip of her coffee and waved a hand dismissively in the air. "It wasn't because he cheated on me or found out he was gay or something like that. We were together for years, and then we weren't. Maybe we got too routine or something, I don't know. I think we finally admitted that we had fallen out of love and were better off not being together. We made good roommates and probably could have lived a life together, but I want more than a warm body in my bed. He wasn't too upset when we broke up either. Makes me wonder if we were ever really in love in the first place. The kind of love that lasts. Know what I mean?"

Owen nodded and sipped his own drink. Bertie seemed genuine in her words, and his thoughts of having to let her down disappeared.

Bertie's hands started folding a paper napkin in quick precise shapes. "Jodie thinks I'm nuts for buying that old farmhouse. Jerry said if we hit it off, I could get some free help with fixing it up. My plan is to turn it into a bed-and-breakfast." She shook her head on a sigh. "I wouldn't do that to someone, and frankly, I'm not ready. When I invite someone into my life again, it will be for me and only me. I hope you're not offended."

Her friendly smile and warm personality had him easing back in the bistro chair. No pressure meant he could relax and enjoy her company with no expectations. "Not offended."

Bertie set the folded napkin in the middle of the round table. She'd transformed the plain white square into a paper swan. Owen reached a finger out and poked it.

"Cute."

She smiled and picked up her cup. "Thanks. Just a little hobby of mine. Jerry worries about me spending too much on what he calls my money pit, but I have plenty. I worked at Star Bank and Trust for the last fifteen years as an investment officer and portfolio manager before moving here. I made a lot of money for my clients and myself, but I needed to do something else. It's hard to explain. I wasn't *un*happy with my career, just as I wasn't *un*happy with Karl, but I wasn't happy either. Kinda like I was existing, but not really living. Does that make any sense?"

Owen thought a moment as he lifted his coffee cup. Yes, he understood all too well. "I get it. Too routine."

Her smile shone brilliantly. "Yes, that's it." She reached for another napkin and began to fold it with quick, precise movements. "I appreciate you coming and being so understanding. Maybe we can be friends with a few benefits?"

Owen choked on his coffee and grabbed the swan to cram against his mouth. Bertie's face turned red and slackened as she realized what she'd said. "Oh goodness, I'm sorry! That's not what I meant at all! I meant that... um... I could hire you to help with the renovation. Not... not… that! Are you okay?"

Owen looked up at the distraught woman and coughed a few more times. The ruined swan sat in his hand.

"I'm so, so sorry. Jodie says I need to think before I speak."

"It's good."

"You sure?"

"Yeah. I'll help."

"Help what?"

"B and B renovation." He grinned at her.

Her face flamed again, but she smiled and laughed. "I guess Jodie is right about my need to filter. Jerry says you do great work and are reasonable about pay. I'm glad to hire you for this job. I need all the help I can get if I'm going to make a real go of this."

She picked up her cup and sipped at it. "I've always wanted to own and run a quaint little country inn. You know, one with a nice flower garden, gazebo, a little lake, lots of white, blue, and brick charm. That's my dream. I turn forty in a couple of years and decided if I was ever going to make this dream happen, now's the time. Karl had no interest, and when we split up, I figured it was a sign to get off my ass."

She reached to her purse and pulled out a folder. "I hope you don't mind if I turn this into more of a business meeting than a date. I have pictures of the rooms and the yard, if you want to look."

Owen set the remains of the swan napkin on the table and reached for the folder. "Sorry 'bout the b-bird."

She waved a hand in the air in a dismissive gesture. "No big deal. I can make more."

He thumbed through the set of 5x7 pictures. The house appeared as a mishmash of different styles and add-ons over the years. The squat original structure sat in the middle of two larger and taller wings. One side had three floors and two gables, and the other side had two floors and three gables. A covered porch wrapped around the entire structure, tying it all together in one unit. The middle sported a rusted tin roof while the other two parts had different-colored shingles.

Owen fingered the picture of the overgrown,

weed-choked garden in the back. The whole place looked neglected, but he could see the potential in it. Bertie's assertion about the workload was spot-on. This would take a long time to complete. Garrett had called him again about finding work, and he really did need to get away from his current situation.

"What do you think?" Bertie scooted her chair into his personal space and pointed to one of the images. "There's a barn on the other side here and a storage shed next to it. Towards the back of the property is a small lake and a larger wooded area. I'm living in the extended-stay hotel right now, but I have plans to move into this little cottage that sits behind the garden. It used to be something called a dodder house, like what Amish people had for their older in-laws, but it has electricity and running water. It needs work too, but for now it's livable enough."

Owen listened to her chatter and lifted his cup again as his brain measured, planned, and calculated. Plain black coffee was his preference, but the tea wasn't bad. He'd ordered it on impulse, to try something new. Briefly, he wondered what Melanie would order. Some sort of complicated latte that took an hour to order and another to make.

The universe decided to play a joke on him, and the object of his thoughts suddenly appeared in his vision.

She stood at the edge of the dining area with a bunch of shopping bags hanging by her sides. Her eyes were glued on him, and her mouth hung open. She looked pale against the red of her jacket. She looked drawn, weak, vulnerable; three words he would never have associated with Melanie Miser.

Owen froze. His brain locked up tight, and no words came to him. A sheen of sweat broke across his brow, and his eyes hit Bernadette's in a panic. She was oblivious to the turmoil rolling through his gut. He glanced back up, and Melanie had fled.

"Owen, are you okay?"

Owen closed his eyes as a sense of doom flushed over him.

***

I DROVE AWAY FROM THE MALL WITH MY HANDS WHITE-knuckled on the steering wheel. Owen was with another woman. They'd sat close together, drinking coffee and looking like any other couple out for a day of shopping and being together. The stuff on the round bistro table made it seem they were making more plans. I saw her smiling face as she talked away to Owen. It had to be a date, based on the nicer shirt he wore. First? Second? Third? From his obvious comfort level, he must have known her for a while.

A sense of betrayal bubbled up inside me. My head told me I had no right to feel like this. Owen MacAteer was a free man and could see whomever he wanted. He had no obligation or commitment to me. Too bad my heart didn't feel that way.

My stomach burned, and I swallowed several times as I reached for my stash of Tums. Throwing up sounded like a good idea, but not in my car.

My car. I needed to look at new cars. I pulled a sharp U-turn, probably pissing off several other drivers in the process, and drove straight to the car dealership where Jerry worked. It didn't take him long to find me. I put on my brightest smile and hoped the raging storm in my head stayed hidden.

"Hey, Jerry! I'm so glad you're here today. How's Jodie and the kids?"

If he heard the brittleness in my voice, he ignored it. "I'm good, Miss Miser. Family's good too, thanks for asking."

"My students call me Miss Miser. I think we've known each other long enough that you can call me Melanie."

His chin wobbled a bit as he nodded and shook my

hand. "Thank you so much, Melanie. Is Owen here too?"

"Why would he be here?"

"Uh… I just thought maybe he'd come with you to look at cars."

My laugh came out loud and high enough to shatter glass. "Nope. I don't need him or anyone else to pick out a car, and besides, he's occupied with someone else at the moment."

Jerry's mouth formed a perfect round shape. "Ohhhh, I see. Um… well, what did you have in mind?"

"I need a baby car. Not like a minivan, just a bigger one than what I have. More like a family sedan. Whatcha got?"

TWO HOURS LATER I PULLED OFF THE LOT IN A CAJUN RED Chevy Equinox. Even if I had to drive a bigger SUV type vehicle, I could still have my favorite color. My account had taken a big hit with the car, and I still had the house to deal with. The papers sat next to me and a quick glance through them had assured me that Robert did not have the power to stop my mortgage loan. He might be able to make trouble for me, but I could either rent or sell my condo if I needed any extra income. If I guessed right, closing for the new house wouldn't happen until after Thanksgiving, as there were inspections and official stuff that had to be done. My plan was to put a whopping big down payment that made the mortgage easy to make even with my teacher's salary. The car, I paid for in full, which I was sure my brother and father would say something about if they had the chance. So far none of them, not even my mother, had called or contacted me in any way since the disastrous Labor Day party.

Bevvie's ringtone started up, and I pressed the Bluetooth button on the dashboard. Damn, this car came with all sorts of bells and whistles.

"Yo, Mellie-Jellie, you up for an Italian night? I'm doing spaghetti and salad for the horde. Abby's friends are coming over for a girly night, and Connor is planning on taking the boys to the new Marvel movie. Dinner's gonna be early, around five tonight. See you then?"

Most of my weekends now were spent over at Bevvie and Connor's place rather than at my condo alone. Often, it would include hanging and playing games with the kids, watching movies, painting toenails, hearing the gossip about the boys in school, and of course seeing Owen. More than once, I ended up on the couch, curled up next to him for his body heat and falling asleep to whatever trending movie came up on Netflix. If I went to Bevvie's house tonight, would that still be an option, or would a cute brunette be there to take my place? Visions of this other woman sitting on the wide sofa, barefoot with her knees under her, leaning against Owen danced in front of my eyes. I could hear her laughter and imagined the soft look he gave her as he lifted his arm to place around her shoulder and draw her against his body. Bev and Connor would be sitting similarly. All four people in couples' bliss while I, the single fifth wheel with rounded stomach, sat alone to the side.

"Oh, shit, Bev, I actually have different plans tonight. Sorry for not telling you sooner."

I heard the surprise in her voice. "Oh. Okay, then. Do you have a date?"

My hands tightened on the steering wheel. I wasn't about to tell her any lies, but I couldn't tell her the truth either. "No, not a date. Just… just… other stuff I need to do. Listen, I'll call you or see you at school next week. Yeah?"

"Sure. Mellie, are you okay?"

I choked back a sob before I answered her. "Yes, I'm fine. Brilliant. I just bought a new mom car and I want to drive it around. You know, put some miles on it."

"So, your plans tonight are driving around with no destination and no real purpose."

When she put it like that, it didn't sound like that great an idea. "Um… yeah."

"What's going on?"

Fuck, I've never been able to fool her for long. "Nothing I can't handle. I need to run. I'll catch you later."

"Melanie?"

Meltdown imminent. "Bevvie, I can't. Please. Not now." *Not ever.*

I heard her sigh. "You know I got your back no matter what."

The first tears tracked down my face, and I struggled to keep the sobs from coming out. "Yes, I know, momma PITA. I promise on a stack of Bibles that if I need you, I'll call. I just… I need… space."

I knew my words were lame, but it was all I had. I also knew she didn't believe me in the slightest.

"Okay, Mellie, but will you stand by as the cavalry in case Abby's group has a crisis tonight? Like if they run out of blue nail polish or emery boards?"

I gave a watery laugh. "Sure. Love you, Bev."

"Love you too, Mel."

I clicked off and drove up to my condo. Maybe I could get some preliminary packing done tonight. I had a freezer of frozen dinners, a pint of my favorite

Ghirardelli triple chocolate ice cream, and a can of Redi-whip. There, plans completed. I could simply forget about today's events and put them out of my mind.

Junior kicked, one foot in my right side and butt pushing against my left.

"Yeah, yeah, kid. Rough day. Really rough, but nothing we can't handle, right? I've got this. I promise."

I had the feeling I'd just lied to my child.

CHAPTER TWENTY

"*X* EQUALS THE SQUARE ROOT OF *A* TIMES THREE." THE three other mathletes groaned as their teammate recited the answer.

"So close!"

"How did you get three?"

"What theorem is that? Not Pythagorean, right?"

I listened to them discuss and figure out where they went wrong. We had about fifteen more minutes of practice. This was our final session before the first math meet, and we were having it on a Wednesday night instead of Thursday because tomorrow was the Thanksgiving holiday. My mother had called and left a message saying I was invited to dinner, but I'd erased it. No way was I going to sit at that long table with my parents and Magnus. Especially since she'd mentioned Robert and Kiki would be there. He and I in the same house? That house? No. Just no.

A sigh escaped my lips. I'd missed Halloween with my favorite family because of work, fatigue, and other things. Those things mainly being Owen. I'd seen him twice at Bevvie's since the mall spotting, and both times my heart hurt so much I couldn't say much to him. He didn't say much back to me either, reverting to his usual short sentences. I didn't sit next to him on the sofa and tried not to make a big deal of it. I thought I covered it well, but Bevvie gave me sympathetic looks.

"Okay, people. Last round. Write the expression for the volume of a thick crust pizza with height a and radius z." I grinned, waiting to see who would get it first.

Jimbo didn't disappoint. A big smile burst across his face. "Ah, Miss Miser, that's so lame."

"Is not. What's the answer?"

He rolled his eyes and recited with his eyes heavenward as if asking why he had to put up with such antics. "The formula for volume is pi times radius squared times height. In this case, pi-z-z-a."

"Absolutely correct, and if we stay here much longer, I'll order us a few. I'm getting hungry."

My kids moaned at the math nerd joke but perked up when I mentioned one of their staple food groups.

"Miss Miser? Mr. Bradshaw is here with two police officers." Coral Blakely, a student teacher, stood in the doorway. Her timid voice sounded uncertain. She played with one of her long dreadlocks. I already knew that to be a nervous tic of hers. She spent a lot of time in my classroom, as she would be graduating in December and taking over for me as a long-term sub in January.

"Can he wait until we're done? It's only a few more minutes."

Two police officers? What the hell was going on? None of my students acted out, as long as you didn't count their drive-thru math prank of making weird change for the attendant.

"I'm afraid not, Miss Miser." The principal strode in my classroom with a confidence I'd never seen in him. His smirk covered his face from ear to ear, and he practically bounced with glee.

A cold dread hit my stomach. If something made him this happy, chances were it was bad for me.

"Miss Miser, you're under arrest."

What the fuck? The roaring in my ears almost covered the rest of his words.

"For inappropriate sexual contact with a student."

The collection of my mathletes surrounded me.

"No, you're wrong!"

"You can't do this!"

I stared at the diminutive man with the smug look on his face. "What the fuck are you talking about? I've never fucked one of my students, and I never will. They're kids, you fucking pervert! Who are you even talking about?"

"Ashton Fordham said you made inappropriate comments and touched him."

I shook my head in disbelief. "Are you kidding me? You've not done your homework, have you? Ashton Fordham has been gone for a long time. Remember his dad put him at some military boarding school after the party he threw at his father's house? He hasn't been my student since his freshman year, and he never joined the mathletes team. I've not laid eyes on him in a long time, and I sure as hell never laid hands on him either."

"Nonetheless, it has come to my attention that he has claimed he's the one who got you pregnant." His shit-eating grin freed my tongue, and I let loose. Probably not the best scenario for my students, but I'd had enough. More than enough.

Of all the statements that man could make, that one took the fucking cake! "You are out of your goddamn mind! Ever since I came to this school, you've spent years, *years*, trying to get me fired or make me quit. You damn well know this trumped-up crap is false, but you'll jump at anything to fuck with me. You've gone too far with this stunt, you fucking asshole. This is one paternity test away from the biggest lawsuit you've ever seen."

"Please turn around, ma'am."

Fuck, they're really doing this. They're putting me in handcuffs in front of my students. "Is this necessary, Officer? I'll be glad to drive over to the station and clear up whatever shit this toad has smeared."

The officers didn't budge. "Sorry, ma'am. This is just procedure."

What else could I do? Two of my girls were crying, and two boys looked like they were thinking about it. If I put up a fight, it would make that worse.

"As you can see, Officer, I am pregnant."

He sighed. "Please, ma'am. Turn around, and we'll get this done a lot quicker."

I shook my head. "If you have to cuff me, don't you do it in front for safety reasons?"

The second cop lost patience. He grabbed my arm and twisted it behind my back. "Quit resisting, bitch. I ain't got no time for this shit."

I cried out in pain, and my students renewed their yells of protest.

"Stop, you're hurting her!"

"No, you can't take her away!"

"Ashton is a liar!"

One of the kids rapidly typed something on his phone. "Don't worry, Miss Miser. I posted a video of this on Facebook. I bet it will go viral, and you'll be out in no time."

Fuck, that's all I need right now. "George, please don't."

Another boy piped up. "Yeah! Make it shareable. I'll post it on my page. It'll spread like the flu. We'll make some posters and storm the police station in protest."

Oh, shit! "Aaron, not a good idea."

The rest of the team joined in, chanting, "Free Miss Miser! Free Miss Miser!"

Principal Bradshaw clapped his hands in sheer delight. "See what you started, Miss Miser? Disrupting student activities. Encouraging them to misbehave. I hope you're proud of yourself."

Really? I'm so done with this! One look at the gloating troll's face change my mind. "You're actually happy about traumatizing these kids. You know what, post away, Aaron. It's gonna be real funny when dipshit here finds out he's out of a job."

"The only one out of a job is you, Miss Miser. Let's hope you're out of jail before you give birth."

The click of the handcuffs brought reality crashing down. Shit, I was going to jail tonight, and there wasn't anything I could do about it. Even worse, Bevvie, Connor, and the kids had left for Disney World early this morning. The drive took about eight hours, which meant they should be pulling into Mickey's place about the same time I arrived at the police station.

My students looked to me in horror. "Does everyone have rides home, either waiting or driving yourselves?" Several nodded. "Good. Please make sure you get home safe, try to have a good holiday tomorrow, and don't forget to study for the meet next week."

"You'll be in school Monday morning, right, Miss Miser?"

"You bet I will."

The officer jerked my arm forward, and I almost stumbled. "What the hell is your problem?"

He sneered in my direction. "Fucking sluts, that's what. You got the right to remain silent, so why don't you shut the hell up?"

He finished spitting my Miranda rights at me as he directed me to the police car, lights flashing red and blue. My clumsiness in getting in the car irritated him further, but the first officer had his act together and even fastened the seat belt for me.

I took the dickwad's advice and stayed quiet throughout the drive to the station. All the episodes of *Law and Order* I'd watched hadn't prepared me for what I faced. I thought I'd get put in a room for questioning. Instead, they took my personal information, mug shot, and fingerprints. I kept it together when they took my purse, jewelry, and phone. When I had to strip out of my clothes completely and put on the beige-colored prison garb, I lost it.

"Dammit, I'm pregnant. Don't you have special circumstances for this?"

The female officer ignored me. Humiliated, hungry, and forced to be naked under the watching eyes of two strange policewomen. It was too much. Tears of frustration flowed down my cheeks and I held my breath in an attempt to stem the flow. "This isn't happening. When do I get my phone call? When can I see a lawyer?"

"Be lucky to see one o' them 'fore the weekend. Erbody's out for the holiday. Getchoo a phone tomorrow. Lucille brung some punkin pie in the break room, and I'm gettin' me a piece 'fore it's all gone."

They led me to a small single cell that smelled of Lysol and puke. I had to step inside and hear the crash of the bars as they slammed the door shut. The only other person there lay passed out on the cot in the cell across from me. I had a similar cot, a metal sink, and an open toilet. Fuck, this was real.

I'm sitting in a jail cell, and no one knows I'm here. I knew the charges were completely bogus, and one little DNA swab would prove it, but still, facing tonight and perhaps more nights in here just might break me. I sat on the edge of the thin mattress and let my sobs out. Once I got to call someone, who would that be? Bevvie and Connor weren't around for several days. My parents wouldn't bother coming, probably preferring to stay away from any scandalous mess. Magnus would show up just to take pictures and revel in my disgrace. The only other person I could call was Owen. I knew he would come get me even it if meant dragging a date with him, but until the officers bothered to bring me a phone, I was alone.

No support. No help. No one around to care. I'd been alone most of my life, but this absolute sense of abandonment shook me to my core. The yawning black pit of depression opened in front of me, and I stood at the precipice. The last time I'd felt this alone was years ago when—

Junior flipped and did his four-limb stretch, reminding me of his presence. The distraction of his movements helped bring me back to myself. I stepped back from the void and wrapped my arms around my belly.

"I got you, melon-head. I got you." My whisper came out jagged, but I think my little alien understood. I rocked back and forth on the edge of the cot and cradled my unborn child. "We'll get through this. I know what's right and wrong, and so do you. Timing sucks, but that's all it is. Just time. Best thing about time is it's always moving forward. People say time heals everything. I'm not so sure, but I know enough time makes everything more bearable, even if it doesn't seem like it."

I didn't know how long I sat in that cell rocking my child until an officer came to release me. Several hours at least. She clanked open the cell and stepped back to let me out. "Free t' go."

Does a law officer application come with a personality test? I got up and followed the woman to the changing room where I got to change clothes again. They handed me back all my stuff and led me to the front of the station.

It turned out I didn't have to call anyone. Owen stood at the desk with his twin, Garrett, and another man who looked vaguely familiar. I didn't think I had anything left in me, but water filled my eyes again.

More forms to sign plus some half-hearted apologies, and I was free.

The stranger spoke first. "I'm so sorry for this, Miss Miser. Believe me, my son is going to regret the mess he started. It's my fault for indulging him so many years and letting him get away with so much. I thought parents were supposed to hand their kids life on a silver platter. I was wrong and still paying for that mistake."

It didn't take me long to find out what happened. Apparently, Ashton had posted on his Facebook page a list of his favorite TILF (Teachers I'd Like to Fuck). My name sat at the top. This happened years ago, and I had no idea about it, as I made a point of not associating with my students on Facebook or any other social media platform. Somehow, one of the school parents found the old post and decided that meant my child was the result of an affair between Ashton and me. They reported it to Principal Bradshaw, and instead of verifying the outdated information, that troll had me arrested by some of his cronies in the local police. They didn't bother to verify anything, just come to the school on that asshole's word. When Aaron posted the video of that horrid event, it did go through the student body like the flu. Abby showed it to Bevvie, and a few phone calls later, Owen showed up at the police station with Garrett and Ashton's father. All charges were dropped, as Ashton's dad explained the impossibility of his son having an affair with me. Ashton had lived five hours away at a military boarding school before he graduated this past May and now lived even further away at another higher education military academy in Virginia. He hadn't been in this city for months.

"You want to press charges against Principal Bradshaw, ma'am?" The first arresting officer had his pen poised over yet another form. He seemed to be sympathetic and ready to make amends for the shit he put me through earlier or maybe he only wanted to make sure I didn't press charges on him. The younger hotheaded guy wasn't around.

Fatigue hit me. Extreme fatigue and my brain shut down. "Absolutely, but I can't right now. Maybe tomorrow or Friday?"

"Sure, ma'am. You just ask for Officer Dillon, and I'll get you sorted."

"Thank you, sir."

Only then did I turn and faced the two MacAteer brothers. Garrett hugged me lightly. "You okay, darlin'?"

"Been better. Good to see you, G-man."

Owen stood rock solid when I moved in front of

him. "O-man?" God, I hated the whine in my voice. When the fuck did I get to be this little timid mouse of a woman? *I'm a fucking lioness. I'm a mighty warrior princess. I'm a lean, mean, goddamn fighting...*

The moment he put his arms around me, my knees buckled. I clutched the lapels of his jacket in two hands and held on for dear life. I imagined I stank from the sour jail cell, and any makeup I might have left was probably smeared across my face in a spectacular fashion. I didn't care. His scent. His strength. His heat. It surrounded me, and I soaked it up like a greedy dry sponge.

He didn't speak a word as he bent his knees slightly and scooped me up. My weight didn't slow him down as he strode straight out of the station into the cold air, and he didn't stop until he placed me in the cab of his truck. Owen heaved himself in the driver side while Garrett got in, effectively sandwiching me between two hard protective bodies.

"Hungry?" Owen's barked question broke the silence.

"Yes, I should eat something."

He pulled into Cook-Out on the right side of the double drive-thru so Garrett would order for us. The thought of a greasy burger made me a little queasy, but that was the quickest option.

Owen stayed silent.

"Thanks for coming to get me."

He grunted.

"Um… thanks for the food, too."

He nodded.

"Are you taking me home? I really want to take a shower."

He nodded again.

Garrett broke into the conversation. "What he means is, you're coming home with us. Beverly will have our hides if we leave you by yourself. Plenty of room at her place with them gone for the weekend. Lots of time to just chill and figure out what to do next."

I tried to come up with a smartass answer or quip, but nothing came to mind. "I had no idea you were coming down for the holiday. Everything good in your world?"

Garrett gave a short laugh and looked out the front window at the strip of road illuminated by the headlights. "It will be."

I let that cryptic answer go as we pulled into Bev's driveway and into the backyard. Rain started to fall as we exited the truck. Not the pretty soft rain at the end of a romantic evening. Wet sheets of it came down in a hard, punishing rush that soaked us in freezing cold water before we got to the front porch. I remembered the forecast had said the whole weekend would be full of scattered thunderstorms and heavy rain. *Fuck. The perfect ending to a super shitty day.*

Muttface met us at the door with his excited barking. Garrett kept the food bags dry under his jacket and put them on the kitchen counter. "Jesus, Mary, and Joseph, what a gully washer, eh? I'm gonna go change real quick so you can have your shower time in the guest room." His feet made clomping noises as he went upstairs, leaving me and Owen alone for a minute.

"Be back." Owen's muffled words came to me as he headed out the back door to his camper. Muttface followed him.

I guess that's that. Not sure what else to do, I pulled off two paper towels from the hanging roll and blotted my face. I expected if I went into the powder room, I'd scare myself. I was sure my face was blotchy and swollen from so much crying. Puffy eyes, red nose, leaking sinuses… yup, tonight sucked big-time, but at least my ass sat in my BFF's kitchen instead of in a jail cell. My eyes started up again at that thought.

Goddammit, Mel, stop this shit! Get your act together!

Owen came back in, still dripping water from his

face and clothes, carrying a white garbage bag. "Sweats and T-shirt. Maybe big. Least dry."

I had some spare clothes in the guest room closet, but Owen didn't know that. The kind gesture made me want to wear whatever he brought me, even if it meant putting on a burlap sack.

Garrett came back down, rubbing a towel briskly over his longish ginger hair. "Ah, much better now. Food, then shower?"

As uncomfortable as my clammy cold clothes felt, hot food sounded better. The burgers and fries disappeared with little conversation between Owen and me. Garrett kept up the flow of words.

"Da's over his head again. Booked a renovation at a pub up in Pennsylvania and didn't check his manpower. Patrick and Angus are working the site, but they need more hands and they've already gone over budget. Patrick said the next two jobs have already cancelled, and there's a third that is on the fence. We've been saying for years now, Da needs to retire. I think something else is going on with him. He can still build with the best of them, but he can't remember shit anymore. Last week, he got mad as hell at the job site because he couldn't find Connor. It's been almost three years since Connor worked a site with us. Little things like that keep happening. Makes me worry about him."

Owen ate silently, only making a few timely acknowledgement noises.

I excused myself as soon as I could. "Well, MacAteer people, it's been a helluva day, and I'm ready to end it."

Garrett gathered the trash and dumped it while the dog whined. "You take the guest room, Mel. I'll crash in one of the other rooms tonight." He grinned. "Which kid will freak out the most when they find out Uncle G slept in their bed?"

"Abby for sure, G-man. Thanks for rescuing me tonight."

"No problem."

Once I got upstairs, I stripped and showered. The hot water sluiced over my head and face, washing off the day. I imagined it taking all the bad shit and gurgling down the drain. *You got this. You got this,* I repeated over and over in my head. I hoped I did.

Owen's T-shirt came down low over my hips, but I left off the sweatpants. I had dry panties, and that's all I needed. I left the bedroom door open and could hear the muffled voices of Garrett and Owen as they talked. They were fraternal twins. Their looks were similar, but enough differences presented that they could be identified. Garrett's body was slightly smaller than Owen's. Not quite as broad and bulky. They shared the same green eyes and ginger hair, however Garrett wore his long and kept it tied back at the nape of his neck. Owen kept his beard and mustache trimmed, while Garrett preferred to be clean shaven.

My mind drifted as my head hit the pillow. *You got this. You got this. You got this.*

CHAPTER TWENTY-ONE

HOMECOMING. WHAT A BEAUTIFUL, MAGICAL NIGHT! I BET this is what Eliza Doolittle felt like in My Fair Lady, or maybe Cinderella when the prince came to take her away from her nasty stepfamily. Pretty dress, perfect hair and makeup, lots of attention from everyone during the dance; all I needed was a tiara, and my status as a princess would be complete.

My parents weren't at home, and Bee-Dee had gone to see her sister in Black Mountain. I had the whole house to myself, therefore, when the after-party at Colin's house got shut down by his parents, I invited everyone to mine. My classmates had raided the liquor cabinet already, and someone had set up a boom box. Music pounded through the walls, red cups littered every surface, and the furniture had been moved around to make room for more dancing. I didn't care. I might worry about cleaning up tomorrow, but tonight, I got to be the princess.

I pirouetted in the hallway of my house, still floating on cloud nine. Vincent got me a really pretty wrist corsage, and his eyes stayed on me the entire night. He said over and over again how pretty I was and how much he liked being with me. He held my hand, put his arm around me every opportunity he found. We danced the fast dances, and I moved my hips in wide circles with lots of hair flips and chest thrusts. When we did the slow ones, he pulled me in so close I could feel his hard body moving against mine. I liked it! I got all jittery and flushed. Turned on. A giggle escaped my lips.

"What's so funny?" Cassie had a marshmallow vodka cooler in her hand. I snatched it and took a drink of the overly sweet concoction. Ugh! How could anyone stand the stuff? I'd had some of my mother's wine already, and my head spun pleasantly.

"Nothing. I'm just having fun!" I tipped my head back and turned in a circle to enhance my first buzz. I loved my party!

"Well, look who's here. Nice dress."

I stopped spinning at the loud, unexpected voice. Robert tipped back the glass of whatever liquor he was drinking and took a healthy swallow. By the way he was swaying, this wasn't his first. He, Archie, and Magnus attended the same college now. Even though this was their first year and technically they were still underage teenagers, just being at a university instead of high school made them seem like mature men and not boys.

"Lookin' real good there, Mel." His gaze went pointedly to my displayed breasts.

The night suddenly didn't seem as wonderful.

I'd bought a special water-filled padded bra to lift them up and out of the white bandage dress I got for homecoming. They were so high, one big breath would make my nipples pop out. The way Robert stared at my chest made me want to cover myself. "What are you doing here?"

"Fall break." Archie made an appearance in the hallway with Magnus right behind him.

My brother took one look at me, and his lip curled in disgust. "You better hope Mom and Dad don't find out about this party of yours. In fact, you need to get these people outta here now. When the fuck are you gonna grow up?"

Indignation rose up in me. "It's homecoming, and we had the dance tonight. I have just as much right to invite my friends here as you do."

"You don't have friends. You have sycophants."

"Who didja go with?" Robert's words slurred as he took another drink.

"Vincent Ziglar."

Robert laughed and snorted "Ah, did Ziggie-boy get him some?"

Heat flushed through my body at the implication. I wasn't stupid and knew exactly what he was talking about. "None of your business."

"Ah, come on, Mel, fess up. No way with that gorgeous body and those tits are you still a virgin."

Any buzz I had from the wine disappeared, leaving a headache behind. "Still nun-ya, Bobby."

Robert's lip curled. I knew he hated to be called Bobby as much as Magnus hated to be called Mags. "Well then, I guess you're not as mature as I thought. Still a little girl playing dress up, eh, Mel? No drinking. No fucking. Just a little high school Barbie princess."

Indignation rose in me. "I'm plenty mature."

"No, you're not."

"I am too!" Shit, I sounded like a whiny little girl stamping her foot. Pull it back, Mel.

"All right then, prove it. Come party with us in the library. You know you want to."

"No, I don't."

He smirked at me. "Like I said, little girl playing dress up. Wanna go get your dolls?"

"I'm not a little girl, and I never played with dolls."

"Then come hang with the college crowd. With the men and not the boys. Just one drink." He turned to look at my brother as if making a challenge. "Magnus, you care if she drinks with us?"

Magnus snorted. "I don't give a shit about her or what she does."

Robert grinned. "See? Big brother is cool. Come on, Melanie. Show us you're not a little high school girl."

The look in his eyes should have warned me. His teasing bugged me as much as Magnus's indifference. Little girl? Immature? Nope, not me. I was all grown up now and as sophisticated as any of the girls in college.

He opened the heavy door to my father's study. I seldom came in this dark room with the heavy furniture. Magnus closed the door, and the volume of the music cut in half.

"Let's get this party started, shall we? Archie, go make Melanie a drink."

I wrinkled my nose. "Ugh, make it a little one."

Robert laughed, and the sound filled me with unease. I glanced at the door and thought about leaving, but it would take a big chunk out of my pride to have to retreat.

"Come on, little girl. Little princess. Prove how mature you are."

Archie held out a chunky glass half full of amber liquid. I took it and, without thinking, took a big swallow.

Fuck! The burn of the liquor slid down my throat, leaving a trail of lava in its wake. I choked back the tears and struggled not to cough out the fire that erupted in my gut. I didn't know what type of alcohol he gave me, and I didn't care. That shit tasted nasty, and I never wanted to drink it again.

Robert threw back his head and laughed at my suffering. "Ha-ha-ha-ha! That's it, baby. You're drinking like a pro. I'm impressed."

I glanced at Magnus. He curled his lip at me and turned his head away in a deliberate snub. I may have been drinking like a pro, but my brother considered me beneath him. I should be used to it by now, but it still hurt. Robert's words of admiration actually meant something to me, and I smiled at him. He looked at me with glazed eyes and took a big sip of his own drink.

"That's it, baby. Drink up. Show me just how old you are."

I tipped the glass back with a flourish, showing off my new talent. The liquor didn't burn quite as bad. I giggled and flipped my hair. Robert's attention had me thinking he might not be so bad, or maybe he was sorry about the way he treated me growing up. He was so handsome even when he was being an asshole to me. Now he saw me as a mature woman, and his equal. Someone who at last, believed I had value as a person.

"Finish it up, Mel, and Archie'll ged choo anudder won."

My head got swimmy, and Robert's voice sounded like a record on slow speed. Something was happening to me. The *glass slipped from my hand, but I blacked out before I heard it hit the floor.*

The next memory I wish I could forget.

I had no control or choice. My consciousness faded in and out, but I knew what Robert did to me. The pain he inflicted on me while Archie and Magnus watched. Decent people stepped in to help strangers every day, but no one was there to rescue me. My parents were gone, and so was Bee-Dee. My friends were too busy at the party tearing up my house. I had no idea where Vincent had gone, or if he would have helped me. My own brother let it happen. How could he? He really didn't care. No love lived in his heart for me. No sense of protection. Robert hurt my body. Magnus hurt me worse in my heart.

When Robert finished, he got off my prone body. "Toldja that shit works fast. Arch, you want a turn?"

"No thanks, man." Archie couldn't look at me. He seemed nervous and a little grossed out, like he couldn't believe what he just saw.

Robert peeled off the condom and knotted it. "I hope you're not plannin' on runnin' off to Daddy. This was payback for getting me in trouble with Coach that one time. You tell anyone, I'll come back and do it again. This time in your ass."

I believed him. I was alone. Nobody had my back.

Nobody would stop him if he chose to follow through with his threat.

"Why do you hate me so much?" I could barely get the words out.

Magnus looked down at me, his eyes cold. "You were born."

CHAPTER TWENTY-TWO

"Melanie, wake up. Wake up!"

I fought. I clawed. I slapped and punched the body that loomed over me.

"Melanie, it's me. It's Owen. Wake up."

I didn't know how long I struggled until I recognized the concerned face above mine. I gasped for breath, and my chest jerked with each hard pound of my heart.

"Owen?"

"Yeah, I'm here."

"Where are we?"

"Guest room at Bevvie and Connor's house."

"I'm… I'm… safe?"

His face turned to granite. "Yes, you're safe. Always."

"I had a bad dream."

"I could tell."

"A nightmare."

"Yes."

"Did I wake you?"

"You were screaming."

"I'm sorry."

"Nothing to be sorry about. It sounded pretty real. You sure it was just a dream?"

I couldn't lie to him. I couldn't tell him the truth. The adrenaline rush hit me, and I started to shake. "D-d-did I wake Garrett?"

"Garrett can sleep through an earthquake. He's fine where he is."

My teeth clicked together, and I clenched every muscle I had to try to bring myself under control. It didn't work. Owen made a noise and settled himself to spoon me from behind, molding the shape of his body to fit. His legs crooked into my knees, his hips and torso tucked against mine so I felt every shift. His heavy arms went one under my head and one over my chest and shoulders, locking me in place. Not an inch of space remained between him and me. My shaking subsided, and my cramping muscles slowly unlocked.

"Who was it?"

God, he knows. Somehow, he knows. What the fuck did I scream? "Wh-who was what?"

"Who did this to you?"

"Why?"

"Because I'm going to beat the shit out of him. Then I'm going to let Garrett beat the shit out of him. Then Connor. Then Bevvie. Then I'm going to start it all over again."

Big neon flashing sign! He spoke in whole sentences, which told me his mind was back with me. That, or his anger was focused to a razor-sharp edge. "It happened a long time ago."

"It doesn't matter if it happened yesterday or twenty years ago. I'm still going to beat the shit out of him."

"Owen."

"No. You… Fuck, Mel, I heard your scream before I could get you awake. You said stop. You said no. You said it hurts. You said I'm bleeding. You begged for help. You fought me when I woke you to stop the nightmare. I don't have a college degree, but I'm not stupid."

No, Owen was not stupid. He was actually one of the smartest people I knew and had a depth not many people understood. This new knowledge of me, I couldn't walk back, nor hide from him. "It happened a long time ago, and I never told anyone. It was my intention to take it to the grave, but I guess that's impossible now. I'd appreciate it if you'd keep this to yourself. I don't want anyone else to know."

His whispered breath brushed across my cheek and his voice rumbled with emotion in my ear. "Christ, Melanie. You've carried that shit with you for fucking years. There are people in your life who love you that are more than willing to help you heal."

I had the impulse to deny, deny, deny. It was on the tip of my tongue to say I was over it. That I had already healed myself and didn't need anyone. It didn't matter anymore. Hiding behind false bravado and a smart-ass attitude had taken me this far and if needed, I could fake it for a lifetime, right?

Heat flushed through me and I took a big breath to calm my nerves. "That's too much to ask of anyone. I know Bevvie and Connor and the kids care about me, but I can't dump my problems on them."

Owen tightened his arm, and his heat burned into me. "What about me? I care about you too. A lot. More than you think."

Oh, shit! Dangerous waters ahead. His words thrilled me and scared me at the same time. It was easier to make confessions at night where faces could stay hidden in a layer of protection. In the daylight, all thoughts and feelings became visible. Then it got complicated. Here in the dark, hearts can be laid open and words said that cannot be spoken when face-to-face. "I know you care about me, Owen. I don't want my shit to fuck things up between us."

"I LOVE YOU."

Those three words hit me like pointed shards of ice. In my favorite romance stories, when the man made his love confession, the woman melted into a big pile of emotional goo. Then they had the best sex of their lives, full of descriptive adjectives for several pages. Owen's declaration didn't fill me with fluffy feelings and thoughts. I was totally and completely scared out of my ever-lovin' mind.

The truth was harder to face and there it was, standing right in front of me. Even in the dark I saw it with a clarity that left me as one big, raw, open wound. How many fucking times in my life had I sought one-night stands just to feel something? Anything. How many times had I let someone touch me and not known his last name? How many times did I mistake lust for love? Was I worthy of it? Would I ever be good enough for someone's love? How could I even recognize it?

"I don't know how you can love me."

"Yes, I can."

"You shouldn't."

"Why not?"

"Because I don't deserve it. I'm so fucked-up, I don't deserve anyone's love."

Owen's voice growled in my ear as he proceeded to gut me completely. "No one deserves to be loved. It's not something you have to work for either. You don't buy it like you do milk in a grocery store. It's not about clothes or looks or money. I know your family thinks that way, and I've seen firsthand that being rich doesn't mean shit when it comes to loving someone."

Owen's lips pressed into the spot just under my earlobe. "Listen well, Melanie. You know I don't bull-shit. Ever. There's nothing you can do to *make* me love you. Nothing you can say, nothing you can buy. Not sex or the promise of it. Not a house or car. You do not and cannot *make* me love you. I just do. Something else you should figure out. You can't make me love you, and you can't stop me from loving you either."

I couldn't contain it. I let the torrent free and totally flooded the shoulder underneath my cheek. My fingers dug into his skin as I clung to his strong arm. I didn't know how long it took for me to empty. It might have been a few minutes. It might have been an hour. He stayed there throughout the entire deluge, holding me, breathing into my hair, kissing my skin, and murmuring *I love you* over and over. The shakes subsided at last. I should have been exhausted from the roller coaster emotions of the day. I wasn't. I felt alive. I felt lighter. Freer. More open. I felt… I felt… I felt pure need.

"Owend?" Shit, my nose was plugged up.

He knew exactly what I asked and offered. "If I touch you now, I'm not going back to friends only. I'm committed and I'm not leaving. Are you ready for that? If you're not, I can wait."

"Yez, I'b ready. I'b zo ready, I'b scared shidless. Whad if I fuck this up? I don't thinck I can take it."

He chuckled as he shifted and moved me to my back. "You heard me, but you didn't understand. You can't force me to love you. You can't make me stop loving you. No way can you fuck this up."

He kissed me. Smooth lips rounded over mine, coaxing them apart, and I let him in. His tongue, slightly rough, stroked my mouth. "Is this safe? Won't hurt the baby?"

"No. The doctor said I could have sex right up until labor if I wanted to, as long as it's comfortable."

He kept kissing me as he pulled up the T-shirt I

wore, baring my chest. "Tell me when you want to stop. It won't hurt me, and I'll never hurt you."

I'd done a lot of straight-up fucking. Hard, fast, animal fucking. The kind where bodies pounded so brutally against each other that I was sore for days. I'd had some experimental sex. Blindfolds, bondage, some spanking and flogging. I did anal a few times with one of my short-term boyfriends.

That was the first time I'd truly made love. Glowing coals smoldered in my belly as he moved over my breasts. They had grown more sensitive and my nipples larger. He circled each one gently before drawing a tight peak into his mouth. *Ah, God, that tongue!* Thrills shot through my body with each stroke. I arched into him, and he answered by cupping my other breast and playing with that nipple with his thumb. I heard a low, keening moan and realized it came from my own throat. Just before the pleasure became too much, he switched sides and treated both my breasts equally.

I was one big mass of finely tuned nerves. I felt everything ten times more than I normally did. His hands on my body, fingers on my skin, mouth on my breasts, neck, lips—there wasn't a place he didn't touch or explore as he learned the intricacies of my body. At last he lowered his head between my legs, stripped my panties, and spread me open. He didn't play, tease, or tickle. He went right for the gold with a long, hard swipe across my clit that nearly sent me through the roof.

"Oh, fuck! O-man!"

I swear he smiled against my sex. Nibbles, strokes, hard sucks, light flicks; he played with me, sending me up the steep climb of a roller coaster and letting me slide back down before cresting the top. If he went any slower, I thought I would have a heart attack.

"Please, Owen. Please let me come!"

One long finger pressed around my entrance.

"Ahh!"

The digit pushed inside and pressed upward. His lips fastened over my clit, sucking it inside his mouth. His tongue rapidly flicked over the tip. Just as I thought I'd lose my mind, he pulled his finger out of me and reached lower to press it against my anus. I gasped at the unexpected intrusion. He only got the first knuckle in before I gave it up.

I fell over the edge in one long, continued wave of pleasure. He kept playing me, driving me through those coaster curves until I came a second time. Maybe it was a single nonstop orgasm. Whatever it was, it was good, and I wanted more.

He finally released me and moved to stretch out at my side. "Good?"

My laugh was breathy. "You couldn't tell? Incredible, O-man. You have some serious talent, baby. Your turn."

"I don't know if that's a good idea. I'm fine with waiting."

God, this man! "And waste that hard-on? No way."

The backs of two of his fingers stroked my shoulders. "It'd be awkward for you."

"Not if I'm on top."

Those fingers stilled. "Are you sure?"

Was I sure? Not of much in my chaotic life, but in this moment, right here, right now, I was sure I loved Owen MacAteer, and I wanted him inside me with a fierceness I'd never had before. I rolled up, pushed his shoulders to the bed, and straddled his hips. My hand snaked down between his legs and mine to find the big beautiful dick I'd seen and held once before. Big indeed. I grasped him and stroked the head across my pussy, coating him in wet. "This is mine. You made it for me, and I'm claiming it."

His hands came to my hips as I eased myself down. The broad head breached my opening, and he slid inside. His eyes stayed on mine as I took him all the way. Sensation flooded my body, and words flooded my mind. Tight fit. Full. Stretched. Wonderful. Home.

This connection went much deeper than physical contact. He moved, flexing and making me gasp at the intensity of his touch.

"Owen." I had no other words. I didn't need them. He held my hips as I rocked on top of him. He let me set the pace, easing in and out of my channel. God, he felt good! So fucking good. I leaned back as he slipped a hand between my legs and his thumb slowly circled my clit.

"Mel, I can't hold back much longer." His growling tone vibrated in the room. I felt his quivering body as he tried to slow down. "Come with me."

He flexed inside me, pressing on my magic spot. My breath rushed out of me as I came. Half a second later, I felt his final push, and he came with powerful pulses, buried deep, filling me with everything he had.

In the aftermath, Owen got up and went into the bathroom, leaving me in the bed with a tender kiss to my forehead. The light from the bathroom and the noise of the faucet running made my brain kick in, and I started to think.

Oh my God, I just fucked Owen MacAteer. Not fucked. Made love. Owen MacAteer made love to me. This is the real deal. I can't go back, can I? Do I want to?

Owen came back in the room, his naked form outlined for a moment before he turned off the bathroom light. He walked over to me and gently eased my legs apart to clean me with a warm cloth. His ministrations made me feel loved, respected, treasured—all the feels I could ever want from a man. I reached a hand up to stroke his bearded cheek. The faint moonlight made his eyes glitter as he looked into mine. I pulled his face to me for a kiss and whispered against his lips. "I love you too."

CHAPTER TWENTY-THREE

BEVVIE WAS RIGHT WHEN SHE TOLD ME I'D NEVER FIND another man to have my back like a MacAteer man. They should come with warning labels. No thirty-day trial period, no try it before you buy it. No returns or exchanges for a different size. Once Owen decided he was my man and I was his woman, he committed one hundred percent. We became a real couple who spent every waking minute together outside of work. He came to my house every night to paint rooms, hang blinds, and install a new water heater. I unpacked, hung pictures, and watched my stomach grow bigger. We went grocery shopping together—or rather, I went grocery shopping with him, since he did almost all the cooking. We hung out at Bevvie and Connor's house. He took Bevvie's place at the birthing classes, coaching me to breathe and pant. He went with me to pick out Beatrix Potter themed baby bedding with Peter Rabbit, Mrs. Tiggy Winkle, Benjamin Bunny, and other characters from those classic children's books. He built me a bunny lamp and bookshelves for the nursery and painted them to match the theme. He installed himself in my life so thoroughly, it was hard to think of a time when he wasn't there.

And the sex. Oh. My. God. The sex was incredible! Once we got started that first time, it became a feeding frenzy. I couldn't get enough of the man and craved his touch like I did my next pair of high heels. Owen was just as generous in bed as he was out of it. I had free reign over his body anytime I wanted him. I loved sucking him off while we watched TV at night. Because of my shape, we did it doggie style for the most part or spooned. He never complained and always asked if it was safe for me and the baby. My pregnant body didn't turn him off or deter him in the least. Sometimes we'd start the day with morning sex, sometimes we'd finish it making long, slow love. Whenever we came together, the level of personal intimacy between us reached a depth I'd never had and never thought possible. Every time he touched me, he gave me a piece of himself as well as took a piece of me, until I didn't know where he started and I ended. Pure. Magical. Love.

He told me he loved me. Often, and I had no doubt he meant it. My life with Owen had become so good and so perfect, it was more like a Hallmark movie than reality.

Garrett only stayed around a few days during the Thanksgiving weekend from hell and then left to go back to his life. The few bits I heard from his conversations with Owen centered on their father's deteriorating health and the woman Garrett lived with. Neither were doing so hot. Sooner rather than later, some decisions needed to be made about Fergus MacAteer and the best way to take care of him. I got the impression that none of the man's kids particularly liked their father and his future care was borne more of obligation than as an act of love. I could relate, and I found the willingness of the MacAteer men admirable, in that they really didn't have to take care of their father. If a similar situation cropped up in my family, and my brother got put in the position where he had to take care of me, I'd be out on the street or he'd try to euthanize me like an old dog.

Owen willingly came with me to the police station Monday after Thanksgiving. The legal advisor I talked to said that filing the charge of a false police report might stick, but Principal Bradshaw had friends and cronies in high places. Even if he ended up getting found guilty, he would probably just get fined. It pissed me off to think that bastard could get away with doing that shit to me with not much more than a slap on the wrist, but I still planned on going through with it. If I decided to drop the charges later, I had that option. I probably would, as I imagined it would be one big hassle and ultimately a waste of time, but for now I wanted that asshole to squirm a little.

Owen put up a Christmas tree in my house, but we spent Christmas Eve over at Bevvie's. We attended the candlelight church service and watched the kids perform their parts in the play. Owen sat next to me in the pew and held my hand through Bevvie's beautiful solo. Jeez, my BFF could sing! Connor thought so too, from the rapt expression on his face as he watched his wife. Total, complete adoration.

The one mood killer happened during the candle lighting. The entire congregation had little handheld candles and passed the flame from person to person. The lights turned out, leaving only the tiny pinpricks of fire to light the large sanctuary. I thought the sight was beautiful and turned to Owen to share my thoughts, and my eyes crossed with Robert's. A hard thud punched my gut as our gazes locked.

Shit... uh... I mean, shoot! Of all places tonight, why in the hell... heck... is he here? It didn't take me long to figure it out. This church was one of the biggest in the city and a large number of high-ranking businessmen and council members attended. Even the mayor came to tonight's service. On holidays, the attending congregation more than doubled as this building became the place to be and be seen. Bevvie referred to them as CEOs. Christmas and Easter Only.

Kiki stood next to him, resplendent in gold and glitter, oblivious to his attention wandering to me. I froze at the menacing glare he gave me. He didn't lick his lips, grab his crotch, or make any gesture other than to stare, but I still got that vibe from him. The vibe that if given the chance, he'd be all over me... again.

I was so focused on Robert that I almost failed to see Magnus standing with him as well. He nudged Robert's arm and sneered at me. I heard an angry growl next to me, and Owen's body grew stiff. He saw them too, and if we'd been at any other location, a massive testosterone-fueled fight would have already broken out.

Junior took that moment to wake up and did his usual four-way stretch. My attention shifted to my kid moving around and reminding me of his presence. I broke off the stare-down with Robert and Magnus and covered my rippling stomach. The dress I had on fit well and somewhat minimized my protruding belly, but my pregnancy still showed. Owen moved his candle from one hand to the other and put his arm around me, pulling me into his sheltering body. He didn't have to say a word for me to get his meaning. If either Robert or Magnus tried to mess with me, I had someone to protect and defend me. Warm fuzzies crowded my belly next to my kid, and I leaned against Owen's side, sniffing his light cologne. He responded by kissing the top of my head.

I covered up a giggle and whispered, "I don't think you're supposed to kiss in church, sweetheart."

He did it again and answered, "God's house is a place of love. He won't mind."

***

AFTER THE SERVICE, WE ALL WENT BACK TO BEVVIE AND Connor's house for presents, hot chocolate, and food. Owen and I walked into a house smelling of rich beef stew, yeasty bread, cinnamon-sweet sugar cake, and total bedlam.

Abby and Beverly were arguing in the open kitchen area.

"That's so unfair, Mom."

"You're too young."

"I'm sixteen!"

"That's too young."

"No, it's not. I just need parental consent."

"You're assuming I'll give you consent."

I looked at Connor with questioning eyes, and he explained. "Abby's found a new boy she likes. This one is big into Japanese anime and cosplay. Abby wants to get a tattoo of some cartoon character I've never heard of on her side for Christmas. Bev is against it."

I stifled a laugh. No doubt who would win that battle. I could hear Abby's wail through the house.

"You're so mean!"

Beverly pulled bowls and plates from the cupboard while ignoring the teenage meltdown. "Yup, I'm the terrible mean mom, now and forever."

"It's all I want."

"Too bad. I already bought you socks and underwear."

"Why? Why can't I get a tattoo? Harvey's parents let him have one, and it's soooo cute!"

"It's a Pikachu Pokémon. I agree, they're cute."

"So why can't I get a matching one?"

"You've never been into Pokémon before."

"I'm into them now, and Harvey thinks it will look really cool."

"If you're still into them when you're eighteen, you can get one then."

"You're just prejudiced against people with tattoos."

I had to admire Bevvie's patience. I was sure there was a special place in heaven for moms of teenage drama queens. She lifted the top from the huge crock-pot, and fragrant steam rose from the bubbling stew. "I'm not against tattoos, Abby. I'm against the reason you want the tattoo so bad."

"Why?" Bevvie was not the only stubborn female in the house.

Bevvie paused, stirred the stew, and placed the large spoon on a rest next to the pot. "You're talking about going through a painful and permanent experience just because a boy you like says he wants you to. Do you not see what's wrong with that?"

Abby crossed her arms and huffed. "I don't see your point at all. Connor, make her stop."

Connor barked out a laugh as he rejoined Bevvie in the kitchen. He unwrapped two round loaves of homemade bread. "Sorry, Abby. Your mom is right. You shouldn't have to get a tattoo for this Harvey fellow to like you. No woman, young or old, needs to twist herself into knots and become something she's not in order to keep a man interested. If he can't love you for just being you, then he's not worth your time."

Abby still wasn't ready to give up the argument. "I like Pikachu."

"Enough to have him on your body for life? Suppose you and Harvey don't work out and the next guy you like can't stand Pokémon. Are you going to go through a laser removal because of that?"

Abby hesitated and then rolled her eyes before she flounced off. "Ugh, I hate it when you use logic."

Connor's chuckle followed her, and he turned back to the task of slicing the bread on a cutting board. Mattie, already in pj's, surfed through the kitchen. Sarah sat under the tree, sorting the gifts into separate piles for each person. Jacob started a medley of Christmas music playing on his phone.

Good food. Good family. Good man at my side. How could it get any better?

It did in the form of a breaking news text alert.

Former Principal Garland Bradshaw has been arrested this evening on charges of possession of child pornography and solicitation of a minor. Details to follow.

Bevvie got the same alert I did. Our bugged eyes met, and both our mouths formed perfect Os. "Holy shit!" I mouthed at her. She nodded mutely.

Neither of us really knew what this news meant for the future, but we both knew one thing for certain. Principal Bradshaw no longer worked for the school system and wouldn't be coming back. *How in poor taste would it be to offer a high five to my best friend?*

We ate the filling stew, nibbled on sugar cake, and watched the kids open presents. Jacob got his own soldering iron and other electric gizmo stuff I couldn't quite figure out. Sarah got her own Kindle plus a lot of Amazon gift cards for books. Abby got a new smart phone with a blinged-out case and wireless earbuds. Mattie ignored the clothes and concentrated on the trick skateboard. Fortunately, knee pads, elbow guards, and an industrial strength helmet came with the gift.

I had only one small gift for Owen, but it meant a lot. At least, I hoped it did.

Connor and Bevvie gave themselves a gift of concert tickets and overnight resort accommodations at Harrah's casino. It didn't take a psychic to see Owen and I would be spending a weekend with the kids while Bevvie and Connor got it on with some slot machines and great music.

Owen handed me a Christmas card covered in candy cane and Santa Claus stickers. Mattie danced around us. "I helped decorate your card, Auntie M. Ain't it pretty?"

"Isn't. Not ain't." I opened the card, and several pictures fell out. A beautiful handmade crib of dark mahogany wood, a sturdy changing table, and a glider rocker met my eyes.

"Connor designed them. I built them." Owen's rumble filled me ear. "Too big to wrap. Sitting out there in the shop, ready to be moved in."

I bumped his arm and snuggled under it next to his warm side. This routine and position had become a habit, and I doubted it would ever get old. "These are beautiful. Thank you, O-man."

He looked at me with those gorgeous green eyes of his, and my breath disappeared. God in heaven, how did I get so lucky to have this man? I brushed at my eyes. "It's just a bit of wood dust."

Mattie broke the moment. "Ewww, they're gonna go all kissy face!"

Sarah tapped at the screen on her Kindle. "That's what you're supposed to do when you're boyfriend and girlfriend, doofus."

"It's still gross. I'm never getting a girlfriend if I have to do that."

"Might change your mind someday, boy-o." Connor remarked as he unwrapped Muttface's present. The dog spun in circles at his feet until given the ginormous rawhide chew bone.

Only my gift to Owen remained, and I handed him a huge wrapped box. Mattie had helped with this one too and fidgeted while Owen carefully slit the paper with a pocket knife.

"Just tear it, Uncle Owen!"

Inside that box, he found another one, wrapped just as prettily with bows and ribbons. He gave me a wry look as if saying *I know this game.*

Four wrapped boxes later, he pulled out a small gift bag filled with paper and confetti. From the bag, he lifted a snap ring box. He popped it open to reveal a house key.

My stomach fluttered. "What do you think, O-man? Wanna move into a house instead of living in a camper?"

He held the key in the palm of his hand and stared at it for several moments. I held my breath. *Too soon? Maybe he wasn't ready? I hope I didn't just fuck this up!*

"Guess I n-n-need to add more closet space."

My eyes grew wet. "I guess you do."

He smiled and hugged me. The Grinch was not the only person at Christmas whose heart grew three times as big. Happiness burst and overflowed inside me. Junior flipped in agreement.

Later that night, we lay together in Bevvie's guest room. The kids had zonked out immediately after presents and coming down from the excitement of the holiday. The whole house settled into post-Christmas lull. Owen snuggled behind me, spooning me in what had become our favorite position.

"Was that the man?"

I had been drifting into sleep, all warm and comfy. "What man?"

"The man at the church next to your brother. You stiffened up when you saw him."

Owen's voice sounded calm and rather nonchalant. His body stayed relaxed against mine, and his arm was secure around my front, holding me close. Safe. I felt safe.

"Saw him at the party at your parents' house. Saw you react to him then too. He's the one."

I saw no reason to deny or confirm what Owen accurately guessed. He'd already heard the entire story of that horrible night.

"Yes. That's him."

Owen kissed my hair. "You scared of him?"

Am I? "I don't like being around him and wish he lived somewhere else, but I'm older now and know better. When it happened, I was a kid who didn't know how to handle things and I was by myself. I'm not alone anymore. He can't hurt me."

He can't hurt me. Those four words made my heart grow light and my head giddy. It was true. He could stare, make rude statements, try to fuck with my accounts, even resort to physical intimidation. He could do whatever he wanted, but he couldn't hurt me.

Owen moved my hair to kiss the back of my neck. "No, he can't and won't. He comes around, he has to go through me to get to you."

His hand moved over my breast, and he lightly thumbed the nipple. "I move in, I'm not moving out. Not in a month, not in a year, not ever. This is it for me, Mel. I've waited for it a long time, and I'm not giving it up."

I slipped off my panties and raised my leg to hook his hip behind me.

"I love you, Owen MacAteer."

He freed himself from his boxers and pressed the head of his dick against my opening. He slipped in like a well-fit glove. Christ, I would never get tired of this!

His hips flexed as he slowly made love to me, moving in and out of my pussy at his leisure. Each stroke pressed against my G-spot, drawing a gasp from me every time he flexed. He filled me not only with his dick, but with his love, until I couldn't tell where he ended and I began. His hand shifted from my breast down between my legs, and his fingers plucked at my clit, rolling it gently between them.

I came breathing his name. He came breathing mine.

CHAPTER TWENTY-FOUR

God save me! How did this kid plan on getting a good SAT score when he didn't have basic math concepts? He needed to scrap the idea and take a remedial course instead of wasting my time and his parents' money. This was my last tutoring session for the evening, and I couldn't wait for his mom to come pick him up. My back had been aching all fucking day, and I was ready to put my swollen feet up and relax. That was, if I still had feet. I hadn't seen them in a long time.

Owen texted to ask if I wanted him to pick up food on the way home. I smiled and texted back my latest craving for Panera Bread potato and bacon soup.

It was mid-January. New Year's Eve had come and

gone. School started back, and life had settled into a new norm. Owen moved in the day after Christmas. It didn't take much time, as he mostly owned his clothes and a few personal items. The rest of his belongings consisted of his tools. The camper stayed parked at Bevvie's, as it was a pain in the ass to move and Garrett would be using it for a while. He showed up at Bevvie's on Christmas Day, having broken up with his girlfriend. Owen didn't say much about it, but I got the impression it was a bad scene and Garrett needed time to heal and figure out his next steps. I'd listed my condo as an Airbnb rental and planned to keep it that way for a few years. If Garrett planned to stick around, maybe I'd offer it to him to use.

I was also nearly two weeks late and on the verge of having labor induced. Junior just didn't want to join us in the big outside world.

Coral had taken over my classes at the school, but I still did some nighttime tutoring to help some of the more challenged students, Gary Tharpe being one of them. His lanky build, towering height, and prowess on the court put him in the perfect position to earn a basketball scholarship, but he had to score well on the SATs. That possibility diminished bit by bit the longer I worked with him on his limited math skills.

I stood from the spot at my kitchen table and felt

rather than heard a weird pop. A moment later, a small flood gushed from between my legs.

Oh shit, my water just broke!

"What's that?" My genius student gawped at the puddle that formed at my feet. "Did you just piss yourself?"

"No, I'm in labor."

"Huh?"

"The baby is coming."

The kid's brain cells finally fired up, and his mouth formed a perfect O. "What do I do?"

"Call your mom to come get you."

"She goes to the grocery store when I'm here gettin' tutored."

"That has nothing to do with the price of eggs in China."

"Huh?"

He missed my sarcasm completely, and I was out of patience. "Call. Your. Mom. Now!"

He pulled out his phone and dropped it twice before he was able to place the call. My phone was on the counter, and before I got there, a low pain twisted in my stomach. I puffed and counted while my student panicked.

"Oh, shit! I mean shoot! Uh... no, not you, mom.

Miss Miser. She's having the baby. Right now. Can you come get me?"

I didn't pay attention to him as the pain faded and I took a full breath. Fuck me, if this was the beginning, I wanted drugs. Lots of them.

I texted Owen twice before I figured out he was probably driving and couldn't answer me. I tapped his icon to call him, and another contraction hit me as the line connected. Owen got an earful of my hee-hee-heeing breaths.

"Almost eight minutes apart. Fuck, this is a lot faster than the book said it would be. Hee-hee-hee. Where are you?" I hated the whine in my voice, but dammit, that fucking hurt! It felt like a big fist just grabbed my abdomen in a vise.

"Driveway."

A moment later, he was there, holding me and pressing into my back.

"Gary? Are you ready?"

Thank God his mom came quickly, or else I would have left his ass alone at my house.

"How did he do tonight? Do you want me to pay you now or next week?"

This woman gave birth at least once. Did she not recognize what was going on here? "Next week, please," I gasped out as the contraction eased.

Owen glanced at his watch and frowned. "Go now."

The woman blinked as her son gathered his books and papers and stuffed them haphazardly into a backpack. "That's a little rude, doncha think?"

"I'm in active labor, Mrs. Tharpe."

She flipped her hand. Actually flipped it. "Oh fiddle, you've got hours before that happens."

Owen didn't bother mincing any more words. He wrapped his arms around me and took my weight against him as we hobbled to his truck. I panted the entire short trip, hoping either mother or son had enough sense to lock up when they left.

The ride to the hospital was cut in half with Owen driving. I huffed and puffed and moaned the whole time. He hit the Bluetooth icon, and the cab filled with the buzzing ring of the phone.

"Hello?"

"Bevvie!" I cried out, "I need you, I… oh shit… *hee-hee-hee.*"

"Hospital. Now." Owen contributed.

"Got it. I'm on the way. I'll text Connor to let him know. Abby will stay with the kids tonight. Have you called the hospital to tell them you're on the way?"

"Not. Yet. Would you mind?"

"I can do that for you. How far apart?"

Another conctraction hit me. Fuck, this *hurts!*

"I… hee-hee-hee… think maybe… hee-hee-hee… five minutes?"

"Shit, that was fast."

"You're telling me! I thought this was supposed to take a day or two. I… hee-hee-heeeee!"

Owen pulled up to the circular drive of the emergency entrance and parked.

"You can't… hee-hee-hee… leave the truck here. It will get towed."

"Don't care."

One look at me was all it took for the nurse to send us straight to the back. They plopped me in a wheelchair and whisked me away. No forms, clipboards, insurance cards—my red face and puffing breaths was enough. Owen followed me to a partitioned-off spot, and the nurse whipped the curtain closed. Two more nurses appeared, and I was unceremoniously stripped of my clothes and draped with sheets.

Another pain ripped through my belly. *Fuck me sideways, this is cramps on super steroids!* "Owen!"

He was right there by my side, holding my hand, his lips to my sweating forehead, hee-heeing with me. "Don't leave me, please don't leave me," I cried.

"Never."

"I mean it. *Hee-hee-hee.* I need you."

"Always here."

A steel band wrapped around my middle and tightened. I had no control. "I need some goddamn drugs! Where's the fucking guy with the spinal thingy?"

It was a wonder I didn't crush Owen's hand. He held on for dear life as I hee-hee-heed through another hard contraction. Tears fell down his face and dripped to mingle with mine. "I'm sorry, Mel. I w-w-wish I could take some of this f-f-for you."

The on-call doctor finally showed up, and from his appearance he graduated school sometime last week. High school, that was.

"Okay, Miss Miser, I understand we're having a baby today?"

I'd left my patience back at my house along with my hospital bag. "No shit, Sherlock! *Hee-hee-hee!* You might want to join the party, like now!"

Owen growled.

The Doogie Howser wannabe calmly pulled up a stool and lifted the drape between my spread thighs. His startled yelp was the last thing I wanted or expected to hear. "Oh my God, you're crowning already. Too late for an epidural."

Crowning? What the fuck? No drugs? I thought labor took hours. Days, even. I puffed and puffed and puffed. "I need to push. I gotta push."

"Yeah, okay, Miss Miser. At the next—"

My cry cut him off as the tightest, hardest contraction hit me and my entire body strained with effort. I left permanent impressions in Owen's hand as I gripped him. I might have even broken a few bones. He placed an arm around my back and helped me bow in half as I was ripped apart.

"Love you, Mel. Love you, baby. You got this. Breathe."

Other voices in the room faded into background noise as the entire universe focused on one event.

"Oh my God, the head's out already."

"Textbook always said it would be more."

"I suspect neither she nor the baby read the textbook. Check the cord. Quick before the next contraction."

"Get ready to catch."

"Damn, this one is fast!"

"Here it comes."

I felt a giant lump slide from my body, and my internal organs shifted. I took the first full breath I'd had in months as my body returned to me. The pain disappeared into a dull ache, and my muscles relaxed. A sense of euphoria washed over me, and for a moment, I floated in the air.

Then the mewling cry of a baby reached my ears. My baby. My baby boy.

"Eight pounds, two ounces. Sixteen inches long. APGAR test nine. Jeez, he's a big one!"

A wrinkled little alien covered in cheese was placed on my softened stomach. His scrunched-up red face and open mouth announced to the world he was here and not happy about it. I didn't blame him, as I'd be upset too if I was forced out of a cushy warm place where I got constant room service. I touched his back, and he quieted into little whimpers.

My world had arrived. I had a son. My son. My little boy. The little boy I would teach, nurture, and bring into manhood. *This is my son.* I couldn't contain it. The emotion poured out of my eyes. I turned them to meet Owen's beautiful green ones. I had no words. None.

I didn't need them.

Owen leaned down and brushed his lips over mine in what was not just a kiss. It was more. It was a promise. A promise of being by my side. A promise of dinner at home, lawn maintenance, chaperoning, babysitting. A promise of a lifetime commitment.

He loved me. This wonderful, quiet man loved me and loved my child.

The kiss was light and brief, but it burst in my heart with a bazillion sparkles of light.

"Ryan," Owen whispered brokenly. He still held my

hand while his streaming eyes were on the perfect little human lying on me. "Ryan. Little king. Once he made up his mind, he hurried to get here."

I smiled. "Ryan. I like it."

The nurses took Ryan to clean him up, and the doctor finished taking care of me. Fatigue set in. Damn, no wonder they called it labor. That shit was serious work.

I didn't make it to the fancy delivery rooms with all the pretty pictures of babies on the walls. I delivered right there in an emergency room bay. The nurses kept remarking about how quick my labor went as they wheeled me up to the maternity floor, baby Ryan wrapped in a sheet and sitting in my arms.

"Damndest thing I ever seen. That baby wanted to be born somethin' fierce."

"I think you done set a record here at the hospital. First timer, too."

I didn't know how to take that sentence. "Um… thanks?"

One nurse had rich brown skin and long micro braids with translucent and raspberry-colored beads hanging from the ends. She tossed them with a rattle over her shoulder. "I'm not too sure about hospital records, but you were only active for about forty minutes or so. Might be, you were in labor a couple days and didn't know it."

"Maybe. Where's Owen?"

"Your husband stayed downstairs to sign some papers."

"We're not married."

"Oh? Shoot, anyone can see that man is a husband whether or not there's a ring on his finger."

God, am I ready for that? Nope, not yet. I just truly became a mom. I'd think about wife later.

It didn't take long before I got settled into a room. It had a portable wheelie box that looked like an under-the-bed Rubbermaid container for Ryan, but I held him in my arms and watched his movements in fascination. My heart overflowed with sheer joy.

Bevvie came in, and both of us boo-hooed at each other. "Oh, Mellie-Jellie, you're a mom now."

"Yeah."

"He's so pretty."

"He's my little boy."

"I'm gonna cry again."

"You haven't stopped since you came in the room."

"I'm not going to either."

We sniffed, snorted, and cooed, while Ryan made baby faces and squirmed. He made a grunting noise and suddenly stretched out all four limbs in a very familiar action.

"Oooh, I see you now, booger," I told him as I recognized his favorite move.

Owen walked in the room with a plastic bag of complimentary hospital stuff and came right to me. He kissed me and took my hand as Bevvie and I continued our blubbering.

An administrator followed him in with a giant-sized clipboard. "How are you feeling, Miss Miser?"

"I'm good."

"Wonderful, and congratulations on your baby. I heard you set a record for the fastest delivery in this hospital."

"I'm expecting a call from Guinness records any time now."

Confusion appeared on her face as she didn't get my joke at first, and then she finally barked out a light laugh. "I'm sure they will contact you soon. In the meantime, I need your signature on some forms."

Bevvie sniffed one more time. "I'll leave you alone to get your business done and then get some rest. I'll run by your house to get your bag and be back tomorrow. Okay?"

I nodded while the forms woman stood patiently. Owen didn't say a word but leaned down to gently pick up Ryan out of my arms so I could sign. After the woman left, he continued to hold my baby, cradling my son's tiny form in his huge arms. I watched as one tiny hand grabbed an offered finger.

"Do you want him back, or do you want to nap a bit? Bevvie's right that you need rest. Ryan and I will be here when you wake up."

Fatigue suddenly made my eyes droop. "I think that's a brilliant idea. Please wake me if you need to."

He brought Ryan over to me for a quick cuddle and kiss. I noticed my baby's eyes were drooping too. "Being born is hard work, isn't it? Love you, Peanut."

Owen laid the drowsy baby in the crib where I could see him and came back to sit with me on the bed. He took my hand in his and held it softly. "I've never had many words to say to anyone. I should probably have words to say now, but I can't think of any other than I love you." His eyes rose to mine. "I love you, Melanie."

I sleepily smiled at him. "I love you too, Owen."

***

OWEN LEANED BACK IN THE HOSPITAL RECLINER. HIS large frame barely fit in the flimsy piece of furniture, but no way would he leave that room until Melanie did the following day. Connor, Bevvie, and the kids planned on going to the house first thing later this morning to check the readiness of everything. Diapers stacked, new baby clothes washed and in the dresser, sheets on the crib, food in the fridge, and whatever else they would need for the next few days.

He looked over at the sleeping woman, who gave a light snore and rolled over. The nurse had removed the IV earlier to make the rest of the night more comfortable. A pamphlet of aftercare instructions lay on the oblong table near the baby's crib along with a how-to card on breast feeding. Giving birth in real life was not nearly as pretty as in the movies, and Owen's respect for women deepened further after watching this miracle firsthand.

Ryan squeaked and shifted, catching Owen's attention. He rose from the chair and walked as quietly as he could to the plastic crib. The newborn's eyes were open, and his face scrunched up as if trying to decide whether to cry or go back to sleep. Owen squirted some hand sanitizer in his palms and rubbed them together before lifting the tiny bundle. He figured this would be the first of many long sleepless nights that he and Melanie would have. Ryan smacked his lips and stretched as Owen stood in one spot and swayed.

A slight creaking noise had Owen looking up from

his perusal of the infant's face. He assumed it would be a doctor or the night nurse coming to check on Melanie. Instead, it was the last person he ever expected to see again.

Martin Miser entered the room. He didn't blink an eye when he spotted Owen holding the tiny bundle.

"I heard she had a boy."

Owen continued to sway, but his protective instincts kicked into high gear. He dipped his chin. "Ryan."

The man looked at the sleeping form of his daughter and visibly swallowed. "May I see him?"

Owen hesitated before leaning over and allowing the man to see his grandson.

The man gazed silently at the next generation of his family. His eyes shone wetly, but no tears fell. He sniffed before he spoke. "I planned on leaving Deloris. I married her because of Magnus and stayed because of Melanie. I blamed her for decades because her birth made me stay in a loveless marriage. No prenup meant if I left my wife and two children, Deloris could take me to the cleaners. Leaving now would be no different. I spent a lot of time cheating on Deloris and made no attempt to hide it from her. She has all the proof she needs to take half of every-thing we own, but she still wanted to stay married to me. Not from love. More for appearances and reputation."

His eyes stayed on the tiny bundle in Owen's arms. "When you pointed that finger in my face and said 'your daughter. Shame on you' I started thinking. Yes, I do have a daughter. I've never thought of Melanie in that way before. I always considered her Magnus's sister or the second child, but she is my daughter. One I ought to be proud of. I don't know if reconciliation is possible now, or if she would even welcome me into her life. The only reason I found out she started labor is from a colleague in the ER."

Hearing the man's confessions didn't rank high on Owen's list of priorities, but he continued to sway with Ryan in his arms and listen to the older man.

"I can't make up for the past. I can, however, do something for the future. I'm not so stupid to think you'll take any money from me, so I set up a trust for the baby. Melanie is named as the custodian, and she'll have access to it should the need arise. Keep the money for Ryan's college or whatever might be needed someday."

Owen bristled. "Don't need your money."

"I know that. I still want you to take it for the baby. He's my only grandchild and likely the only one I'll ever have."

"Magnus."

Martin shook his head. "Not many people know this, but Magnus is gay. I never accepted it and spent so many of his childhood and teenage years trying to force it out of him. I was wrong, and now I've turned him into a bitter, unhappy man who hates everyone around him. Especially his sister."

The man, once a powerhouse in the world, suddenly looked old and defeated. Owen could relate, as his own father showed signs of aging and becoming something other than the tough old bastard he grew up with.

Martin took a big breath let it out slow. "You'll take care of her?"

Owen gave one nod. "Getting a ring. Want more kids."

"You going to adopt this one?"

"Yes. Ryan Miser MacAteer."

Martin's jaw flexed as if fighting for control. Owen couldn't blame him too much. How else did you react when finding out your family name was being replaced? Owen had no sympathy for him, though. After all, you reaped what you sowed.

The older man finally spoke. "You'll make her happy."

It was a statement, not a question. Owen didn't

think he needed to respond, but he did anyway. "All my life."

Martin swallowed again and nodded as if affirming what he already knew. "Please tell her I came by and I'd like to visit again." He left the room and quietly clicked the door shut.

Owen looked at Melanie, still sleeping soundly, completely unaware she'd had a middle-of-the-night visitor. He noticed Ryan had fallen back asleep. Owen placed the baby back in the crib and sat down in the recliner. He closed his eyes and let his brain drift.

Melanie MacAteer. Ryan MacAteer. Mary MacAteer. Regan MacAteer....

CHAPTER TWENTY-FIVE

"Who's got a stinky butt? Who's got a stinky-stinky butt-butt?"

Ryan grinned up at me with his two miniscule bottom teeth showing and waved his hands. My son had some serious talent when it came to pooping. He had an astounding variety of colors, consistencies, and volumes. This beautiful calm Saturday morning, Ryan had had a fecal explosion. It overfilled his diaper, shot up his back, leaked out of his onesie, and totally coated the baby swing chair. Coincidentally, it was the first time I'd ever seen fear in Owen's eyes. The man's face went white as a bleached sheet, and he had to leave the room.

"Owen MacAteer, don't you dare abandon me."

I heard a muffled set of words that included "yard"

and "hose." A few minutes later, I spotted Owen spraying off the swing next to the driveway.

"Hmph. I guess we can let this one go, since he is helping with poop patrol after all. Right, stinky-stinker?"

"Ngahd!" my little man declared in agreement.

Spring flirted with the weather, bringing cold April showers mixed with ice one week, and warm, sunny temperatures the next. Owen had spent the winter weeks gutting our kitchen. He put in new countertops, bigger cabinets, a new dual sink, and new flooring. Next, he planned on redesigning the large unfinished area downstairs into a family room with a big play area for Ryan. If I'd learned one thing about Owen, it's that he liked to work. A lot.

A low *lug-lug-lug* sound came to my ears, and I watched a motorcycle with two riders approach. Connor and Bevvie had come for a visit without the kids. Eva, Connor and Owen's sister, had married a man who was a member of the Dragon Runners motorcycle club over in Bryson City. Connor had a motorcycle but had never joined the club. He and Bevvie just enjoyed riding from time to time. Owen said he liked motorcycles and had handled them in the past but didn't have one. I kinda wished he did as it looked like a lot of fun. Maybe someday, I'd buy him one for his birthday or on our ten-year anniversary.

I glanced at my ring as I lifted up the freshly cleaned and sweet-smelling Ryan to my shoulder. "Whatchoo think, stinker-boo? Is it weird for Mommy to get Daddy a motorcycle, or weird to think Mommy and Daddy will have a ten-year anniversary?"

"Gah."

"Yes, Mommy plans on a ten-year. And a twenty-year. And a thirty-year."

"Melanie! Get your ass out here!" Bevvie's yell came through the walls as I walked down the steps to join the other adults.

"You bellowed, ma'am?"

She rolled her eyes in perfect imitation of her oldest daughter. "Have you seen the new curriculum report?"

"Not yet. I've been having a blast with a Ryan MacAteer poop-fest. How the hell does someone so small produce so much shit?"

Bevvie waved off the question with a flick of her outstretched hands. "That's their job. Gimme."

I placed Ryan in her arms.

"Hello, my little munchkin. *Boo-jee-boo-jee-boo-jee.*"

Her gibberish words made me laugh out loud. "We have four degrees between the two of us and countless hours of professional development seminars. We've lectured students and other teachers, led faculty meetings, and served on every kind of education committee the school has ever established. We get around a baby and forget how to speak English."

She lifted her nose in the air and raised her eyebrow. "I'm bonding with my godson. Go away."

"Your godson just had a major blowout."

"Even better. He knew Aunt B was coming and didn't want to spoil any time with her. Right, *boo-jee-boo-boo?*"

Owen and Connor shared an amused look before getting down to business. "The Bowers called me about their house this morning. Apparently, they've had a leak in their upstairs bathroom for quite some time. The subflooring has completely rotted under the toilet and collapsed last night. Mrs. Bower said there's a pile of moldy wood chips, and the toilet itself is hanging halfway through the ceiling. I know you wanted to get started on the deck off your back porch today, but Mrs. Bower is rather upset. Mr. Bower is willing to pay extra to keep Mrs. Bower happy. Care to make an emergency house call?"

Owen grunted and turned to me with a question in his eyes.

"Go ahead, O-man. Sounds like Mrs. Bower needs a superhero today."

He smiled and pointed at his truck. "I'll drive."

Maybe I should scratch the idea of getting him a motorcycle for our ten-year. Perhaps a cruise instead.

The men took off, Connor on his bike and Owen in his truck, and Bevvie and I moved to the kitchen.

"Coffee?" I asked as I reached for the pot.

"Why are you asking? Just pour." Bevvie settled Ryan in the bouncy chair in the middle of the dining room table and sat in one of the chairs. I pulled down two mugs and filled them for our morning gab session.

"How's the driving lessons coming?"

Bevvie leaned over and pointed to her scalp. "See these new gray hairs? Abby's gift to me. I so wish I could get her father to do this."

"Doug still MIA with the kids, then."

Bevvie sighed and stirred creamer and Splenda into her coffee. "Yup, and not a thing I can do about it. He's missing out on some of the best years of the kids' lives and someday he may regret not being a part of it." She tapped the spoon against the side of the cup. "I can't help him, and I don't want to. He's an adult. Speaking of adults, I think Garrett is finally coming to terms with his ex. Connor and Owen gave Garrett the bulk of the big restoration job on that bed-and-break-fast place, and he's been spending a lot of time out there. I'm glad he's able to help take on the workload, but Connor is still getting piles of calls for work."

I took a big sip of my own cup. "Really? Even with Patrick and Angus coming down from Pennsylvania? Owen said they plan on sticking around at least for the summer to help with the overload."

Bevvie waved a hand in the air as she swallowed and cleared her throat. "I'm glad they're here, but I don't know that they'll stay long-term. They never really do."

I hummed and gently bounced the chair. Ryan, gurgled a bit and tried to eat his fist. "An old friend of mine is opening a yoga studio, and the guys are taking on the job of designing it. Between the B and B, the yoga place, and all the deck jobs Owen's got booked, they might want to consider something long term. We should check out the yoga thing soon."

"I'm game, but don't you make fun of me when I break something by bending over to touch my toes. How's the baking coming along?"

I stuck my tongue out and put a square plastic container in front of her. "Here. My latest batch of chocolate chip cookies."

She popped off the top, took one of the lumps

inside, and looked at it dubiously. I shrugged. "Yes, they are the consistency of hockey pucks, but they make great teethers and aren't so bad when you dip them in your coffee."

She dipped and managed to gnaw off a chunk. "Mmm. Yummy."

Her expression absolutely did not reflect her words.

"PITA."

"You love me. I'm the godmother to your son."

"Still a PITA."

"Love you too, Mellie. Have you heard about the job yet?"

Ryan started fussing, and I plucked him from his bouncy chair and opened my shirt and nursing bra to feed him. He latched on like a limpet and kneaded my breast with his tiny hands as he nursed. "I've heard I'm in the running for the position, but I'm not sure I want that right now. I have plenty of my own money, so I don't really have to work. Owen brings in quite a bit with all the work he's doing. We're not hurting at all financially, and I'm really thinking I'll take a step back for a few years until this little booger is in preschool before I go back to work. I'll keep tutoring a few nights a week, to keep my chops up, but that may be it for a while."

Bevvie nodded. "I get it. I didn't have that option and had to use a church day care 'cause I had to work. My kids turned out pretty damn good, but I would have loved to stay home with them. You're a great mom, Mellie-Jellie."

"Thanks, Bevvie-Levvie. Here's a thought. Why don't you apply to be the principal? You have the administration credentials, right?"

"Yeah, but that's from years ago."

"Still valid."

She wrinkled her nose. "Me as a school principal? In charge of everything and everyone? I'm not sure I can handle that."

I laughed out loud, and Ryan made a sound of protest as he let go of my nipple. "That's too funny. I've watched you handle your four kids with all their activities, balance a full-time job with a part-time one, work out the logistics to take your choir kids to competitions, and still make time for your husband. Running a high school should be a piece of cake."

She turned thoughtful. "Maybe. The pay increase would be welcome, for sure. It would be nice to put aside some money for the kids' college so they don't have to take out huge loans. It's still a lot of respon-sibility."

I shifted Ryan to my shoulder and patted his back.

He grunted some baby noises, then let out a huge burp. "That's my little man. Bevvie, I have every confidence in you. Apply for the job and see what happens. You have my vote."

"It's not an election."

"I'll vote for you anyway."

She laughed and sipped at her coffee. I switched Ryan to my other breast, and he latched on again.

"You look happy, Mellie. I always thought you were happy with your life, but now there's something more every time I look at you. There's a radiance around you that just glows with contentment. Like you found yourself when you weren't even looking. I don't know who's luckier, you or Owen."

I paid attention to Bevvie's words but watched my son's hands as they pressed and grabbed my skin. Ryan MacAteer, the first one to carry the family name in the next generation, and if Owen got his way, there would be many more.

"Me, Bevvie. Definitely me."

CHAPTER TWENTY-SIX

Owen moved closer to me and wrapped me in his big arms as we lay in our bed watching the evening news. Ryan slept in his crib in his own room, blissfully unaware of the turmoil brewing in his mother's head. Even with the volume low, the words from the reporter drilled into my brain like spikes. A film clip played over and over again, showing something I never thought in my wildest nightmares would happen.

"The city of Asheville is reeling from the arrest last night of Mr. Robert Corrigan for the sexual assault of a college intern at First and Trust Bank. The victim alleges Mr. Corrigan drugged her and tied her up before raping her multiple times over a ten-hour period. Sources say investigators have discovered the date rape drug Rohypnol in the

bank president's car along with text messages between him and the victim. Since the arrest, several more women have come forward claiming to have experienced an assault by Robert Corrigan from as far back as his college days. Their stories are eerily familiar and show a pattern of predatory sexual behavior, and it has been speculated there could be more victims. If convicted, Mr. Corrigan will face up to forty years to life for each count of aggravated sexual assault."

The clip showed a handcuffed and belligerent Robert struggling and yelling as several police officers wrestled him from the main bank building to a waiting squad car.

"Brave women," Owen commented as he kissed my temple. "Not easy to step up and tell everyone that kind of personal trauma. Big risks involved."

A knot in my chest formed as I thought about the implications. This would be a long trial. A lot of garbage would be exposed and thrown out for the public to pick over and gossip about. Reputations, names, families, and more would be affected for years.

"I'm a member of that club. I hadn't thought that there would be others like me. Ones he terrorized and assaulted for years. The statute of limitation is probably long over in my case, but some of those women are in that boat as well. They're telling their stories anyway."

He squeezed me in the circle of his arms and kissed me again. "I can't tell you what's right for you. Keep quiet and see how this plays out or talk to those lawyers. He's facing a lot of shit and will be tarnished for life no matter what. I'll be surprised if he doesn't end up in prison whether or not you tell your story. You feel the need to add your voice, you're not alone anymore. I got your back. You got Connor and Bevvie, Garrett, the kids, and a pile of students you've taught over the years. You have an army behind you if you want it, but it's up to you."

The news switched over to another story, but my mind kept sifting through possibilities. "Robert will fight it. He's arrogant as hell and always been that way. As long as I've known him, he always thought his shit doesn't stink and rules that apply to the rest of us, don't apply to him."

"Assholes are assholes. He's just a rich one."

True, he had lots of money and the best lawyers it could buy.

So did I.

I thought about the sword tattoo on Owen's back and the saying about how the quiet pig gets the acorns.

I'd been quiet a long time. Maybe I didn't need to be any longer. Owen was right. I had a fucking army.

"I think I'll make a phone call tomorrow morning. If those other women can find the guts to stand up for themselves and what's right, I can too." Just saying those words out loud gave me a sense of peace. "I'm ready for it."

ENJOYED MELANIE AND OWEN'S STORY? IN THAT CASE, be sure to check out the next book in the series, *Hold It Close*—Garrett MacAteer's sweet and sexy story.

A man recovering from a toxic relationship and slowly healing. A woman recovering from a divorce and seeking a new life. When their worlds collide, will Garrett and Bertie finally heal and find their happily ever after?

Check out the complete Dragon Runners MC series too, starting with the incredible *Mute*.

GLOSSARY

moje dítěmy - daughter

mo rúnmy - love

amadán - fool

ACKNOWLEDGMENTS

Thank you for reading Ready For It. This book was my nod to the #MeToo movement that affected so many women during its inception and still carries weight now. It is my hope that the more people are aware of this issue the more support will be offered where needed. The upside is I believe there are many Owen MacAteers out there. Wonderful and respectful men who know how to treat a woman right. I hope you've found yours, and if not, keep looking. Never forget, you deserve the best.

A big thank you to some wonderful women who helped me keep my words on the right track. Rebecca Allman, Andrea Robinson, Virginia Gaylor, Barbara Hoover, and the always fabulous Olivia Ventura, you ladies rock!

Another shout out to the wonderful Becky Johnson and all the wonderful people of Hot Tree Publishing. Some years ago, they took a chance on a budding author and here we are today, with seven published books and more to come. I'm so glad I hit 'send'.

ABOUT THE AUTHOR

ML Nystrom had stories in her head since she was a child. All sorts of stories of fantasy, romance, mystery and anything else that captured her interest. A voracious reader, she's spent many hours devouring books; therefore, she found it only fitting she should write a few herself!

ML has spent most of my life as a performing musician and band instrument repair technician, but that doesn't mean she's pigeon-holed into one mold. She's been a university professor, belly dancer, craftsperson, soap maker, singer, rock band artist, jewelry maker, lifeguard, swim coach, and whatever else she felt like exploring. As one of her students said to her once, "Life's too short to ignore the opportunities." She has no intention of ever stopping... so welcome to her story world. She hopes you enjoy it!

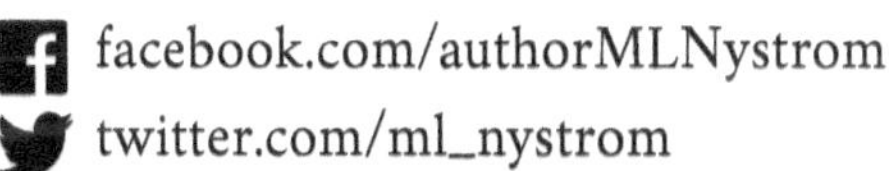

facebook.com/authorMLNystrom
twitter.com/ml_nystrom
instagram.com/mlnystrom
bookbub.com/authors/ml-nystrom

ABOUT THE PUBLISHER

Hot Tree Publishing opened its doors in 2015 with an aspiration to bring quality fiction to the world of readers. With the initial focus on romance and a wide spread of romance subgenres, Hot Tree Publishing has since opened their first imprint, Tangled Tree Publishing, specializing in crime, mystery, suspense, and thriller.

Firmly seated in the industry as a leading editing provider to independent authors and small publishing houses, Hot Tree Publishing is the sister company to Hot Tree Editing, founded in 2012. Having established in-house editing and promotions, plus having a well-respected market presence, Hot Tree Publishing endeavors to be a leader in bringing quality stories to the world of readers.

Interested in discovering more amazing reads brought to you by Hot Tree Publishing? Head over to the website for information:

www.hottreepublishing.com